UNMASKING A COWGIRL

Rachelle Paige Campbell

Published in the United States of America

GET THE WHOLE SERIES TODAY!

PRAISE FOR RACHELLE PAIGE CAMPBELL:

"A clean wholesome read romance fans will enjoy."
-In'd Tale Magazine
"I love Rachelle Paige Campbell's writing style."
-Long & Short Reviews
"A sweet story."
-Paranormal Romance Guild

CHAPTER I

Some days, Abby Whit forgot she was hiding behind an alias. After two years and change of living in Herd, Montana, she fully embraced her cover story as a food truck chef, passing through town. To anyone who asked, she was working for herself after stints being the sous chef for chefs from Kansas City to Las Vegas. Her family didn't put down roots. Those were the kernels of truth. But she'd arrived with a plan.

Determine the public's perception of her family and assess the feasibility of taking back her land.

On the frosty March morning, she parked her food truck in the gravel lot behind the bright red barn on the Kincaid ranch. Against a snowy backdrop and overcast sky, the new construction building popped amidst the open land that had been owned by one family for over a century. Credited with saving the local economy by modernizing their ranch into a cowboy spa, Hank and grandson Ryan Kincaid were undisputed winners in the town's founding families' feud. Her family, the Whittiers, were the first losers. The good citizens of Herd considered her ancestors the villains in the town's history. If she had given her full name on arrival, she'd have been kicked out of the state.

Hating the Kincaids on principle, given her history, would have been expected. Prejudice hadn't suited her. They had never questioned her sudden appearance and purpose in the tight knit community. They'd supported and encouraged her. Their kindness was the reason she continued to debate finally making her legal claim to the small patch of land near the church where she parked her food truck. The deadline approached.

The hum of the idling truck wasn't loud enough to silence her whirring thoughts. Helping out others in the community had been equally about establishing good karma for herself and treating others with the kindness she valued. No one had been better to her than the Kincaids. She didn't think she'd done nearly enough to redeem herself in their eyes once they learned the truth.

Joe would be sure to highlight her villainy.

She shuddered. Joe Staunch, middle school teacher and ranch tour guide, was her very vocal critic. She was careful to never cause anyone offense and yet she'd somehow made an enemy of him.

He either ignored her or complained about her—often within her earshot. Some people rubbed each other wrong. She accepted that fact. The trouble was that she liked him. Her heart wouldn't be reasoned into submission.

She cut the engine and exited the truck, leaving the vehicle unlocked.

An icy breeze whipped past her, burning her ears, and carrying the scent of a nearby fire. She crunched the gravel under her feet as she made her way to the barn.

While she agonized over the decision, she only had two choices. Either she claimed her inheritance, or she gave up on it forever. Security lingered so near she could almost smell the roasting meat in proper ovens and feel the stability of the solid walls and roof from her own restaurant on her land. She couldn't stall much longer. But she didn't want the town to feel she'd betrayed them. She hadn't told bald-faced lies. Neither had she shared the complete truth.

The side door stood slightly ajar. Muffled, deep voices carried out.

She slipped inside and rubbed her hands together. "Hello?" she called, her teeth chattering, from nerves and the low temperature.

"We're here," Hank Kincaid replied.

She blew on her icy figures and approached the men standing in the center of the room.

"Sorry, the new furnace arrives by the end of the week," Ryan Kincaid said. He stood next to several toolboxes and a stack of drywall.

"No bother," she said, waving off any concern like she didn't notice the unfinished walls with wires poking out and gaps visible in the boards. A little spray foam insulation and a working system would solve the heating problem. "I hope the first week in June is warm enough and we won't have to be concerned with turning on the heat. I don't want to add *fix furnace* to either Hank's ninetieth birthday extravaganza or the wedding budget." She plastered on a smile to stop her teeth from chattering.

"Bad luck to replace the furnace twice in one year." Hank Kincaid shook his head. "Makes me worried what the third calamity will be."

"Doesn't the fire count as the first strike of poor luck?" Ted Stirling frowned. "Rebuilding this barn from the ground up is at the top of my list of bad things."

She darted her gaze between the three cowboys.

As the oldest, white-haired, and permanently tan, Hank Kincaid often touted tired cliches and old wives' tales as guiding life principles. "No, that was last year's number two after my trip to the hospital."

Hank's grandson and heir, Ryan, rolled his eyes. Standing well over six feet and with a perpetual scowl, he was the town's stalwart visionary. Practical and forward thinking, he had revitalized his family's legacy and the entire community through a clear and unexpected plan. He didn't waste time looking for signs of divine intervention.

The third, Ted Stirling, was the thoughtful ranch hand turned trusted confidant. Often found stroking his jaw in consideration, the slim man with thin streaks of silver threading his dark hair didn't jump to conclusions. He'd been hired to work cattle and, over the past decade, switched direction to managing people.

Abby had overheard the stories enough from Joe. She almost imagined a first-hand recollection despite only living in town for two years. For the past decade plus, the three men guided the town to an unprecedented economic recovery thanks to their varying character qualities, forming a strong pyramid. If one side wobbled, the other two assumed the weight of the struggles and balanced the load.

What would they do when her revelation rocked them all?

"Was there a number three last year?" she asked.

Hank tapped a finger against the deep cleft in his chin. "I don't think there was unless you count Colby's trip to the vet after she ate that pan of brownies."

Colby, a rescue mutt, was arguably more human than dog. She hadn't been shaken by her life-or-death accident over Thanksgiving weekend. Meg, her owner, and Ryan's fiancé, however had been an emotional wreck.

"No more of this talk." Ryan held up his hands. "Don't even put the energy out into the universe. We have too much going on in the next few months for anyone to go looking for a curse or believing in superstition."

Hank nodded and turned, flashing crossed fingers behind his back.

Abby glanced at Hank's crossed fingers and snorted. She rubbed a hand over her face. "Sorry. Must be allergies."

"Why did you need us to stop by today?" Joe Staunch asked, his voice carrying from the sliding glass doors in the center of the back wall overlooking the deck behind the building. "Couldn't this be a phone call or email?" he asked as he approached.

Abby gaped. She was well-versed in his curt words but had never heard him so short with his friends and bosses. In the summer, Joe served as a tour guide for groups interested in historical excursions on the ranch.

"Yes, keep us on task. Thanks, Joe," Ryan said, glaring. "I wanted you both to get a sense of the space. Abby, we have added a small prep station but besides the sink, dishwasher, and single oven, it's not a fully functioning kitchen."

She nodded, pleased for the prep area. "Can I park the truck close to that space?"

"Yes, we have a service door leading to a spot for you with hook-ups," Ted said. "The plan for Hank's ninetieth birthday and the wedding has expanded."

She widened her gaze and met Joe's. As reluctant partners, she hoped for a second of commiseration to thaw his icy demeanor.

He shook his head and glanced away. He wore his disapproval and doubt like a pair of well-worn jeans. Whether he liked it or not, they were tied to each other.

They were stuck together in planning the event. For the better part of ten months, she had been working on her contribution, catering, and communicating mostly by email to Joe. She trusted him to carry his weight, not that he shared much of his progress.

"Meg and I have decided since we are only getting married once, we need to do it right," Ryan said. "No more simple ceremony. We want a full weekend of events."

"Oh." Abby tipped her head to the side unsure she followed what that meant. Ryan's fiancé, Meg, wasn't the sort to make a big fuss. A full weekend could include multiple events on each day. She'd have to carefully plan the menus if she was expected to cater everything. She wouldn't want to repeat any meals.

"The birthday celebration remains on Friday night. Saturday will be the rehearsal dinner. Sunday will be the wedding," Ryan said.

Abby nodded. Including one more event, the rehearsal dinner, wouldn't zap her creative spirit. Her worst-case scenario had been avoided but didn't alleviate all of her concerns. She would be doing a lot of cooking in a short amount of time. She couldn't turn down the opportunity. To stay in town, she needed to expand her business. She'd started a catering side-hustle on the ranch to pad her bottom line.

With more events, she needed more space and capacity. Her truck didn't have the refrigerator space to store enough food for three-days of events. She'd have to use what space she could find at the Kincaid's house and ask her friend James Rabbitt at The Golden Crown saloon, the only full-service restaurant in town. She knew he'd agree for the special, one-time-only weekend. If she wanted to be the go-to caterer for the ranch's new wedding and events business, she needed a better plan.

I have one. But it'll make everyone hate me.

"Let me see what I can do." She smiled until her cheek twitched. She hated the chicken and egg predicament she'd landed herself in but neither could she turn her back on the easiest solution. Claim her inheritance and build. Of course, if she was black-listed in town for being a Whittier, kitchen space wouldn't matter. "Do you have any ideas about the food for the rehearsal dinner and wedding? I can cook whatever you like. Ian is almost finished with my new traveling smoker. Depending on the wedding start time, I could be out here all-day roasting meat."

Hank licked his lips. "Sounds good to me. Now I regret asking you to cook all those fancy little things for my birthday."

She chuckled. "I can switch. I haven't put in the order yet. You let me know what you want. Canapes and small plates or a sit-down dinner. Or buffet. I can do barbeque or Tex Mex or steak."

"Could you send me a few sample menus for both options?" Ryan asked. "I'm in charge of the food."

She pulled her phone out of her back pocket. The lock screen flashed with a reminder. *Meeting with lawyer.* She'd hoped for some sense of moral clarity before facing the attorney in the next town over, but wasn't likely to discover it here while the Kincaids were being so considerate and kind. She unlocked the screen and typed in the note. "All set, I'll send you a mock-up in the next day or so. How many guests are you thinking?"

"We've set aside enough rooms for a hundred guests to stay on property," Ted said. "Give or take. Would you mind including Stephanie in the email exchange? She's taken up the wedding planning. She can coordinate with you and Joe."

"Of course." Abby smiled. The simple project was twisting and turning into a complicated knot with each additional person. Maybe that was a good thing. She could work closely with Stephanie, a kindergarten teacher and one of Joe's colleagues, at the local public K-12 school. Stephanie knew how to handle Joe and the bubbly woman remained nonplussed by anyone's moods. "I'd better head into town and discuss the changes with James."

"If you say so," Joe muttered.

Abby spun and faced her partner slash nemesis. "What does that mean?"

"Nothing. If you think you can't handle a big event, you need to get help. Sounds like you already know your limits. At least in this instance." Joe folded his arms over his chest and stared her down.

Her cheeks flamed and red-hot anger bubbled up inside her.

She'd been careful to be overly nice to him. He was an interesting person, rattling off more facts about the town than anyone else alive, including walking encyclopedia Hank Kincaid. If anyone could uncover her secret, it was him. While pursuing her own research about her family, she'd often bumped into him at the library. Despite the need for self-preservation, she was curious about his work and asked questions.

History wasn't immune to bias. Joe's outspoken search for truth heartened her. Whatever happened with her position in town, perhaps he would save her family's reputation. But she'd never won his friendship or even a bare level of grudging respect. Trying to make a success of her business on her own, she was plenty used to naysayers. She prided herself on her thick skin. His comments were typical of his conversation with her. But the cumulative effect meant each word cut her a little deeper. Death by a thousand papercuts.

"I know what I'm doing. I'm very good at making things happen. In case you hadn't noticed?" she asked.

Joe dropped his arms to his sides and turned his gaze away.

His response wasn't a victory, as far as she was concerned. He'd needled her into a verbal spat in front of people she respected and counted on. With any luck, she hadn't disgraced herself too much. Yet. She faced the trio of cowboys once more, blocking Joe from her line of sight as best she could. "If you don't need anything else from me?"

"Thanks for coming out on such short notice," Hank said.

"Yes, we really do appreciate you and all your help with the ranch." Ryan's smile crinkled the corners of his eyes. "We're here for you, too."

"If you need any assistance with loading or unloading your truck, you can always call," Ted added.

She glanced between the three and saw pity in their pinched expressions. They felt bad for her because of Joe's poor treatment. She prayed her one-sided crush wasn't public knowledge. As long as these men didn't pity her ill-fated attraction, she could walk away with her head held high.

She rubbed a hand over her tickling nose. She'd pretend she hadn't noticed their solemn expressions. "Thank you for..." Tears stung her eyes for a different reason. Guilt and shame for her secret. "Thanks for everything. I'll start menu planning immediately." Spinning on her heel, she crossed through the barn, her snow boots leaving a slushy trail behind her on the thick pine boards. As she slid the door open a crack and slipped through the opening, she heard Hank berate Joe.

"What is wrong with you, boy?" The old cowboy's gravelly voice carried through the opening as she carefully shut the door.

Stuffing her hands in her pockets, she dropped her chin into the collar of her coat. With each step, she crunched gravel and snow under her boots. Maybe she just imagined what she wanted Hank to say. She spent enough time lost in her thoughts, preparing herself for the worst. Before long, she'd have to face facts and she wasn't sure she was creative enough to prepare mentally for the town's reaction to her real identity.

If I don't take the land, nothing will change.

Without the land, she couldn't move forward in a meaningful way, and she'd have to leave. Life didn't stand still. Whether she liked it or not, everything was changed by the mere passage of time.

She wished her goal wasn't so tightly wrapped around her secret. But if Joe hadn't figured it out by now, she was in the clear. Probably.

Joe studied the thick pine boards under his boots, searching for the grain in the wavy patterns like he'd uncover the secret of life. He'd do anything to stop from tracking her as she blessedly left the barn, taking the faint scent of butter with her. A cold gust of air swept through the barn. After last night's snow, they were due for a reprieve from precipitation. Not that anyone in Herd or the surrounding area would complain about snow or rain. Last summer's drought had caused major issues for the prairie including a wildfire that consumed the historic barn on the Kincaid ranch.

"Hey, did you hear me?" Hank said.

Joe glanced over his shoulder.

Ryan took a step back and held up both palms.

"What is *wrong* with you, boy?" Hank asked again.

Joe poked his chest with his index finger.

Hank nodded.

Joe flinched. He'd assumed Hank mean Ryan. Joe wasn't addressed as *boy*. Hank saved the moniker for his grandson. Joe gulped. He must have really messed up.

"Well?" Hank glared.

If Joe knew the answer, he'd solve a lot of his own problems. He wasn't sure exactly what it was about Abby Whit that grated on his nerves only that her presence—no matter how pretty she was—set his teeth on edge.

He was being unfair and unkind. He prided himself on being the opposite, treating others with a magnanimity he wished in return. But he couldn't stop his displeasure with her and in turn only grew angrier at himself. It was a vicious hamster wheel he wanted to leap out of but hadn't figured out how.

"I'm sorry. I'm just…" Joe ran a hand through his hair. He'd had big plans for how to spend his spring break. Giving up time to argue with his nemesis wasn't part of his schedule. He let his frustration with himself and his lack of progress on his passion project, a history tome on the town, spill over. "I was wrong."

"Hmm." Hank grunted. "I'll leave it to you to apologize."

Joe nodded. He knew better than to try to explain himself anymore. Hank had eased up on matchmaking Joe and Abby over the winter. With the wedding and upcoming birthday celebration, his attention was directed elsewhere. Joe was glad for the break. And one morning of a walk-through wasn't going to throw off his schedule for the rest of the week. He had interviews lined up and appointments scheduled at the county records office. "Is Stephanie really on board with the wedding planning?" He turned to Ted. "What about her other commitments?"

Ted shrugged.

Joe read the resignation in his friend's shaking shoulders. Stephanie was always busy. If she didn't have three jobs at once, she claimed boredom. This summer, however, she had plans to continue her education with the goal of becoming a school administrator. She'd also be teaching a yoga class on the ranch and running the town's summer festival. Joe supported his friend's ambition whole-heartedly but wondered if she was taking on too much. "Does she have time?"

"Does she ever?" Ted asked. "I've stopped asking her if she needs help and jump in. She won't give up her responsibilities."

"Someone has to be in charge. Meg really wanted to get married in a field." Ryan sighed. "I want to give her the day of her dreams, and she's giving me nothing to work with."

Joe met Ted's wide-eye gaze. Meg was the sort of person who knew her own mind and wasn't shy about letting it be known. If she said she wanted to stand in a field and recite her vows, she wanted to do exactly that. Joe appreciated her frank, up-front personality. He never had to guess around her. *Unlike other people.*

On the surface, Abby was everything sweet and smiling. Eager to please, she pitched in at every town event and joined almost every club. He hardly went a day without running into her at some group. He'd spotted her planting annuals in the reused oak barrels up and down Main Street the week before Memorial Day in the past. He'd nearly been impaled by her knitting needles as she barreled out of the saloon. And, of course and most unfortunately, she asked him incessant questions when he was researching on the second floor of the library. She had no reason to be there, quizzing him, unless she was trying to aggravate him.

"Okay, groomzilla. Calm down. We'll make sure your big day fills every one of your childhood dreams," Joe said.

Ryan raised an eyebrow and widened his stance. The twitching muscle in his cheek flashed a warning.

"If Steph is on board, are you sure you'll still need me? She can probably take over my side of the planning, don't you think?" Joe asked. He tried to keep his words modulated but couldn't completely eliminate the hopeful tone of up speak.

"No. You know what I like," Hank said. "You're practically an expert on everything Kincaid ranch."

Practically but not officially. Joe smiled. The old cowboy knew how to cut straight to the heart of the matter. Earning undeniable credentials, elevating himself from the anecdote guy to indisputable historian was his ultimate goal. After five years, he wasn't any closer to achieving his dream. Of course, the past two and a half had added the distraction of the sudden appearance of Abby Whit and figuring her out was his go-to distraction.

"Meg wants to make a go of weddings and events. She has already worked with Stephanie on pulling a lot of the tasks together. She's developing master lists for the future," Ted said.

"You must unify and execute our visions of the event. You'll know what to do," Hank said.

"Besides you won't be totally on your own. Stephanie will function as a wedding day coordinator," Ryan added. "Her focus is on the ceremony. You can't believe how much needs to get squeezed into such a short amount of time."

The field sounded better and better to Joe. But Ryan was nothing if not a meticulous visionary. He'd have some exacting image of what he wanted. Stephanie might be the only person up to the task. "Is my timetable for the birthday celebration still adequate? Parade, cook-out, fireworks?"

Hank nodded.

"Will we need to hire more staff for clean-up?" Ryan turned to Ted.

Ted shook his head. "All taken care of. If you can support the coordination with the town council, I'd be in your debt."

Joe drew back his shoulders. If he'd earned anything on his own merits, it was the respect of the council. "Of course. We should be set. As long as the new herd doesn't cause too much calamity in town, you shouldn't have too much to worry about."

Ryan scrubbed a hand along his jaw. "We'll find out in a few weeks."

Initially settled at the end of the nineteenth century on a false claim of gold in the creek, Herd was named for the overwhelming number of bison in the area. The eradication of the animals within a few years of the founding was one of many stains on the past. At one time, three ranches surrounded the town. Only the Kincaid family remained, absorbing all the land in the process. Ryan sought to reintroduce the bison. Many remained skeptical about the impact.

"How's the research going?" Ted asked.

"Slow." Joe exhaled a heavy breath. He found himself so easily distracted by the personal stories that he'd lost his main thread of the book several times in the process. He'd refocused around an unshakeable through line, the Kincaids. Betrayals littered the past, but the family found strength from ingenuity. Ryan was only the latest in a long line of smart, risk-taking businessmen.

Joe felt the direction of the book, an undeniable American story, would resonate with readers across a broad spectrum of ages and backgrounds. If he could only finish. "I'm heading to the library, unless you need anything else from me?"

Ryan shook his head.

"I'll walk you out." Ted strode forward, clapping a hand on his shoulder.

The decisive grip was unshakeable. Joe wouldn't fight. Of the three, he'd least expect a lecture from Ted. Maybe he was that far gone that only his friend's warning would suffice. "Sure, thanks." He waved to the Kincaids and followed Ted out of the barn via a side-door.

Joe stepped onto the deck and raised a hand to shield his gaze against the bright glare.

The door shut behind him with a dull thud.

Pristine snow covered the wooden boards and sparkled in the faint sunlight of the overcast day. Beyond the railing, the prairie rose and fell in gentle undulations. With the snowfall, drifts created drama and mystery. In the summer, wildflowers grew amidst the tall grasses, brightening the otherwise monochromatic view.

Joe hated to wreck the pretty winter picture with his booted steps. But if he was going to be yelled at, he didn't want an audience. He lifted one foot and then the other into the eight inches of snowfall, trudging across the deck.

"I keep forgetting to add *shovel the deck* to my chores." Ted chuckled.

"I can't even imagine your list." Joe raised his hands to his mouth and blew on his icy fingers. "Did you want to talk?"

"Are you okay?" Ted tipped his head to the side.

No. "Same as always." Joe forced a grin. He hoped the twist of his lips was more welcoming than the grimace he felt. "Maybe a little more pressure this year with the events and the end of school coming. Why do you ask?" While considerate, his friend wasn't the type to poke around another person's private business. Until recently, stoic Ted had been allergic to feelings. But then everything changed. The life he'd seemingly left behind crashed into him.

Joe was happy for Ted. The cowboy of a few words might argue otherwise, but no man truly wanted to live alone. With the arrival of his sister and niece, along with opening his heart up to love again after a decade plus as a grieving widower, Ted couldn't seem to escape the influence of one woman without being under that of another. And he never scowled anymore.

Ted flushed.

Shaking his head, Joe stuffed his fists into his coat pocket. He wasn't against love. But he was actively anti-manipulation. Why Hank decided to pair him with the most suspicious woman in town, Joe would never understand. "I'm okay. Feeling a bit impatient to hurry up and prove myself. If I'm being honest."

"All in good time. You don't have anything to prove. You're valued."

Not to me. Joe was tired of feeling so out of sync with himself. Abby was the only person who seemed interested in hearing his history tidbits and facts. She'd quickly become part of the fabric of the community and wasn't leaving. He'd have to deal with her for the rest of his life.

"If you want off the project, I can probably talk to Steph about it."

Joe shook his head. "No, don't do that. I didn't realize how high-maintenance Ryan was going to be about the wedding. She's going to have her hands full with his demands."

"Okay. If anything changes, let me know. I've got your back. Good luck with your work this week."

"Thanks, Ted. See you later." Joe strode across the deck and jogged around the side of the building to his car parked nearby. Shielded from the worst of the drifts by the barn, the gravel lot was exposed. Joe unlocked his car and hopped inside, turning over the engine.

His love of history was rooted in learning about personal connections to important moments. What seemed small to someone at the time ultimately became a barometer of a broader sentiment.

And if he didn't hear someone else's tale, he often filled in the details on his own. Storytelling was embedded deep in Joe's soul. He'd never met a dog without developing a backstory for the creature or witnessed an event without stringing together motivation for what unfolded.

He backed his car out of the parking lot and coasted onto the two-lane road heading to town. He needed distraction from Abby Whit. Her unexpected arrival bugged him over two years later. With each passing day, the chance of uncovering her secrets grew more unlikely. He couldn't shake the burning questions that simmered at every encounter.

Who was she, and why was she here?

CHAPTER 2

On the raised wooden sidewalk outside the rough-hewn stones of The Golden Crown saloon's façade, Abby crunched the remaining layer of snow and ice under her boots. The pathways around town were neatly shoveled. Road salt was avoided to protect the integrity of the wooden boards that comprised a big part of the Old West charm.

She snorted. The town was founded on a murky tale. A hopeful prospector claimed to discover gold in the creek now located on the Kincaid ranch. In truth, he had only found a gold tooth. The mistake wasn't caught until long after three families from the East Coast were well into their ranching operations, dividing the land between them in a decades long campaign of backstabbing and betrayal.

With the toe of her boot, she pressed against a patch of ice, cracking the thin sheet. Completely clearing the wooden sidewalks was almost impossible without the help of portable outdoor heaters. Near the saloon's front door, where warmth had escaped, the snow had melted and reformed as ice.

If she went inside, she wouldn't have to bother with the chill or the slick patch. She drew back her shoulders and filled her lungs with a deep breath. Asking for favors never got any easier for her. She did her best to offer her help and support whenever and wherever she could. She especially was proud of herself for those moments she anticipated someone's need and offered before being asked.

How many good deeds must she accomplish to wash herself clean from her deceit?

A lie by omission was still dishonesty even if it wasn't malicious. And strolling into the building that ultimately pushed her family out of town never got easier. Long ago, on one drunken night, her family's fate was sealed. Hoss Whittier had kicked over a kerosene lamp and set this entire side of Main Street ablaze. And then, after the buildings had been rebuilt, he did it again.

Shipping stone this far out on the prairie bankrupted the wealthiest family in town. Hoss's father sold the ranch to the Hawkes and Kincaids, splitting the land that had been the barrier between them down the center. The Hawkes wasted no time and built a pretty clapboard house on their newly acquired property, inching closer to the Kincaids. A few outbuildings remained, but the Whittier home was razed. If the Hawkes and Kincaids were determined to eradicate the Whittiers from the land, they had been successful. Only a spot of land, two acres, near the church at the far end of Main Street remained under Whittier control.

She'd often wondered why. If the townsfolk were so determined to push them out, why had her ancestors held onto anything? Since her arrival, however, she was grateful. Because Herd was the sort of place a person longed to call home.

For good measure, she rubbed the sole of her boots against the historic iron boot scraper. She pushed inside the swinging door and blinked, her vision adjusting to the interior. With the snow almost blinding under the gray sky, she needed a second to recollect herself under the replica kerosene lanterns hung throughout the open dining room.

"Abby?" A deep voice called.

She turned toward the bar, a polished walnut relic that ran the length of the western wall. "Hey." She waved and approached.

Behind the smooth counter, James Rabbitt, owner and proprietor, wiped glasses with a cloth. Dressed in shirt sleeves held in place with garters and a striped waistcoat, he complimented his historical dress with a neatly trimmed, waxed moustache. He was known for his friendly demeanor as much as his facial hair. He never kept one look for too long. Switching from mutton chops to an Imperial from one week to the next.

"Are you here for knitting club?" He tipped his head toward the tote on her arm.

She glanced down at the bag, almost forgetting the other purpose of her visit. She held onto the strap. "Yep. I'm still not ready to get off the loom, but my scarf is coming along."

He chuckled.

"Actually, I'm glad to bump into you." Her voice cracked, and she frowned. The words were stilted, awkward, and rehearsed. The last point was perhaps the one she feared the most.

When the truth came out, because even if she didn't claim the land someone was bound to uncover her real identity eventually, she didn't want to be accused of acting her way through the past several years of her life. She'd been honest and real about everything except her name and purpose.

She cringed. How much worse would the truth sound out loud?

"Do you need to pick up a few more shifts?" James asked.

She shook her head. James and his wife Heather, had been big supporters. As the only restaurant in town, they had welcomed a little friendly competition and sent business her way during the busiest time of the year. In the winter months, when she could not operate her food truck, they employed her in their kitchen. Without their help, she wouldn't have lasted more than the first summer in Herd. Once she opened her restaurant, she wouldn't need to burden them so much. She could be their friend and equal. "I came from the ranch. Ryan's wedding sounds bigger than I initially assumed."

James shook his head, lifting the corner of his mouth in a grin. "I told you. He never does anything small."

"Isn't the wedding day supposed to be all about the bride? I thought for sure Meg would win out with her intimate ceremony."

"I subscribe to the happy wife, happy life mantra. Heather told me where to be and when. But I think Meg doesn't want to fight. Besides, it's a good chance to launch their new business. Can't overlook that."

Abby nibbled the inside of her cheek. No one could ignore a single opportunity. While Ryan redeveloped his land, he could not have revitalized the town on his own. Every business had to step up and take charge of their future. Weddings and events at the ranch promised Abby a good deal of business growth. She couldn't lose the opportunity, or she'd never get the chance again.

"Are you here to ask for more refrigerator space?" James threw the cloth over his shoulder and crossed his arms over his chest. "Do you need another oven?"

Yes, and yes. She couldn't throw herself on his mercy without showing she was determined to help her career on her part as well. "Ian should have the new smoker ready well before June. I won't need all of your ovens. But yes, I definitely need more refrigerator space. I'll tap into everything I can at the ranch but the new barn doesn't have a fully functioning kitchen, just a prep space."

"We'll come together and help. It's a big weekend for the town. But if the weddings do take off at the ranch, you'll need to find another solution."

"Thank you, and yes, I know." She nodded. Her budget wouldn't stretch far enough to purchase property in town. She barely had enough to build on the land she already owned.

"Looks like they're here." He pointed behind her.

She spun and spotted Heather and Kelly Strong, one of the local kindergarten teachers.

The pair waved and strode toward their usual table next to one of the thick structural wooden beams with a light positioned directly above the circular oak, table.

Turning back, she met his gaze. "I'd better not be late. Thanks again, James."

He smiled.

She crossed the room to the table. Since coming to town, she started a wide variety of hobbies in an effort to get to know her neighbors and figure out if she wanted to settle here. She decided long before she arrived that she wouldn't claim the land and immediately sell for top dollar. The Whittiers already had a poor reputation. She didn't want to solidify them as a scheming, inconsiderate, money-grabbing family. They had left town because they lost the faith of the community. She wouldn't twist the knife and make the wound irreparable. Claiming the land and using it was less likely to cause backlash.

"Good morning." Abby pulled out a chair and sat, setting her tote bag on the table. "Meeting up during the day to knit is always such a treat."

"Spring break never feels like much of either," Kelly said, her eyes sparkling with humor. "Until I get together with you ladies."

"You'll make me blush," Heather said.

No nonsense Heather wasn't the sort to be embarrassed by anything. Abby laughed. She wished for some of that self-esteem. Rifling through her bag, she retrieved her circular, plastic loom.

While the others worked with knitting needles, she stuck to the knitting hook. She'd made good progress, considering how many times she'd started the scarf. With ten inches of teal hanging off the loom, she traced the accidental rectangle she'd created near the bottom edge. On her second day, she'd hurried to get started and e-wrapped the wrong way, making the yarn double the thickness and almost breaking her hook as she attempted to loop the yarn over the loom.

Once she realized what she'd done, she could have undone the knitting and started for the tenth time. Instead, she wanted something different. She would leave this error in plain view as a reminder of what she screwed up.

Inevitably, during every project, she lost track of what she was supposed to be doing and made mistakes from her impatience to plow ahead instead of understanding what she needed to do. Overcomplicating her life and preparing for the worst was just what she did.

She wanted to change. Coming to Herd had been about more than restoring her family's good name. It had been about putting down roots and fighting to belong somewhere. The longer she stayed in town, the more she wanted to have a permanent position.

Her military parents were both children of military parents, and so on stretching far back into the past. They loved to pick up and start something new. She'd thought she loved it too. Until she'd started researching the family history and learning more about the motivation of what became her nomadic family. She was tired of running away. After culinary school, she'd had one-to three-year long stints with major chefs at restaurants around the world.

After a few rows, she stopped knitting and examined her progress. She'd lost track of whether to purl or knit. *Focus on the moment.* This hobby forced her to do that or end up with a bumpy, messy piece. She reviewed the sheet of paper tracking her progress, marked off what she'd knitted, and then studied her companions.

Kelly hummed as she knitted with her needles.

Heather kept her chin down, focusing on her work with a narrow-eyed gaze.

Abby couldn't ever just live in the moment. Her companions were good examples to her of what she could find if she stayed present.

Heather frowned. "Are you stuck?"

"No, just trying to gather my thoughts and set them aside." Abby smiled.

"How's the big event coming?" Kelly asked.

"I think it's getting even bigger," Abby said.

"I'm glad to hear it. It's sort of like our town's royal wedding. The two founding families finally coming together?" Kelly beamed. "I can't wait. I feel like I need to order a new dress and a hat for the occasion."

Heather snorted. "We're not in London. Don't expect to see them drive through town, waving to adoring fans lining the streets. Or to spot commemorative plates and tea towels with their faces in the shop windows."

"That's not a bad idea." Abby crossed her arms over her chest, content to ignore her knitting for a moment as she pondered. "When the British royals have a wedding, it is a huge boost to tourism. I'm not saying we start screen printing every mug we can find with the wedding date. But maybe we do need to play up the town's involvement more. Why not have them drive through town? With a western twist, riding around on horseback?"

"Better call, Stephanie," Kelly said.

"She's already on board but yes, I better run some ideas past her." Abby studied the table, unseeing. Because maybe if the third founding family, the disgraced, shame-faced Whittiers, worked extra hard to celebrate the other two, past sins could be more easily forgiven. This was another shot at redemption. And she couldn't blow it.

Joe paused the recording playback on his phone. Slipping the wireless headphones off his ears and onto his neck, he let the white-noise of the busy coffee shop drown out his inner demons. He didn't often treat himself to sitting around and working in public. Usually, after an interview, he completed his transcriptions in the comfort and silence of his home.

When he left the interview in Miles City, however, he decided on a change of venue. What was the point of a week off if he didn't get out of town? An hour away wasn't exactly the prototypical, tropical spring break destination, but he was glad for the scenery change all the same. Raising his drink, he blew into the lid and sipped the mocha, savoring the rich sweetness on his tongue.

Today's interview hadn't been of any extraordinary significance. He'd met with a family that had moved out of Herd in the sixties. The surviving members didn't have first-hand memories but shared passed-down recollections.

Joe often pondered when the real depth of the project would become clear. Too many of his interviews slipped into myth-making with unreliable narrators. The only consistent thread remained the villainous Whittier family.

With each retelling, he became more conflicted. Hoss Whittier had set fire to downtown twice. Reportedly, he'd been drunk both times. The town had demanded reparations and exile. His father had sold almost everything he owned to rebuild the saloon and post office in stone. Hoss had left.

The family had retained the small plot of land near the cemetery. After Hoss's father died, the family had disappeared forever to become part of the legend of the town's founding. If a person only lived as long as those who remembered them, Hoss was immortal. Joe wanted the rest of the story. He wouldn't mind a pro-Hoss bias if that meant answers.

The door opened and a blast of cold air rushed into the space.

With a shudder, he set his coffee on the table, drew his coat tighter, and crossed his arms over his chest. Leaning forward, he scanned the notes he'd typed so far. The crowded coffee shop meant he increased the volume on his headphones than he should. Scanning the laptop screen, he frowned. He'd included too many question marks in his transcription to continue the endeavor in his current locale. He wasn't saving himself any time or energy. But he doubted heading home would be the relief he needed.

Today's interview was probably a bust. After the reprimand at the barn this morning, he should just write off the whole day while he still could, go home, and do better tomorrow. He wouldn't let anyone down by retreating. *Except myself.* With a heavy sigh, he scrubbed his hands over his face, wiping away the crust in the corner of his eyes. He knew what he was to his friends and neighbors. A joke. He hated that. He wanted to be taken seriously with official credentials.

She takes you seriously. He bristled. Abby Whit's endorsement was hardly his end goal. He needed the rest of the town's support.

"Fancy seeing you here," a feminine voice said.

He drew up his shoulders and then his chin, preparing for an unwanted visitor. And then relaxed when his gaze met his companion. "Hi, Steph. Care to sit down?" He shut his laptop and cleared the small bistro table, putting his computer securely in the messenger bag on the third chair.

"Thanks. I didn't think it would be so crowded in here today. Especially not in the afternoon." She twisted her neck from one side to the other. "Although, I really should have." She chuckled.

The perky blonde sat in the free chair.

He scanned the packed coffee house. Every bistro table was claimed, including his in the front window next to the doorway. He selected the worst seat in the house out of necessity. Eyeing the overstuffed chairs near the fireplace, he fought the longing to move nearer the blaze. "Not many places to go around here during Spring Break."

"Unless you like snow-shoeing." She scrunched her nose. "I definitely do not."

He chuckled. "Were your ears burning this morning? I was at the ranch and learned all about your wedding day duties."

"Oh, yeah."

Her voice was oddly flat. As the town's go-to coordinator extraordinaire, Stephanie handled many major events. If this ceremony gave her pause, how far in over his head was he? "Is everything okay?"

"I'm sure it will be fine." She smoothed a strand of hair behind her ear. "Meg called me in a panic, and I agreed to help."

Meg panicked? His stomach felt heavy. "Did she explain why?"

"Ryan has a very clear vision. She wants him to be happy so she'll go along with whatever he wants. But she needs help."

And maybe an intermediary. Meg was smart and—after nearly a lifetime—she knew Ryan better than anyone else save his grandfather. If she decided to put distance between herself and Ryan's plan, she must have a good reason. Joe wouldn't be the fool to insert himself into the groomzilla's path. But he couldn't exactly turn his back on a friend either. "I'm done planning Hank's celebration. I have a few details to go over with the council." Namely, how big, how bold, and how bright the fireworks at the end of the night could be. Hank insisted on a sky as light as the day. Joe wasn't sure anyone would agree, including the FAA. "I can help you and so can Ted."

Stephanie blushed. "He already told me the same."

Of course, her boyfriend had. Although the relationship hadn't passed the year mark, Ted and Stephanie were a team. They complimented each other. Ryan and Meg's coupling was the sort of inevitable pairing that was easy to take for granted.

But witnessing Ted and Stephanie stirred up something in Joe he hadn't felt before.

Jealousy. He'd admit he wanted someone who had his back and who valued him. He didn't have the time for love but with everyone settling down, he had less time with his friends without their significant others around. He wanted someone to care about and focus on and help him through the mess he'd created.

But instead, he spent his time worrying over the person who drove him to distraction by her mere presence. What was Abby's secret? Was she genuinely as easy-going and charming as she wanted everyone to believe? Beautiful and giving and kind? She seemed too good to be true, but she'd been consistent in all three since coming to town. At what point would her pleasant façade slip, and she revealed her real self? No one was always giving to others without asking for something in return. "Can you manage a wedding? Do you have the time?"

"I'm working on the timetable at the moment but am sure—once I hand that over to Ryan—he'll have some other more elaborate to-do list to tack on. I'm stalling as long as I can." Stephanie raised her mug and sipped. "You are right. I will be busy enough this summer. I don't need to seek out more ways to occupy my time. But I won't give him the opportunity."

Joe chuckled. Stephanie was a master at managing people. The skill set served her well in both her volunteer work and her full-time job as a kindergarten teacher. She needed Ryan to be distracted.

"When does your program start?" he asked, remembering her plans to earn accreditation to move into school administration.

"Mid-May. I'll be swamped with the end of our school year and Frontier Days in addition to the Kincaid events. I'm dreading May. But by mid-June, everything will be in the rearview, and I can focus on learning. Studying will be a relief." She smirked.

With the big events happening at the start of the summer season, Ryan wouldn't have more to focus on until the *I dos* were over. Maybe Joe could help with another distraction. If Ryan didn't have time to obsess over every tiny detail, he'd be happier. *The unclaimed land...*

Ryan had already put him off about seeking to officially lay claim to the several acre property near the church at the end of Main Street. He'd said it was a waste of time. The prime real estate would revert to the town soon as long as no one came forward with a familial claim. The Kincaids told Joe it was an expensive headache to get lawyers involved in taking ownership of the property.

Joe worried it was a ticking bomb, and no one knew the countdown to detonation. He wasn't suggesting the Kincaids add to their impressive acreage total. He hoped the land would become some sort of civic spot like a small park. An area for skateboarders or dogs would be welcome. Any use, as long as the land didn't revert to a Whittier, would be a positive for the community. With the family's history in town, a descendant would just as likely set the ground ablaze as build some sort of terrible eyesore structure. "You've given me an idea."

"A good one, I hope."

"We'll see. Sorry to run off."

She blushed. "Actually, I'm meeting Ted's sister and niece here. I'm glad I bumped into you, or I never would have found a table."

Honest to her core. That was what made Stephanie so easy to approach and befriend. Abby could learn from the younger woman. "Have a nice day." He drained the rest of his mocha, grabbed his messenger bag, and headed toward the exit.

As the county seat, Miles City boasted a more complete collection of historic materials. Both the county records and the library offered information far more thorough to what Joe had access to at home.

Herd didn't have a library until Susie Kincaid and Betty Hawke established one a few decades ago. They had donated their own historical records, dusty boxes of ledgers and journals from their ranches. But the Whittiers were excluded. What could he find in materials from a town established almost twenty years earlier?

Since he was already in town, a visit to the library wouldn't be out of the ordinary or remarked upon. Small town living meant never truly shaking off the eyeballs of his friends and neighbors, not even in the nearest city. He didn't mind. As long as he was in control of the narrative.

CHAPTER 3

Abby tucked her chin into her coat collar as she made her way down the busy street. She hated feeling like she'd answered a summons. The lawyer was working for her and not vice versa. Still, Harrison Wolff was the best around and had taken her on pro bono. She couldn't afford to offend him, or she'd bungle her future.

The drive to Miles City had been blessedly as boring as ever. She hated driving in the winter. Between pot holes, black ice, and snow blindness, she often had car trouble. Or, rather, truck trouble. Two years ago, she had invested almost everything into her food truck. Driving the huge vehicle around was great for advertising but poor for keeping a low profile.

The investment had been sound. She'd earned back her costs and then some, saving a tidy nest egg for her restaurant. A costly auto repair would eat a huge chunk of her money and set her back. Following her complicated morning, she readied for the worst.

As she turned into town, however, her luck turned around. She pulled into a large, parallel spot for two vehicles a block away from the office. She exited the cab and crossed to the pavement, avoiding the slush near the curb. Maybe she could make quick work of her summoning.

She wasn't sure she knew what she'd say to the lawyer. The more logically she approached the situation, however, she couldn't miss the chance. Strolling slowly on the sidewalk, the hairs raised on the back of her neck, and she turned her head from side to side. She had the off sensation of being watched. Glancing up and down the busy street, a few pedestrians passed on either side and cars zoomed past. But no one paid attention to her. She was being ridiculous and giving in to her guilt.

The sooner she settled this business the better. She knew what she had to do, and there was no point in backing down from it now. With her focus on her feet, she didn't look up in time to see the familiar face. Not before a hand reached out and grabbed her elbow. She turned and shot her knee straight up into the offender. "Joe?" She covered her mouth with both hands.

Joe hunched forward, groaning.

She felt bad. Joe didn't like her. Kneeing him in the groin wasn't likely to earn her his friendship. She'd tried so many times for something warmer than his cool disdain. Now she'd caused him physical pain, proving he was right to keep distance.

And yet, she was proud of her natural instinct for self-preservation. She wouldn't apologize for defending herself. He couldn't just grab a woman on the street. He had no right to touch another person without permission. "What are you doing here?"

"Trying to save you from getting splashed by that truck." Straightening, he pointed to the street.

She dragged her gaze to follow his direction and spotted the pick-up barreling down the road. "Oh, I didn't notice." Stepping toward the storefronts, she tugged her knit hat low over her burning ears.

"Clearly." He dragged in a breath and frowned. "What are you doing here?"

She could ask him to answer her since she asked first, but she wouldn't. She wasn't rude even if the man always suspicious of her never gave her cause for being polite in return. Neither would she give herself away. She found her resolve in the face of his harsh niceties. "A little of this, and a little of that. What about you?"

"I had an interview." He bit the words tersely. "I'm stopping by the library."

"Of course. How's your book coming?" She knew asking would irritate him. But needling him wasn't her motivation. She was genuinely curious about his project. During her research into her family tree, she often bumped into him at the library in town and always asked about his work. He was a passionate historian and his fervor pulled her in, piquing her curiosity. She supposed that made her a moth flying straight into a bug zapper.

"It's fine. I'd rather wondered if maybe you had an interview in Miles City."

She widened her eyes. "Me? For what?" She wasn't working on a book. Why would she be at an interview?

He shrugged. "A job. You're talented. You should be a head chef in a big city."

None of his compliments sounded positive. He had a way of delivering *hello* like an accusation. He would've been great during the inquisition of centuries gone by. "I've done the urban center guidebook rated top marked restaurant thing before. I wanted something else. Besides, I've got more business than ever with the events at the ranch, what would they do without me?" She forced a chuckle.

She meant the words light heartedly, but deep down she was worried. She needed the town a whole lot more than anyone needed her. If she showed weakness to the one person always looking for it, however, she'd be kicked to the curb. "Why aren't you a professor of history somewhere? You definitely love research. You could easily be on a university campus. Wouldn't your talent be better served with more history to uncover than in middle school in Herd?"

"It would."

She rolled her eyes. He didn't have a shred of self-deprecation. Why would she expect anything less of the man with the biggest ego around for hundreds of miles.

"I work hard to inspire the kids. We live in a place where it doesn't seem like there are a lot of opportunities for academics. These kids need me."

He wasn't wrong about any of it. And she wouldn't question him further. She was just annoyed that he was constantly finding flaws in her very similar argument. She wanted one meeting where she wasn't knocked off balance. He showed her his annoyance with her presence at every turn. And she stood there smiling like a fool every time.

He lifted his arms, glanced at his sleeve, and dropped the limb. "Look at the time I have to go."

She nodded like he hadn't just pretended to look at a nonexistent watch as an excuse to be rid of her. But at least he was leaving before he could see where she was headed. "Of course I'll see you back in our town."

He tensed, tilted his head, and strode past her.

She counted to five before continuing on her way. She wouldn't turn around to see if he followed her progress. The skin-crawling sensation of being watched was gone. She didn't need visual confirmation he disappeared. Neither could she shake off the grin that hadn't reached his eyes.

She continued to her destination, entering through a communal lobby, and pulling open the door to the lawyer's office. She checked in with the receptionist and sat in one of the tapestry-covered side chairs in the waiting room. Tucking her ankles under the chair, she focused on her breathing, drawing upon her short-lived tenure in the meditation class led by Stephanie.

Harrison Wolff hadn't become the best without playing a few mind games with everyone who bumped into him along his path, including his clients.

She glanced up at the slogan displayed prominently near a muted TV. "Need justice? Trust a Wolff," she murmured.

When researching who could help her, she only had two options. A lawyer with a wide range of expertise in property and estate law. Or an ambulance chaser. While she didn't love Harrison's slogan, it was better than his competitor's catchphrase: *Want justice? Give them the Brass (knuckles).*

After one morning of watching TV, she had decided to go with the former. Over the past six months, however, she learned more about Harrison. Her association with him made her almost as uneasy as their business together.

He had moved to Miles City from Herd and graduated high school in same class as Ryan Kincaid. She'd learned he fancied himself a rival. From him. She'd never heard either Kincaid mention Harrison's name.

But Harrison always circled back to Herd's first family, slinging mud with petty comments. Nothing she could call out. He was too savvy for that. His pro bono help also advised her to bite her tongue. She couldn't afford his legal fees on her own. One internet search informed her of the exorbitant cost of the over-inflated ego.

"Ah, Abby Whittier. Good to see you," a deep voice boomed.

She drew her shoulders to her ears, shrinking like a turtle in a shell as she turned.

With arms outstretched, Harrison approached in his tailored, navy-blue, three-piece suit. "Come on back. Let's get the paperwork settled."

Abby stood, tucking her icy hands into the pockets of her puffy coat. In her salt-stained boots, knit hat and scarf, jeans, and t-shirt, she felt shabby next to the lawyer. She followed dutifully behind him.

He opened his office door and waved her ahead.

On the double-sided walnut desk, paperwork was fanned across with flags marking spots for her signature. "Wow. This is it?" she asked, slightly breathless at the somewhat underwhelming moment. Changing her future and the shape of town as her neighbors and friends knew it should have some sort of trumpet blast heralding the occasion, not a few scratches of a pen on a sheet of paper in an unremarkable office building an hour away.

"Yes, this is it." Harrison boomed. He strode around the desk, pulled out his chair, and sat. Rifling through the top drawer, he reached for a pen and handed it over. "Just a few signatures and you get to take back your land from the Kincaids."

She didn't like the gleeful gleam in Harrison's eye. With a frown, she accepted the pen and pulled out the chair opposite him. She stared, unseeing, at the papers. "I'm not taking anything away from the Kincaids. I'm reclaiming land from the town that is undeveloped. This shouldn't impact anyone."

He scoffed. "The Kincaids are the town. It's one and the same."

She didn't correct Harrison. She hated the comment. She loved Herd and didn't want to ruin anything.

Instead, she grabbed the documents and read, dragging her index finger along the left margin, and tracking every line. She reached the middle of the first page when Harrison interrupted her.

"Oh, now you don't trust me?" He chuckled, low and deep.

His amusement scalded her skin like she grabbed a tray out of the oven without a mitt. She'd always been a slow reader, needing time to digest and absorb every word. She wanted to argue that no matter her opinion of him, she would read every line before signing.

But she met his gaze and froze. Her good girl instincts activated and insisted she quiet down and not agitate anyone by advocating for herself. She uncapped the pen and flipped ahead to the last page, writing her loopy, full signature.

In this instance, she knew that her goals aligned with the lawyer. She wanted a chance to reclaim her good name and redeem her family history. No one in town knew what had happened after Hoss was kicked out of town and exiled from his family. How he devoted his life to God, becoming a pastor in Minnesota, raising a family, and earning the respect of every community he preached in. He worked hard for redemption. In her small corner of the world, she wanted to broaden the narrow understanding of history. "You'll keep my claim anonymous?"

"At the start. But the truth will come out sooner than you might want."

She nodded, swallowing the lump in her throat. *It always does.*

At the library, Joe struggled with focusing on the text in front of him. Research grounded him. Usually. Joe couldn't quite shake off the dull ache after Abby's self-defense demonstration. It wasn't just the physical discomfort from her surprisingly strong reflexes. For that pain, he was mad at himself.

Joe deserved to be kneed. He should never have grabbed her. He wasn't even sure why he had. What did he care if someone he didn't like was splashed by a sloppy, slushy puddle?

But he had.

While he'd been minding his own business striding to the library, he suddenly sensed a shift. The air changed around him, and he caught the faint hint of her intoxicating, no nonsense bar soap and butter scent. He paused on the sidewalk and studied his surroundings. Then he spotted her.

He didn't want to. He would love to not notice her or how she had kind eyes that studied him with too much clarity. But he couldn't seem to block her from his consciousness, no matter how hard he tried. And she hadn't said thank you for his concern.

Why was she all the way over in Miles City? His love of story took the form of filling in the blanks, often where none existed. He knew it was a bad habit. But he couldn't stop himself from inferring an entire back story based off of one clue. The problem with her, however, was that he had never rationalized her presence with a history. She came to town, fully formed, in the middle of the action.

His questions had been delivered from a place of frustrated honesty. She could go anywhere. He wished she would. *Then I won't have someone to project all my imposter syndrome feelings onto.*

While he had been observing her, he felt the deep rumble before he saw the truck. In slow motion, he reached for her and pulled her back. In the end, the truck driver spotted the pothole at the last moment and swerved. For his troubles, he'd been kneed hard. And she hadn't really apologized. No good deed went unpunished.

His valiant efforts had once again been in vain as far as she was concerned. He'd been so annoyed with himself that he forgot why he was studying her so intently. Since childhood, the public library welcomed him like an oasis. He'd always been warmed from body to soul by stepping inside, no matter the location. The hushed tones, the smell of musty books, and the ambient light of research table lamps and overhead fixtures, was a warm welcome. As a kid, he stopped in for books every week. He struggled to read, wanting to be a good reader but taking his time to make sense of each sentence. He wasn't content to memorize and throw a fact away. He wanted knowledge and operated at a slower pace because he wanted to retain every single word.

He began to read faster in college, because he had to. And he found the more he read the better he read. But he still wanted to be as smart as everybody thought he was. Many days he felt like a fraud.

And somehow, with her thoughtful questions, she saw through him. *What if my best isn't good enough?* His greatest fear laughed at him, taunting him every time he extolled to his students the ethos their best was more than he needed. He longed to believe it; a twisted version of fake it till you make it.

Exposing her secret before she could learn his, grew in importance with every passing day. She almost tripped him up today with her smile and questions. He was put off by the sense she wasn't upfront.

Why did he care? He wanted to stop thinking about her with a fervent desperation. He couldn't shake the unnerving sense she hid a huge secret. But what? And why did she seem almost surprised by his logical train of thought that she was interviewing for a full-time job?

Her truck was mostly closed during the winter. She helped the Rabbitts in their kitchen. What else did she do?

He couldn't waste more time caring. He had too much to do on his limited time off school. After spring break, he was on a collision course with the end of the school year. Projects and testing would dominate his days. He pulled out his headphones and queued the recording on his phone. He'd make another attempt to transcribe the day's interview, once again a third hand recount of the epic fallout between the Whittiers and the Kincaids.

Taking a deep breath, he inhaled the scent of paper and dust unique and universal to every library he'd ever entered. He slowed his racing pulse and hit play. His fingers worked almost independently of his mind, quickly dashing across the keyboard. Words appeared as if by magic, from his ears to his eyes.

After fifteen minutes, however, he stopped typing. He paused the recording and rubbed his weary eyes. He'd lost track of the interview and begun to channel his inner dialogue onto the page.

Why didn't the Whittiers sell the parcel in town? Why didn't the entire family leave? Where are their descendants?

Leaning back in his chair, Joe folded his arms over his chest. He couldn't shake the nagging inner voice that had grown from a whisper to a shout. Some big piece of the puzzle was missing and left the town vulnerable.

What happened after Hoss left? His research had turned up nothing. Struggling against his demons, he'd probably lost the battle. But what if he hadn't? Where was his family? Would they come back to Herd and demand payback?

Ryan had advised Joe not to get involved and not to worry about the unclaimed land. But Joe hated a loose end. What happened if a Whittier came back and snatched up the plot and built some awful high-rise or something equally obscene. Then the landscape of the quaint town was changed forever and once again a Whittier was to blame.

Ryan was too busy building his empire and planning his wedding. Joe didn't blame him for not wanting to take on one more task. But what was stopping Joe from taking up the mantle?

On his laptop, he pulled up the website for Tom Brass. The flashy lawsuit lawyer wasn't his first choice, but he was the only option. The more reputable attorney-at-law, Harrison Wolff, considered himself Ryan's high school rival, and Harrison never shook off his second-place attitude. On several occasions, he had returned to town, strutting like a peacock with a snide remark and seeking to somehow dethrone the man that single-handedly brought about an economic recovery. He hadn't been received well at the high school reunion, and he had left just as quickly as he had arrived.

Joe dialed the number and held the phone to his ear. The line rang and rang. Was this a mistake? Probably.

"Tom Brass speaking," a gruff voice answered.

"Hello, Mr. Brass, I had a question about property," Joe murmured. "Can you handle ugh..." Joe scrambled to make sense of his thoughts. How could he say this over the phone without sounding like a fool and a complete waste of time? "Do you handle real estate closings and such?"

"I can when I need to. But mostly that's Harrison Wolff's territory."

"What if there's a potential for a lawsuit?" Joe asked.

"Are you talking about bringing about a lawsuit or preparing to be sued?"

That was a good question, and Joe had no idea. The spur of the moment call was a mistake and each passing second made the error more glaring. For the sake of the other patrons and his own self-preservation, he should hang up.

"Because Harrison Wolff is still the man to talk to about property. Of course, if this has to do with his big case moving forward."

That piqued Joe's interest. "What big case?" He already sounded like an idiot. He wasn't sure he should push his luck that much further. But he had nothing to lose.

"Some unclaimed land."

"In Herd?"

Tom grunted. "Listen I can't talk about a colleague's business over the phone. Should we make an appointment? This could be pretty interesting. Haven't gone head-to-head with Harrison in a while. I'd enjoy it."

Joe shuddered. He wouldn't. "I'll give you a call back if I move forward. Thank you for your time." He ended the call and flipped the phone screen-down on the library table. The loud clatter echoed in the cavernous space.

Had he opened a major can of worms? Was his curiosity about to spell his doom? Was his imagination getting out of hand? Or was something bigger at play?

What were the odds the lawyer mentioned another, distant plot of land in the state of Montana? It was a big state. Tom hadn't disputed or confirmed the location.

What would a legal battle against Harrison Wolff look like? Probably protracted and expensive. No matter if Joe started the suit, he knew the Kincaids wouldn't leave him on his own—no matter how foolhardy the decision to pursue.

If they did nothing, what happened to downtown? He'd urged Ryan to purchase the land on behalf of the town, to be proactive. Ryan hadn't seen the need, preferring to wait until the end of the claim.

How would the return of a Whittier—a family that would have no warm feelings for the community—change the town? He couldn't shake the uneasy feeling his powers of deduction had been too late and definitely too little.

CHAPTER 4

If Abby had learned anything during her time in Montana, she had reached a new appreciation for the beauty of nature. Strolling down Main, she admired the brilliance of the wide-open sky on a sunny day. The blue overhead was almost cobalt, a rich shade that somehow warmed her despite the cold air. The colorful facades of the false front buildings on one side of the street shone.

Would she be able to help the town with its efforts of being a year-round destination? Without mountains, Herd couldn't lure snowboarders. A few intrepid souls had attempted to snowshoe and cross-country ski around the Kincaid ranch once but needed rescue by Ted after mistaking part of the creek for solid ground.

She wasn't sure one restaurant would be enough, but it would be a start. And her contribution to town would make her proud. As long as everyone supported her, including Joe.

Replaying yesterday's encounter, she was sure he had inserted a dig somewhere into their conversation. With the rest of her day devoted to tying herself up into knots about the decision to file her claim, she chose to reflect on the positive of the encounter. He pulled her back from a very soggy fate.

If he didn't care about her, even a little bit, he wouldn't have touched her. Maybe she was making inroads with him after all this time. Which would be great.

Because she needed as many friends as she could find.

After signing all the documents, she insisted on a promise Harrison would keep her name anonymous as the proceedings started. She couldn't hide forever, although she'd done a pretty good job of concealing her identity for the past couple years. She wanted to broach the subject on her own terms, first with the Kincaids and then with her other friends in town. She'd been supported and wanted to continue to keep everyone's goodwill.

At the General Store, she blinked, doing a double take at the crowded room.

The occupancy wasn't quite *standing room only please take a number*, but she stood in line behind another customer at the coffee counter. For the typically sparsely occupied store, any amount of time in a queue was remarkable. The weather hadn't warmed up enough to lure tourists to town. Every head she spotted she recognized, if not by name at least in passing.

She scanned the seating area along the back of the building, past the bakery case and souvenirs for sale. The four booths and six bistro tables were all claimed. The General Store was the nearest thing to a coffee shop and bakery. Their biggest selling food item was their homemade fudge. In summer months, Will Buck, owner, used a marble topped table to work the Wolff 's chocolate into a delectable treat in view of tourists. The rich smell was often enough to drive traffic into the building.

Besides a few muffins and coffee, and the occasional special-order cake, Will didn't sell a meal. So why was the room full? Spring break alone couldn't account for the buzz in the room.

The customer in front of her paid and left the line.

Abby stepped up to the counter.

"Good morning, Abby. Can I make you a Chai latte?" Will greeted with his typical broad grin.

"Hi, yes, please." The coffee shop owner knew her order by heart. Familiarity was one of the perks of small-town living and warmed her from the inside out. She opened her purse and pulled out her wallet. "What's up with the crowd? You giving coffee away this morning?"

He chuckled as he rang up her purchase. "Hardly. We've got other big news in town. It's unverified so maybe I shouldn't say anything."

The hairs on her neck raised. "Is it gossip?"

"I don't think so." He handed over her change. He moved to the gleaming espresso machine and started preparing her drink, heating the milk. "If it is, it's not much to go on," he said, loudly. "And you should know. It affects you most of all."

Her stomach dropped. Oh no. Harrison filed but hadn't kept her name concealed for the time being? "What do you mean?" she asked, her voice cracking.

He finished her drink, secured a lid on top, and slid the paper cup into a cardboard sleeve. "The unclaimed land by the church has an owner. Some Whittier descendant is back and stirring up trouble. You'll be kicked off the spot, I'm sorry to say."

"I will?" She accepted the hot beverage with shaky hands. Raising the cup to her mouth, she blew into the steaming spout. At least she had reason to look concerned with the drink in her grip.

"I haven't heard any details. But the Whittiers were always combative. Get yourself ready for a fight."

"Do you know the family?" She frowned. "I thought they'd been kicked out like a hundred years ago."

He shook his head. "They were. Let's just say they left a lasting impression."

She shuddered. She knew what she'd been up against. Changing an entire community's perception of the past was a tall order. But she'd always had hope. The neighbors she'd gotten to know—Will included—had been so kind and welcoming. Surely, they wouldn't hold onto prejudices that should have died several generations earlier? "Thanks for the heads up."

He nodded.

With one last glance at the full seating area, she decided her next step. She needed to check with Ian on the progress of her new smoker. The town's blacksmith had been a professional welder for years. He had lucked into a job tapping into his hobby of old-fashioned metalwork. She had a destination and a purpose. So why did every step feel like she beat a hasty retreat?

Following the scent of burning metal, she blew into her drink and strode down the covered, raised, wooden walkway. Under the awning that protected this side of the street from the elements, she felt exposed. If she glanced to her left, she'd spot the stone edifices marking her ancestor's ultimate fall from grace. The elegance mocked her.

She couldn't stop her plan now. She had no choice but to move forward. She'd meet with an architect in a few weeks to discuss how to build on her property. At the end of the street, she jogged through the intersection toward the blacksmith shop.

The clanging of metal on metal punctuated the air as a wave of warm air filtered out from the open doorway. The dirty smell of burning fuel mixed with the earthy aroma of hot iron.

She entered and knocked on the door, banging loudly.

Ian pounded the red-hot iron and dropped it in a bucket of water. Steam rose. He slipped his protective mask up and waved. "Hey, Abby. Come on in."

She stomped her feet on the mat outside, stepping over the threshold. With a few seconds in the toasty room, she relaxed.

The building had been built as a replica of the original. Ian hadn't changed dirt floor with anything permanent. He'd been talking about laying a brick floor. If she helped, could she still count on him as a friend?

She couldn't do little chores or pay for upgrades for everyone in town, or she'd be broke in a day. Bribery wasn't an effective way for building meaningful relationships. "What are you working on?"

"Well, maybe nothing. I came up with a couple of brands for the bison."

She widened her eyes. "Does Ryan want to mark them?"

Ian shrugged. "I don't know. He's still thinking about how to best keep track of managing the herd. I'll admit, I'm a bit skeptical."

"You are?"

"Sure. The Kincaids have plenty of land for the animals to roam. But that doesn't mean the bison will stick to the ranch."

Abby crossed her arms over her chest. "The Kincaid ranch is partially fenced. Ted does a good job of maintaining the barriers."

"How well can you explain the rules to wild beasts?" Ian snorted. "If an animal that big and strong decides to break down a split rail fence, the wooden posts have no chance against it. I don't want to find myself in a stand-off trying to get in or out of my store."

Had he shared his doubts with others in town? She never questioned any of the decisions Ryan and Hank made. Of course, what they enacted wasn't restricted to their kingdom alone. Consequences could be felt far beyond the borders of their ranch. She was living proof. While she hadn't stepped foot in Herd until adulthood, she'd been shaped by her ancestor's exile. Since Hoss had been kicked out, the Whittiers never stayed in one place for too long. "It's not just a split rail fence," she said. "Ted installed a tall square wire fence along the closest section to town. And besides, I don't think they'll be a disruption. What would buffalo want with town? It's full of people."

"And food."

"I thought bison eat grass?"

Ian shrugged.

If Ian was set on his opinion, she couldn't dissuade him. Still, she had to try. "Won't the noise be a discouragement? Loud voices? Trucks?"

He shook his head. "Let's hope so. The best-case scenario is once they get settled to our community quickly."

She nodded. Maybe she should work the angle of the new animal arrivals and redirect everyone's attention and energy off her claim. But that felt disloyal and she added shame to her list of the day's woes.

"Did you hear about the land? Can't believe a Whittier is coming back to claim the last scraps." He whistled.

"Scraps?" Heat crept up her neck and burned her cheeks. She'd been proud of her location in town. While the sidewalk didn't extend to include the spot, she had high hopes of being able to encourage the development with time. In the summer, she often had a line around the cemetery. But her property was the leftovers? The assessment stung.

"Sure, hope this won't hurt your business. That would be a shame. But really, what would you expect?"

"Well, I don't know what to think." Her voice cracked. She dried her clammy palms on her jeans one at a time and sipped her tea. She needed another angle with this ally. He prided himself on being a free-thinker. Why conform? "I'm surprised you have that opinion. You're a transplant too. Have you been totally indoctrinated in the town's old beliefs?"

"Good point, maybe I have been guilty of falling into line too much. I'd better do something reckless soon, or I'll get a good reputation," he said. "The smoker is ready to go. Just let me know where to drop it off."

"Until I get an eviction, I'm keeping my truck where it is." She lifted her chin.

He smiled and nodded. "Sounds good."

It sounded fake. She was pretending to be brave against some unknown foe. When, in reality, she was up against herself. Her own worst enemy? Yep, that fit.

Joe held the legal pad full of questions and concerns he'd heard around town about the bison. The herd wasn't due for another month, but he liked to stay ahead of a problem, especially when he had the time to do so. With the week off from both of his jobs, he leaned into his other projects. He'd met with frustration about his progress for his history of the area.

He wanted a new angle. Every interview only reinforced long held beliefs. The oral history had turned more into a recounting of local legend than illuminating town tales. After his frustrating day at the Miles City library, finding nothing of importance for his project in the census records, and leaving with an unshakeable sense of doom about the call with personal injury attorney Tom Brass, he was almost glad to think out worst case scenarios and anticipate questions about wildlife.

He jogged across the gravel drive and climbed the front steps of the ranch house. Every time he approached the house, he marveled at the strength and beauty in the old construction The solid stone foundation held the timber frame of the two-story home. A low hanging roof covered the wraparound porch.

The house rose from the land rather than fighting for attention.

Lifting a fist, he knocked on the door.

"Come in," Hank's deep voice called.

Frowning, Joe twisted the knob and stepped inside. The Kincaids spent most of their time too busy to monitor the comings and goings at the ranch house. Had they waited for him with bad news? His stomach clenched. "Hello?"

"We're all over here in the war room," Hank called.

War room? Joe shut the door and wiped his boots on the bristle mat inside before slipping off the slush covered footwear. In his socks, he slid over the slate tiles, passing the staircase and heading into the front room.

With a large couch facing the fireplace and a pair of wing-back chairs in the window overlooking the front yard, the room hadn't been transformed into the make-shift lobby for the summer season yet. At the moment, it was still a comfortable family living space.

Ryan leaned against the fireplace, glowering.

Ted stood perfectly ramrod straight on the other side.

Hank turned around on the couch, Colby the black and white mutt at his side. "Come on, Joe. We need all hands-on deck."

Joe gulped. Was he on trial? He'd only meant to give an update on the rumblings he heard around the saloon and school. He hadn't intended to alarm anyone. "You didn't have to go to so much trouble for me. I didn't make photo copies. I thought we'd keep this causal."

"Huh?" Ryan asked.

Ted shook his head.

"Hard to keep it casual when the whole fate of the town is at stake but come in and sit down," Hank said, smoothly, ever the statesman.

Joe approached the group, standing near one corner of the couch.

"If you want to tell me you told me so, you're out of luck," Ryan said.

"About what?" Joe asked, meeting Ted and Hank's serious expressions.

"You haven't heard?" Hank asked. "A claimant has come forward for the Whittier land in town near the church. You told us to get it handled. You were right."

"We'd almost run out the clock, too," Ryan said.

A shiver tickled Joe's spine as a pair of thoughts emerged simultaneously. He'd guessed the cryptic warning from Tom Brass was about the land. Was this the secret Abby hid? He had no reason to jump to the second conclusion except his own ever-present feeling something was off about her.

He'd bumped into her downtown. She could have been on her way to Harrison Wolff's office. He hadn't spared her a glance after he'd righted her. He wanted her out of sight out of mind.

If only that actually worked, he'd be better off. "Harrison Wolff is involved?"

Ted nodded.

Joe really didn't like Harrison, always flashing his fancy cars and nice clothes, displaying his perceived superiority to those he left behind. To Joe, the man's attempts were sad. No one seemed to care about the high school popularity besides the attorney. Everyone else had grown up.

"That's about all we know at the moment. The heir is keeping their anonymity for the time being. Can't imagine what will happen once they are officially announced," Ryan said.

"Do you think it's someone in town? Someone we know?" Joe asked.

"Why else would the person insist on not being named? Why would we care about someone we don't know?" Ryan added.

Joe considered that. With the last name Whittier, everyone in town would have their opinion pre-determined. "I doubt that. If it's someone in town, why wait all this time?"

By that logic, I can rule out Abby. She'd been in town for years. He breathed a little easier. While he couldn't shake an uneasiness about her, he didn't want her to be so duplicitous. He wanted her secret to be inconsequential like she was a secret millionaire living in town to bestow money onto unsuspecting good Samaritans. Not that he'd ever had any such hint. He didn't want her secret to bring her downfall.

"What do you need from me? How can I help?" Joe asked. He'd keep the news about reaching out to Tom Brass to himself. Luckily, he hadn't divulged any identifying information besides his phone number.

"We don't have time. I'm frustrated. I was warned. You were right to do that but I still don't think it would have been worth the cost. Guess we'll have to wait and see," Ryan said. He hunched forward, looking defeated.

Joe had never seen him less than absolutely certain. In good times and bad, Ryan held himself with a stoicism and seriousness fitting for his role as the head of a major business.

"I worry about Abby," Hank said.

"Abby? Why?" Joe tipped his head to the side.

"She'll be kicked off the land she parks her truck on. We'll have to see if we can give her more space out here to help make up for her lost revenue," Hank replied.

A pang of guilt burned him. Joe looked away. If he hadn't dissuaded Ryan from an idea to build a restaurant for Abby, he wouldn't be complicit in pushing her out of town. He knew she wasn't telling him—or the community—everything. But he had a heart. He didn't want her ruined and destitute to prove a point.

"I wonder if I can convince the new owner to put in a pickle ball court," Hank said, stroking his chin.

"Pickle ball?" Joe asked.

"It's the hot new sport everywhere but here. I had my eye on campaigning to the city council to develop a court," Hank said.

Ryan snorted and rolled his eyes.

"Maybe I'd be better off discussing it with the new owner. Since some members of the community are set against getting with the times," Hank added.

Colby whined and laid her head in Hank's lap.

"She hates it when I'm unhappy," Hank said, petting the dog's belly in long strokes. "I am worried about Abby, pickle ball or no."

"The events might help her out," Ted said. "We'll have plenty of catering jobs if the bookings sell well."

"Speaking of," Ryan said. "I have to head to a meeting with a vendor for the wedding. Are those the notes about the complaints in town?"

Oh, right. The reason for his visit. His succinct plan felt silly in light of the news. He'd spent hours thinking of problems only to be dumbfounded by a real issue. Joe held up the legal pad. "Yep, more concerns than anything. We can't anticipate the problems, can we?"

Hank snorted.

"Thanks, Joe." Ryan stepped forward and grabbed the legal pad.

Ted nodded and followed his boss.

As the pair left the room, Joe considered the new information. Would the descendant provide the direction he needed for the book? If he could meet the person, he had plenty of questions. Perhaps he'd finally get the answers—and a direction—he needed.

"What's wrong?" Hank asked.

"Just feeling a little off-balance," Joe said. "Guess I'm not sure how to take any of that news."

"Agreed. All I know is, I won't join the mob that is forming in town. Whoever it is, I won't make them an enemy before learning the motive and goal. The whole thing could be overblown with fearmongering," Hank said.

Joe wanted to agree. Too many odd occurrences aligned recently to tie everything together as the result of coincidence alone. "Do you really think we know the person?"

"I'm not the one who solves the mystery's around here."

"I was a kid detective," Joe said. Had Hank been paying attention every time he claimed his former hobby?

Hank huffed. "Coulda used you when Ryan and Meg were young. Can't tell you how many pies were stolen, and no one was ever brought to justice. The only time those two ever worked together was to steal my dessert."

"And you're sure you want to move forward with their wedding?"

Hank grinned. "Oh, yes. They can't walk off with a multi-tier wedding cake. I'll have the photographer guard it until they cut it at least."

Joe lifted the corner of his mouth in the closest approximation of a smile he could manage.

"Let's get coffee in the kitchen. You have time for my interview today, right?" Hank asked.

"Yes, sir. I blocked off the whole morning."

Hank pushed off the couch. Colby nimbly jumped to the ground at his side. "Good girl, Colby." Hank smiled at the dog. The pair ambled around the couch.

Joe followed. Was the obvious answer, right? Or was he doubling down on his prejudice against her? Was Abby tied into the whole mess and in a bigger way than losing her spot in town?

If she was the descendant, she'd definitely want to tell her side of the story. But why hadn't she made her claim years ago? He couldn't ignore that he'd bumped into her in Miles City. He never paid attention to Harrison Wolff's business address and for all he knew, she had been in the neighboring city for an innocent reason.

He'd focus on what he could control. His interviews and his work with the town council regarding the bison. He'd deal with people later. Or better, never.

CHAPTER 5

Abby frowned at her rudimentary sketch. Her artistic skills and penmanship remained subpar even when she applied her best effort. At least she could afford to hire an architect because no one would be able to make sense of her work.

Sitting on the hard oak chair on the library's second floor, she shifted but found no comfort. Worry caused her physical pain she couldn't escape no matter her position. After meeting with Ian, she was left more uncertain than ever. Her instinct was to head home and hide out. Her truck was closed today. No one expected her anywhere. She could spend the rest of the day under the covers in her bed, cozy and snug and pretending her life wasn't on the verge of implosion.

While she wasn't particularly passive aggressive, she avoided conflict with every ounce of her soul. Throughout her life, she'd been insulted and snubbed, but she never rose fought back.

Maybe that's why she'd done so well being partnered with Joe for so long.

She sniggered and glanced about the empty space. Instead of retreat, she sought sanctuary. Only after she'd climbed the spiral staircase to the second floor had she realized she headed to the ultimate site of her undoing. If she was spotted in the genealogy section, would someone put the pieces together? If she wasn't in town, would anyone notice and question why she was avoiding her neighbors?

Understanding her current state of paranoia didn't alleviate the fears. Her claim was progressing as she'd been told. No one suspected her. She'd spent too long daydreaming—with the help of the library's collection of interior design magazines—about her new building.

She was going forward. She was putting down roots with a property she could live and work on. Some of her friends would still believe in her and understand her motivation. She just needed a plan to deliver the news with care.

Heavy footfalls echoed off the metal risers.

She turned toward the staircase and spotted Joe.

Warmth spread through her from head to toe. Maybe this was a sign. She had the overwhelming urge to tell him everything. Since he already judged her, he'd be the easiest person to confess to. She couldn't go any lower in his opinion.

Joe turned and spotted her, waving a hand. "Oh, hi. I didn't realize anyone else was here."

"Yep, just me, don't worry," she said. *No one that matters to you.*

"Did you hear the news?" he asked.

She stiffened and glanced over her shoulder. The second floor was empty. He was pursuing a conversation with her. His tone was warm and genuine. She held a hand against her churning stomach. A total change in character didn't happen overnight. Unless he'd had a dire news-inspired epiphany.

With his shoulders back and his chin lifted, he strutted toward her. The smoothness of his gait shouldn't be possible with heavy outerwear. As winter lingered, she moved slower, trudging through her days in worn snow boots and puffy coats. *Stop staring. He asked a question.* "I'm sorry. News? What's going on?"

He dropped his messenger bag at the table next to hers and leaned against the top. "Apparently, some Whittier is coming back to town. You'll have to find a new place for your truck."

She stared. If she didn't know any better, she'd assume a certain level of friendliness in the warning. For once, he delivered a sentence to her that didn't drip with condescension or suspicion. How did she respond?

"I already spoke to the Kincaids," he continued.

Her jaw dropped. She was stunned into silence. He brought up her welfare to the Kincaids? He spoke on her behalf? She couldn't feel her face. The muscles in her jaw and tongue were frozen liked she'd been injected with anesthetic.

"I was up there about something else." He shrugged. "They mentioned letting you park on the ranch more often. Right now, their offer wouldn't be very helpful. Over the summer, you'd have a steady stream of business."

"That's really nice of them," she murmured. And so typical. Ryan and Hank were kind. If she was lucky, the animosity between their ancestors hadn't carried over to the present.

Joe had no longstanding roots in town, but he carried the torch against the Whittiers like so many others. He was practically the leader of the movement, stoking and recording beefs for posterity. Joe's project would ensure no one ever forgot the Whittiers were the bad guys. Once Joe knew the truth, she feared he'd regret his moment of kindness.

"I heard some talk." She wouldn't compound her sins by pretending to have learned the information today.

Joe crossed his arms over his chest and stared.

She broke away first. She had to act normal. But how when he was behaving so unusually? His steady gaze unsettled her. He looked like he wanted to speak. She longed to get out of his way. "Why were you up at the ranch? A meeting about the celebrations?"

"No, just reviewing a few concerns about the bison."

"Oh, right." She almost sighed. "You'll have your hands full. I don't think everyone is on board with the latest plan. I've heard concerns about the town being overrun by the animals. I know it's highly unlikely to happen. I tried to defend the plan."

"While I appreciate your help, I can promise you I have every-thing well in hand." He tipped his head to the side. "Why are you changing the subject? Don't you want to get your future settled? Aren't you more worried about what will happen to you?"

"Am I changing the subject?" she asked, her voice squeaking. She cleared her throat. "I guess I don't want to anticipate prob-lems. I'll deal with it when it comes. The thing that comes out of worrying is stress."

"Is that your usual M.O.?"

Why do you care? She shrugged. "More my family's motto."

"Where did you grow up?"

With a shaky hand, she tucked a strand of hair behind her ear. She forced a laugh. "Are you actually interested? I thought I was far off your radar for your project."

"Everyone has a story."

Unfortunately, she had quite a history to tell. Not regarding her immediate family. Growing up as a military brat, with her family in the armed services as far back as anyone could remember, she learned not to let herself get overwhelmed about tomorrow. Because the future inevitably meant change.

She both lived for and loathed the chaos of uprooting her life. As an adult, she finally got to make the decisions for herself. While her siblings continued in the family tradition, she had been happy to travel around from kitchen to kitchen. Until she actually went looking into the past and found Herd.

At the moment, she had nothing else to offer that would placate Joe. She wasn't sure what was standard for her anymore. She hadn't been actively deceptive over the past two and a half years. She'd pursued her standard, putting off something bad for another day, techniques, becoming an expert in delay tactics.

"Sorry, I shouldn't interrogate you." He scrubbed a hand over his face. "Old habit I guess."

"Why?"

"Excuse me?"

She gulped. She knew enough of his opinion that she didn't want actual confirmation. But some nihilistic side pushed her. If she was going down, she might as well burst into flames and leave only a pile of ash where she once stood. "Why is it your habit to treat me with open disdain?"

"I wouldn't say disdain." He flinched, breaking away from her gaze to study the floor.

At least he had the decency to show a little embarrassment. *Once he learns the truth, he'll only feel vindication.* She should stop talking while she was ahead. She gained nothing from their stand-off. "I would," she said, forcing the issue. "I've been nice. Other people like me."

He lifted a shoulder. "Do you want the truth?"

No. She swallowed the sharp metallic taste in her throat, pushing down her fears, and nodded.

"I have this sense that you're holding something back. Maybe it's just my love of story-telling. You pop up with considerable skills in the middle of nowhere. I try to fill in the blanks. For projecting onto you, I apologize. We're almost done with the party planning and then you don't have to deal with me ever again."

I don't want that. She pursed her lips and dropped her gaze to the table. She skimmed over the pile of incriminating papers strewn across. She'd had enough fight and now was flight time. She gathered her papers, clutching them to her chest and swinging her purse onto her arm. She'd never taken her coat off, the second floor boasted a legendary draft year-round. "I'll get out of your way."

She turned nearly bumped into him. He had taken a step forward and stood too close. The papers slipped from her grip.

Her cheeks burning from his nearness, she bent and grabbed the scraps of paper.

"What's this?" He reached down, grabbing a sheet off the floor. "A map?"

She widened her eyes. Why couldn't he have found her poor building layout or list of punny business names? No one would expect anything nefarious from *Home Skillet.* Why did she have the worst luck? *Because I'm a Whittier.*

He met her gaze. "It's you?!"

Joe rubbed his eyes, blinked, and then squinted. Was seeing believing? Or did he believe so he saw? In this instance, he hated being right.

Abby hadn't changed in the past few seconds. Her appearance remained the same. Her hair was still a mop of brownish reddish curls. Her green eyes flashed with a startling clarity, demanding his attention. She remained completely herself, the woman he didn't care for because of an indefinable something. The one person he couldn't stop thinking about and noticing. He felt like she should have morphed into an entirely different person. Or at least pasted on a cartoon villainesque moustache.

He wanted her to change from the person the town loved to a grotesque monster.

Because how could the woman who—he grudgingly admitted—earned the town's friendship have betrayed everyone so thoroughly? Couldn't she whip off the curls like a wig and take out the color contacts and be some other person hiding underneath? Hiding in plain sight—and lying by omission—was so much worse. "I was right?! This whole time. It was you?"

"Shh." She furrowed her brow, snatched the paper out of his hands, and scanned their surroundings.

The spiral staircase terminated in the center of the room. With shelves on the perimeter, the second floor was one large open space. There was no place to hide here.

She wanted discretion? She'd hardly earned the right to set the terms of her confrontation. But yelling and screaming wasn't his style. Luckily for her.

He pinched the bridge of his nose. Under the flare of anger, he poked at something deeper. He had spent the morning defending her and the better part of two years ignoring every sign telling him the truth. "I've felt bad about something and now you've made me sure I shouldn't."

She frowned.

They were going to build you a restaurant. You wouldn't have had to backstab anyone in the process. Try as he might, he still couldn't quite feel okay about standing in her way and stopping the Kincaids' proposed business partnership with her. Scrubbing a hand over his face, he studied the ground. He didn't want this to be her big secret. He'd grown used to her as a scapegoat but this felt too low. "I hate that you are the heir," he murmured.

A single, deep belly chortle responded.

Frowning, he looked at her. He meant what he said. It might be the most real thing he'd ever uttered in her presence. Her reaction rankled him. "I don't want you to the be villain."

"Why?" She shook her head. "You don't like me. You've never made that a secret. And I know all about secrets."

"I... I..." He had no argument. She was right.

She rolled her eyes. "It's bad manners to call you out. I'm sure you'll chalk that defect up to my questionable heritage."

She stuffed her papers into the tote bag on her arm.

Did he imagine the catch in her shallow breaths? He was wrong to treat her the way he had. But he hated that she could be throwing away everything she had worked for and the community's goodwill. She'd built something for herself out of nothing. Would she stay? Leave?

She strode forward, eyes downcast.

He reached out and touched her elbow with a light press of his fingers against her sleeve. He only felt the down of her puffy coat. It was enough.

She stopped in her tracks and glanced up at him.

He watched her thick lashes flutter. Up close, he studied her. The shiver wracking her body couldn't be hidden. Anger? Or something else? Standing inches apart was madness. "I'm sorry." The words rumbled out of him, low and soft. "It's not that I don't like you. I just felt like you weren't being honest."

"You were right." She lifted her chin and met his gaze. "I wasn't entirely truthful about who I am or why I came here."

"Now that I know the truth, I have a question. What comes next? We're almost done with the wedding and birthday planning. You won't need to worry about whether I like you or not."

Her chin trembled.

What wasn't she saying? He shouldn't push her but why hold back now? "You don't care about my opinion."

"I do. Actually. You're setting yourself to be the go-to expert on all things Herd. You want to tell your version of the town's history." She stepped away, breaking contact. "Not the truth."

"What are you talking about? You know how much work I've put into my project." He didn't want to argue. He was supposed to be taking the high road, but he couldn't. He'd defend his integrity to the end. "I've conducted years of interviews. I'm presenting the most unbiased picture I can."

She snorted. "The town remains very patriarchal. The men in charge aren't bad or wrong, but their view points are limited by their experiences."

She poured salt into the open wound of his imposter syndrome. He was not simply retelling the story of how the Kincaids won. He resented her opinion. How many in town shared her assessment? No, he wouldn't let her flawed judgement hold him back.

Joe knew history wasn't black and white. And in their community, facts were almost secondary to legend and myth. It suited the founding families to be seen as pursuing something greater through hard work, the American manifest destiny dream. But the reality was greed and backstabbing.

Establishing Herd in the early days was more a story of survival amidst constantly shifting allies. In the end, the cleverest among them won. The Kincaid family took a ranch overrun by bison and sold them off at a steep price for every head.

Ryan and Hank understood their luck and attempted to do better by truly putting community ahead of themselves. Joe wasn't sure what they would think of the book once their family's history was printed. He didn't want to hurt anyone, including Abby.

"Isn't everyone's life colored by the stories they've been told and those they tell themselves?" he asked. Hank and Ryan had been her biggest supporters, more than she knew. "The Kincaids will defend you to the end of time. I think the bigger concern is the man you've chosen to partner with."

She scrunched up her face.

"Don't be oblivious. You're being used."

"How do you figure?" she asked.

Joe swallowed the sigh building in his throat and kept his eyes steady. Expressing his annoyance wouldn't help the tense situation. Could he explain her troubles without being accused of using a condescending tone? For the sake of the town, he could. "Harrison Wolff has always been out for his best interests and to take down Ryan Kincaid."

"So? Why tell me that?" she asked.

Joe gasped. He didn't bother to shield her from that reaction. Standing on the top floor of the library, anyone could stumble onto the scene. He almost wished someone would and save him.

"How does an old grudge involve me?" she asked.

Her directness unnerved him. "You're being used."

"Maybe." She shrugged. "Even a broken clock is right twice a day."

"Meaning?"

"I'm not a fool." She readjusted the bag on her shoulder and took another few steps toward the exit.

Had he detected the tremor in her voice? She was firmly on the defense. This would be the easiest of the battles she'd face in the days to come.

"I know Harrison is a viper," she said. "For the moment, my professional interests align with my lawyer's. That's it."

Joe nodded like he understood. But he didn't. The history of Herd reflected much of the greater area. The town had been founded and shaped based on vengeance. If it was best served cold, hers was perfection. Her reveal was glacial.

"How are you going to tell the others?" he asked. He almost hated himself for the question. Her cold demeanor told him to stay away. But he couldn't. He'd been proved right at the expense of everyone he cared about. The victory was worse than hollow.

"What do you propose? What would satisfy you? Shall I pin a crimson *L* to my shirt for liar or tattoo Whittier across my forehead?"

"Will Harrison keep your identity secret? Do you trust him?"

"He's already moving forward on my behalf. What other choice do I have?"

She would experience a fierce backlash. The community was warm and welcoming of newcomers. But they'd feel stupid once the truth came out. In hindsight, they'd wonder if she was laughing at their easy acceptance of Abby Whit without questioning her. Her name wasn't even a major attempt at concealing the truth. Every good lie held at least a kernel of honesty.

Her worry and hesitation were obvious. She must have felt justified in her actions, probably even compelled. If he hadn't stopped at the restaurant, would he or anyone have ever learned the truth? And why throw a jab at him and his project? Striking first?

"Good bye, Joe." She walked away.

He didn't stop her. Her steps echoed in the quiet second floor and her descent on the staircase rang out like a clang of the church bell.

They'd had a common goal but would her ambition drive them apart? He was disappointed. With the mystery solved and the evidence presented, he just kept not believing the truth. He'd let her, or her lawyer, break the news. He wasn't going to intercede. Unless she asked for help.

CHAPTER 6

Over the next couple of weeks, Abby kept telling herself she wasn't a coward. She hated how she had behaved with Joe. He had always provoked her but his faux concern had really pushed her over the edge from civility to hostility.

Why pretend to care about her? After the run-in at the library, she'd been left shaken and scared. He had confirmed her worst fears. That everyone would hate her.

And she'd proved him right.

She wasn't sure which angered her more.

As talk settled down about the big bad Whittier in their midst, the town returned to normal. By the weekend, she hadn't heard any mention of the land she parked her food truck on. Harrison hadn't publicly named her. Neither had Joe shared her secret. The days passed without any change, leaving her in a sort of anxious lull.

As frustrated as she was with Joe, she was also grateful. He'd never liked her but hadn't sought her ruin. At least, she knew that now. She had a lot of respect for him and what he was trying to do with his book. In many ways, she was jealous. He belonged to the community in a way she might never attain. Her name would always create a distance. She was glad to know he held a sliver of the same emotion for her in return.

Her reprieve was temporary, of course. As soon as she was named, she would have nowhere to hide. In big sky country, she would be conspicuous as a skyscraper. And so she steered her food truck to her destination, doing what she should have a long time ago. Telling the truth to Hank and Ryan and letting everything else fall where it may.

The vehicle made her every movement conspicuous. For someone who'd spent so much time hiding, the truck was an unexpected choice. She'd be glad to be done with secrets. She parked her truck and scanned the surroundings for Hank or Ryan as she approached the stone and timber house. The snow had started to melt, patches of dead grass poking up through the pristine white. In other spots, mud marred the sparkly snow surface. Snow was pretty for a day and then a slushy pain for weeks.

She loved all four seasons and couldn't imagine living in a place where the change of the weather didn't provide an opportunity for a fresh start. By the start of April, she was wiped from dealing with the cold and ready for spring. The next two months, coinciding with the lead up to Hank's birthday and Ryan and Meg's wedding, promised no break, unless they fired her for her deception.

She climbed up the front steps and wiped her boots best she could on the doormat outside. The covered front porch that wrapped around the house was a welcoming spot, even on a chilly Monday morning. Fisting her mittened hand, she knocked on the door with muffled thuds.

"It's open," Hank's deep voice boomed.

She smiled and twisted the doorknob, letting herself inside. The house was rarely locked.

The Kincaids' happily welcomed visitors dropping in at all hours of the day. In a few months, the building would serve as the lobby for the resort as well. Maybe after the wedding and once Ryan started a family, they'd want more privacy from the business and their personal lives. But she doubted it.

The family was as wrapped up in their legacy as they were in their individual identities. She had only recently come to appreciate the heavy weight of that responsibility. They were the good guys in the town story thanks to a lot of hard work and sacrifice. And—if anything—the town's opinion was perhaps the heaviest weight of all. A two-ton anvil wrapped around their necks.

Shutting the door, she leaned a hand against the solid oak panel for balance as she slipped off her boots. The wood was warm against her icy palm. A nice welcome she wasn't sure she deserved. "Hello? Hank?"

"I'm in here. We all are," Hank called.

We all are? A terrifying thought. Was she about to be put on trial in front of the original tribunal? Ryan's fiancé, Meg, was the last Hawke in town. Once she married Ryan, she'd consolidate the two families into one for the rest of time. *If I have a kid that marries their kid, then the town would really belong to the Kincaids.* She shook off the thought.

Spending so much time with Joe had scrambled her heart and her brain. He disliked her and didn't pretend otherwise when confronted. She couldn't seem to stop the butterflies fluttering in her stomach with every encounter.

She tiptoed across the slate tiles toward the front room. The surface was uneven from natural flaws and over a hundred years of wear. The Kincaids lived with a permanence in direct contrast to her nomadic upbringing. They weren't leaving. None of them.

In the front room, Hank and Meg sat on the leather couch. Colby the mutt lounged on her back in between them, receiving belly rubs and chin scratches from both humans. Ryan sat on the fireplace hearth, holding a steaming mug of coffee. In the corner, Ted stood perfectly straight and silent. Usually, Abby found the stoic cowboy's presence comforting. He was steady and stalwart like an old Roman statue. Today, she was intimidated.

"Good morning," Ryan said and stood. "Can I get you a cup of coffee?"

Abby shook her head, darting her gaze wildly from person to person. "No, I don't deserve it."

"What?" Hank twisted in his seat, craning his neck until it cracked. "Girl, you don't have to earn your morning cup of ambition. It earns you."

"Are you okay?" Meg asked. "You're pale."

Ryan approached and guided her toward one of the wingback armchairs. "She's right. Sit. Catch your breath. Ted? Can you get her a water?"

Ted nodded and strode out of the room.

Abby sank into the chair's green velvet upholstery like a bag of stones dropped on the ground. Her stomach churned. Her vision clouded. Her head spun. If she didn't blurt out her news, she might be sick. She shut her eyes, scrunching her face to block out her view. "It's me."

"What's you?" Meg asked.

"Come again, girl?" Hank asked at the same moment.

Abby breathed through her nose and opened her eyes. She had to do what her family couldn't. She had to face the other families and ask for forgiveness. After Hoss had been kicked out of town, his father had left without a word. Never acknowledging the epic mistakes that had cost the town families their livelihoods and eventually came for their own. She met the frowning stares of Ryan, Meg, and Hank.

"I'm the Whittier," Abby said.

"Oh, thank goodness," Hank said and exhaled a shaky breath. "That's it? Don't scare me like that. I don't want to spend another birthday in the hospital."

"Whit? Should have seen it," Meg said, shaking her head. She flashed a smile.

"Why didn't you say anything before?" Ryan asked.

"Well..." Abby stared at the glass in her hands. She still felt nauseous, but the bile had retreated enough for her confession. They hadn't demanded she leave their land and never return. "I don't..." She sighed. She couldn't lie. Lifting her chin, she stared at them through her watery gaze. "I was scared. I know how much everyone hates my family. I wanted to see if I could claim the land or if I'd be kicked out of town the moment I set foot in city limits."

"It's been over two years, Abby." Ryan retreated to his spot on the fireplace hearth, pinching the bridge of his nose.

"I know. I shouldn't have let it go on so long. To be frank, I wasn't even sure about claiming the land at all. I might have let it lapse but then with the ranch hosting events. I need a proper kitchen to cater and it just seemed like..." Abby shook her head. Her words came out too fast and sounded accusatory. She alone would accept responsibility for her actions. "I'm sorry. I didn't think I'd love Herd as much as I do. I didn't think I'd want to stay. But the longer I'm here, the more it breaks my heart to think about leaving. I can't afford to buy land and build. But I can afford to build on land I own." Her vision blurred. She sniffed, scrunching her burning nose. "I can't apologize enough. Now that the truth is out, it's okay if you hate me."

"We don't hate you," Hank said. "I worry about what everyone in town is gonna say about your secret. We still support you. We still choose to partner with you."

Abby offered an approximation of a smile. She couldn't move her face much more or she'd loosen the tears in her eyes. She wanted to believe Hank, but he wasn't the ultimate decision maker anymore.

Ted strode into the room, his boots announcing his progress. "Who don't we hate?" he asked, twisting his neck from one direction to the other.

"Abby's the heiress we've been scared of," Meg chimed in.

"Oh." Ted strode toward her with the glass of water.

Abby gratefully accepted the token of kindness and hospitality. She took a sip, cleared the awful metallic taste out of her mouth, and swallowed.

"Everyone in this room has dealt with judgment of our neighbors at one time or another," Hank said.

"We support you," Ryan said. "You're going to need to earn back trust and goodwill. It won't be easy."

Abby nodded. Coming clean to the Kincaids was a good place to start.

"I do have a change I'd like to run past you about the wedding and birthday weekend," Ryan said.

Am I officially fired? Abby clenched her jaw, keeping the cords inside.

"We want to simplify," Meg said. "Or, at least, try to. We are moving the wedding to Friday night. Hank's birthday. No rehearsal dinner. No second event. Just one big night to remember."

"Are you all in agreement?" Abby asked.

Hank flashed a thumbs up. "I'm giving up my parade to make room in the schedule. It's the least I can do."

Ryan nodded. "Not that the change of plans will make the headcount any easier. It's still going to be an educated guess. We want to include everyone in town and any guest at the ranch who wants to join."

"Can you handle it?" Hank asked, his voice soft.

"I'll find a way. I won't let you down," Abby said. If anyone heard the tremor in her voice, they didn't react.

Instead, Ryan turned toward her and smiled. "Don't worry about the other thing. We'll do our best to help smooth over the backlash in town. Herd has a long memory. You have supporters and friends. The community will come around."

Abby nodded. She knew that well enough. She'd have a lot of apologies. As long as she stayed a step ahead of Harrison, she'd be okay. She wouldn't worry about Joe. She'd finally given him a reason to hate her, and she'd stay away.

In the teacher's lounge, Joe blew across the top of his coffee. He didn't need the drink and probably should give up caffeine in general. He hadn't enjoyed much sleep for the second half of his vacation or the few weeks back at school, but he didn't think his diet factored in.

He couldn't stop replaying the moment in the library. Finally, he had been validated. In an instant, he had understood how ridiculous his entire campaign against her had been. He had only sought acknowledgement of being right. The win was hollow at best and petty at worst. Why had he cared so much? Did he really let his ego drive him?

He sipped his coffee, not tasting the brew but only absorbing the heat. On the seat, he shifted forward but found no comfort in the soft padding.

How would the community respond? His worries shifted gear from protecting history to shielding her. He wouldn't mind eavesdropping to get a sense of what was being said in town. Since the initial announcement of the claim, he hadn't heard any a whisper. Talk about the mysterious Whittier had died down. She wasn't safe from discovery. She needed to tell the Kincaids before they found out from Harrison Wolff.

With his connection with the Kincaids, he assumed many would consider his stance against the claim a given and not even broach the subject. His known association made presenting himself as an unbiased source impossible. He would get an opportunity to take the pulse of the community tonight at the last town council meeting before the arrival of the bison herd. The gathering was meant to be a question-and-answer session for the town to present their concerns. He should have spent his free period this morning running through potential rebuttals to possible town concerns. But he couldn't stop thinking about her.

The door between the office and the lounge opened.

He straightened and turned his head. At sight of the newcomer, he slouched in his chair again. "Hi, Stephanie."

"Worried I was the principal?" She chuckled, clutching a stack of photocopies in her arms.

"A little bit," he admitted. "Mostly just worried I was needed."

"Post break blues?" She set the papers on the round table and crossed to the staff fridge, grabbing a bottle of iced coffee. She returned and pulled out the chair, uncapping her drink. "Cheer up. One standardized test is behind us. Only one to go. We're almost ready for the end of the year alphabet countdown, too."

"Something like that." He traced the edge of the particle board table. The white laminate top yellowed over the years and flaked away in sections, exposing the sharp shards underneath. "Just trying to get back in the swing with everything else on my plate."

She widened her eyes. "You and me both. Nervous about tonight? I've heard some rumblings in town."

"Really?" He leaned forward, searching her face for any hint. "About the bison or the mysterious landowner?"

"Both although I think talk has died down about the Whittier descendant. It has to, right? Hard to stay mad at a faceless, nameless entity."

Not as hard as you'd think. In his interviews, he was increasingly disappointed that the townsfolk accepted legend over fact. Abby had a war ahead of her. And he couldn't stop himself from wanting to help. She wouldn't accept his assistance. Not unless she had no one else to turn to. He feared exactly that situation becoming her reality. He didn't want to be the last person left on earth who had her back. He wanted her to choose him.

What? He took another sip of his coffee, cutting through the lump in his throat. Did he like her? He'd spent most of the past year trying to fight Hank's matchmaking. But could the old man have been right the whole time? Was he supposed to be with Abby? Did they have anything in common?

She was an outsider. He fought to earn his place. She struggled against prejudice based on her name. Maybe they did make sense on paper. "Can I ask you a hypothetical question?"

"Of course," Stephanie replied.

"If the Whittier descendant is someone we know, would that change things for you?"

"Is it someone we know?" she asked, crossing her arms over her chest.

"Hypothetical, remember?"

She rolled her eyes. "I guess it depends on the situation. Has the person always known they are a Whittier? Was this a recent DNA discovery? Context is important."

"You wouldn't rush to judgement?"

"You can tell me if it's you," she murmured.

"No. It's not me. And we're speaking hypothetically, remember?" He almost wished it was him. If he could shield Abby from what might happen, he would. Jealousy impacted his behavior from the start. Every day, he struggled against feeling like a fraud. He wanted to be an expert, an undisputed leading figure. She quietly—and competently—showed her talents to any who approached her business. She didn't have to tout her qualifications. The proof was in the pulled pork.

Now her future was at risk. He hated that he couldn't figure out how to help her. She deserved to stay in the community she loved. But how?

"Joe? Hey, are you feeling okay?" Stephanie snapped her fingers and waved her hand.

He shook his head. "Sorry, did I miss something? What were you saying?"

She sighed. "Yes, your eyes glazed over, and you missed quite a bit. But that's okay. I was just saying I might need more back-up on the wedding than I thought."

"Why?" He tipped his head to the side.

"Ryan has very specific wants for his big day. I'm going to need the groomsmen to help run interference."

"I'm sure we can manage him."

She narrowed her gaze. "Well, I'm not."

Joe laughed. The ranch owner had become quite the groomzilla, ruining his reputation for having a cool head with his exacting demands and wedding day expectations.

"Do you want to practice your speech for tonight? Try a mock meeting?" she asked. "I can offer some hard, ridiculous questions."

"Such as?" He was intrigued.

"What if a bison poops in my yard? Should I call Ted to come clean it up?"

"I'd love to see that happen." Joe smirked. Stephanie's light-hearted conversation lifted him out of his mood and re-focused him on what he could control. "Yes, call Ted."

"A bison is standing in the middle of the road. Do I drive around it? Honk?"

"Back-up and detour." Joe was on a roll. "Give me another."

"Can't. I have to get back to my classroom before they finish gym class."

He smiled and nodded, appreciating the difficulty of both their jobs. She had to deal with boo boos and hurt feelings. He navigated around a class half in puberty and the other still in childhood.

Finishing his coffee, he stood and rinsed his empty cup before loading in the dishwasher. The bison might prove a worthwhile distraction for everyone in town. Give the community something else to talk about while she navigated her way through the truth. With any luck, she'd start her explanations before she lost her chance and her nerve.

Because he'd pity her if the truth came out via Harrison Wolff.

While winners recorded history, some villains didn't understand their place in the story. Aligning herself with the town's biggest antagonist since her ancestors would spell her doom for certain.

He liked having her around. Especially as she provided a new insight into what so many took for granted. Especially on the eve of the town's biggest event ever, Herd's very own royal wedding as two legacy families officially became one.

CHAPTER 7

Behind the open windows in the food truck, Abby welcomed the spring breeze snaking past the row of customers and inside her vehicle. Parked on the lot where Main Street intersected with Church Street, she operated steps away from the heart of town. She liked to think Mother Nature provided her with the light wind to cool down her truck's interior from the ovens and cooktops and waft the aromas of her buttered cornbread and roasted meats downtown, luring customers her way.

With her typical steady crowd at lunch, Abby wasn't worried anyone had heard the news yet. She was annoyed with herself for putting it off for so long. The morning conversation at the ranch had quickly steered into the normal business of wedding and birthday celebration talk. Abby was grateful. While navigating Ryan's demands with Meg's more laidback approach gave Abby a headache, she was glad to resume their normal friendship.

At least one hard discussion had gone well. But she still had a whole list of people to apologize to in advance. She'd rather rip off the bandage entirely instead of letting it dangle, but she couldn't rewind time. Her elevated stress levels were her own fault. She'd gone this long without her secret being revealed, another couple hours wouldn't hurt. As soon as she closed for the afternoon, she'd head to the blacksmith shop and then the saloon. Her arrival at the latter would coincide with the start of knitting club. She could have the talk twice more and be done with her apology tour. She didn't owe everyone an explanation, only a few important people.

She served the last customer in the queue, leaned out to scan the lot for any more guests, and pulled down the retractable metal curtain. Locking up the truck, she left it in its spot and exited on foot. Herd's tiny downtown was perfect for strolling, but she needed a vehicle to otherwise get around the sprawling community. She loved walking as much as she could, and today's stroll was calming. The bright blue sky held only a few puffy clouds and shone on the colored facades of the wooden false-fronts on one side of Main Street. Across the road, the stone exteriors of The Golden Crown Saloon, Post Office, and grocery co-op gleamed like they'd been polished.

"Hey, Abby. Are you sure it's okay to leave your truck there?" Will Buck asked.

She smiled and waved at the man standing inside his shop's open doorway. "It's fine. Thanks," she called.

Better not to respond with anything she couldn't take back. Turning her back to her land, she strode with determination. She kept her chin down, tucking it into her coat collar. The brisk breeze whipped past her ears, scalding her, and propelling her forward. She didn't need to lift her gaze to follow her path. She relied on her nose.

Past the last traffic stop, she breathed deep the smell of the forge. In another life, she imagined becoming a blacksmith. She was always cold and would welcome the heat, even in summertime. With her spate of mishaps, however, she'd probably have set her building on fire before getting the hang of handling the irons.

There is a precedent for accidental pyromania in my family tree. She shook off the unhelpful thought. Hoss had had his own demons. She, of all people, wouldn't judge him. He'd more than made up for his shortcomings after his exile. Not that anyone would ever care to listen to his redemption story.

The door stood a few inches ajar.

She knocked on the door twice but received no answer. With her fingertips, she gently pushed the entry open, scanning the interior.

Ian sat on a stool, studying something in his hands. A cell phone? His visor was pushed back, but he still wore his leather apron.

He hadn't heard her knock? He was too engrossed to respond to her heavy, booted footsteps? The distraction didn't line up with the friend she knew. He hated technology and railed against the use of smartphones to any who would listen. For a millennial, he was as staunchly opposed to digital advances as most were in favor. He'd shared his hatred of selfies and social media often and loudly. Why turn to his cell phone now?

"Hello? Ian?"

He lifted his head and stared at her.

She fought a shudder. He looked at her unseeing. Like she was a stranger. Not the best greeting for starting her confession. She stepped deeper into the room, rubbing her icy hands together.

To the side, she spotted the smoker, a gleaming cylinder on a wheeled stand. She approached and lifted the lid, smiling as she glimpsed inside. Staggered racks accommodated maximum production with every use. The smoker would greatly increase her output, enabling her to cater the large wedding. "This looks great. Thanks so much. I should have driven over."

"I'll drop it off later."

His words were flat. She faced him. With several yards between them, she wasn't encouraged to approach any closer. His brow knit together in a solid line and his mouth was almost comically downturned. He looked like he might spit.

Just say it. Her inner voice shouted over the bad vibes rolling off him in waves. "Hey, I wanted to talk about s—"

"I don't have time." He stood and stuffed his phone into his back pocket. Crossing to the mounted hooks above his work bench, he pulled on his thick gloves and lowered his welding mask.

Like a knight shutting out the world as he prepared for battle. Without another word, he turned toward the forge. He stoked the burning embers with a poker, giving his work his full attention. The coals flickered and then flamed, the fire roaring to life.

What had she done? He was never so cold. She'd have to figure out an apology when he dropped off the smoker. To get his attention now could have dangerous consequences. With a nod to his back, she left the shop.

Raising her coat collar, she gripped the lapels with one hand and stuffed the other into her pocket. She headed toward the saloon. School had let out an hour earlier. Kelly Strong would be at the usual table. With any luck, although she wasn't sure how much she'd used up this morning, she could catch the Rabbitts as well.

This time, she focused on her destination and not her feet. With her chin raised, she met the gazes of a few pedestrians. But her smiles weren't returned. She gritted her molars.

At the saloon, she pushed through the front door and froze.

The buzz of conversation immediately cut to silence.

This time she knew what the problem was. Her. Squinting, she surveyed the room.

In the back corner, a few diners ate at two tables.

In the center, the knitting club focused furiously on their work.

She turned toward the bar.

James focused on polishing pint glasses with a scowling determination.

She approached him first. He'd been her staunchest ally. Surely, if she could explain, he'd have her back. She owed him the first and biggest apology. She rested her hands on the smooth bar top. "Hi, James. Do you have a minute to talk?"

"Who am I talking to?" He stared at her, his gaze icier than the wind. "Abby Whit? Or Abby Whittier?"

The blood drained out of Abby's limbs. Any practiced comeback died on her tongue. In the moment, she was colder than a January morning. Because she saw so clearly what she had done. She'd lied to the town. More than that, she hadn't been honest with people who had cared about her and helped her. People—like James and Heather—who treated her better than family. She had proved herself unworthy.

"How did you know?" she murmured. Fear at discovery didn't quiet her voice. Shock subdued her.

"Harrison Wolff officially listed you and your alias on the documents filed at the county clerk's office. You know how fast word spreads, especially about something so inflammatory."

"I... I'm sorry," she murmured.

"I don't understand why you didn't say anything. Aren't we friends? Haven't we supported you?"

She nodded, scrunching her nose from one side to the other. She sniffed and blinked. Tears threatened to spill, but she wouldn't give in to the luxury of expelling the hot emotions stoked up inside her. She did this. She had no one to blame.

"I would have been happy for you to have the land. We all would. But it's clear you don't think much of any of us." He shook his head and grabbed another spotless glass.

Dismissed. She stood in the spot wanting to argue and defend herself. Wanting to trot out the explanation that she really owed the Kincaids the truth first and she'd only just told them a few hours ago. They didn't hate her.

What could she say? She turned and walked out the front door. She'd had over two years to come clean. While she had at first assumed she'd be judged for her ancestors' actions, and she might, she had neglected how many of the people in town would not be swayed by generational prejudice. She could have had a chance to make her case if she'd been honest from the start.

But she'd prepared for the worst and never let herself imagine the best. Fear had controlled her actions from the start and held her back from telling the truth. Responding instead of acting, she'd never given anyone a chance. She understood now.

The whole mess was her fault but she couldn't just give up. She'd have to find a way forward. And it didn't involve hiding or running off. She'd leave Main Street now and avoid making a scene. But she had a bone deep certainty. She was the Whittier who belonged in town, and she wasn't going anywhere.

As a rule, Joe didn't live with regrets. He dealt openly and honestly with everyone, not wasting time on holding a grudge or concealing his feelings. As emotions arose, he acknowledged and handled them. Like an adult.

But then she'd called him out for his behavior, and now he couldn't stop rehashing what he should have done differently. After school, Joe headed home to change and eat before driving to the ranch. Since Ryan had called the town council meeting to discuss the bison, he made it clear he'd host the event. He had plenty of space for parking and a full set-up to livestream the meeting for those at home. At a table in the back of the room, Meg and Hank fiddled with a laptop and camera. Putting that pair in charge of technology was a questionable choice probably made to keep them busy.

Joe began setting up the metal folding chairs in neat rows. He worked to one side of the room as Ted mirrored him on the other. Monotonous work typically calmed his worrying mind, his anxiety settling as he accomplished a task. Tonight, however, he couldn't stop wondering if he'd have the chance to do better for Abby.

"All done?" Ryan called from near the French doors centered on the back deck. A cool breeze snaked into the room as the doors shut.

Joe finished the last chair in the front row and headed towards Ryan. "Yep. You think you'll really get this big of a crowd?"

Ryan nodded. "I do. Although the bison probably aren't the big draw of the night." He shook his head.

Ted crossed to the room. "Did you hear?" he stared at Joe.

"Me?" Joe drew back his chin, twisting his neck to take in both men's expressions of concern. "Hear what? What's going on? What's happening?"

"Turns out the Whittier in town is Abby," Ryan said. "She came here this morning and told us so herself."

Joe nodded.

"You knew?" Ryan asked, leaning close.

Joe's throat closed. Should he have confessed to the Kincaids as soon as he found out? She would have expected that. With his often-childish behavior around her, tattling wasn't out of the realm of possibility. But he had kept his mouth shut. "It wasn't my secret to tell."

"That's true enough," Ted said.

"How long have you known?" Ryan crossed his arms over his broad chest.

"A couple weeks ago." Joe shifted his weight from foot to foot. "Since spring break. I confronted her. To be honest, I probably knew for longer. I didn't want to see it."

"Why?" Ted asked. "You are her number one critic. Seems like this would have proved you right."

No one could cut through to the heart of the matter in less words and fluff than Ted. Joe wasn't sure he liked the categorization as a hater. It bothered him. A rational explanation for his feelings would make him look better. But he'd behaved with prejudice based on nothing. And now he was ashamed. She'd been correct in her estimation of him, too. She'd humbled him about the bias he fostered on his project. "I don't know."

Ryan snorted. "Come up with a better answer if Hank asks you, or he'll think you're softening on her."

Maybe he's right. Joe turned around to glance at Meg and Hank. The older man made no move like he'd heard his name.

Why would Abby's identity be a subject of gossip tonight? Joe spun back and stared hard at Ryan. "Did you tell the town her secret?"

"Never. Harrison Wolff filed the paperwork today," Ryan said, shaking his head.

Joe clenched his jaw, swallowing the swear forming on his tongue. Had the lawyer promised Abby discretion? Had Harrison used her in his war on Ryan?

Worse, had Joe's unfriendliness made him complicit in her destruction?

"I like Abby," Ryan said. "She did right by us, she came and told us the truth. I wish she hadn't been so scared and waited for so long."

Joe nodded, memories niggling the back of his mind. How many times had she questioned him about the Whittiers? He remembered a couple conversations about the continued animosity towards the family. Had he been part of the problem? He'd railed against the family with a venom as if he'd lived the history first-hand. Had she cared so much about what he thought she let his opinion override good sense? Why did he get a slight thrill to imagine his words mattered to her?

The doors at the front of the barn opened.

A low buzz of conversation suddenly filled the room.

"Guess we finished in the nick of time," Ryan said. "Excuse me."

Joe stepped to the side, letting his boss pass. He hung back and observed the scene as neighbors and friends filtered into the room. The neat rows were dismantled as chairs slid forward, back, and sideways. Each scrape against the pine boards did the same to his heart. He could do his best and still have his hard work disregarded by the public. Until she walked into the room, he hadn't realized he'd been holding his breath.

Abby slunk in, her back rounded and her chin down. She didn't want to be here. But she came anyways. If that didn't tell everyone what they needed to know about her and her dedication to town, he wasn't sure what else they wanted. She found a chair in the back on the end of a row, near the table with Hank and Meg. Hank spoke with his typical animation. Meg smiled. And Abby looked slightly less uncomfortable. Joe's heart ached for her. He wished she had believed more in herself to come out with the truth long ago. The town might have bad memories of her ancestors, but they adored her.

"Are you ready?"

With a start, Joe whipped his gaze to Ted, holding the microphone stand.

Ted strode to the front of the chairs. Centered by the sliding glass doors, he set the stand into position.

Joe approached and flashed a thumb's up to Ted's retreating figure. "Yes, thank you." He nodded. "Good evening, everyone and thank you for coming out." The microphone crackled and his voice boomed. He backed up a few inches. Maybe he didn't need to be so close to be effective. "I appreciate you taking the time for this special meeting. And if you're watching from home. That's some kind of miracle given tonight's IT team." He gestured to Meg and Hank.

"Hey now," Hank called.

The crowd chuckled.

Joe hated public speaking and yet he seemed to constantly put into that path. As a teacher, as a tour guide, and as the face of the bison project, he couldn't escape the spotlight even if he wanted. Was it foolhardiness that propelled him or the surge of adrenaline after he accomplished something that terrified him?

"I want to start the evening by addressing the biggest concerns. The bison will be introduced on ranch land miles from town. The animals are wild and can't necessarily be monitored and controlled. But we are not anticipating a disruption to downtown. The occasional animal might wander past a store, but there is nothing of interest on Main Street."

"Speak for yourself," a deep voice called.

The crowd sniggered and murmured.

He scanned the good spirited group, darting his eyes through the friendly faces. He spotted Will Buck and an older lady next to him. The Rabbitts sat in the front row.

Abby met and held his gaze.

He offered her an encouraging smile. He hated seeing her shrink. With her talents, she wasn't meant to hide.

Should he tame the bucking bronco in the room and broach her identity with the crowd? "I also wanted to take this opportunity to talk about the other big news. We now know the land at the end of Church belongs to our own Abby Whit. I'm sure I'm not alone in expressing surprise but also my relief at the revelation."

Frowns marred the faces in the rows. A pretty picture of prairie pride cracked.

"Yeah, what a relief," a sharp voice called.

Derisive snorts of laughter accompanied the jest.

"I am relieved, and you should be as well. We don't have to fear development of some awful skyrise or whatever other fear we've stoked."

"She lied to us," another male voice shouted.

A chair scrapped back.

Ian, the town's blacksmith, stood. "She's pretended to be someone else this entire time. How do you know she won't sell the land to a developer? How can you be so sure she won't take advantage of us?"

"Because I know her." Joe met and held Abby's gaze in the back of the room. He wanted her to hear him and to feel the truth of his words. "She has shown us who she is. She was scared of her last name. Can't say I blame her considering the immediate backlash against her."

"Why go about everything in such an underhanded and sneaky way?" Ian asked, forging ahead. "Her family screwed up and was ruined. Isn't she proving why we can't trust the Whittiers?"

The angry question didn't encourage the same general murmurs of support and agreement as the earlier comments. Joe was glad the room wasn't becoming an angry mob. Abby had lied about her identity, but she hadn't committed a crime. The town's people needed time to process the information and make their own, individual determinations about what to do next. He hoped others would forgive her.

"Everyone deserves a second chance," a female voice called.

Joe wasn't sure if the words had come from Stephanie or Kelly Strong, another kindergarten teacher at the school. He was glad for some assistance outside of the Kincaid ranch network.

"I don't trust Harrison Wolff," Will Buck said, standing and crossing his arms. "I'll give Abby the benefit of the doubt. But he is cunning and crafty."

Joe would concede part of the town's issue was Abby using an outside, big city firm to lay her claim. Harrison's history hadn't endeared him to long-time Herd residents. Joe wasn't prepared for her to be burned at the stake for seeking legal counsel. He held up a hand. "I understand. We considered her one of our own, and she wasn't truthful. Many of us feel used. I won't fault her for seeking a lawyer's guidance and neither would any of you, after you've had time to process and cool down."

"She should have come to us. She didn't give us a chance," James Rabbitt said.

Joe paused and nodded. More than anyone, James and Heather had supported Abby. "Fear makes us do rash, fool-hardy things. She wants to settle and stay. Her actions have always been kind and neighborly. Let's move forward. I know Abby will be able to fill in some of the gaps in our town's history. I look forward to providing a fuller picture of Herd in my book. We accept legend and lore as truth. History isn't infallible. I will give her the opportunity to explain her side. I hope you'll give her a chance to do the same."

Ryan strode down the center aisle between the rows of chairs, his eyes flashing a warning. He stood at Joe's side and clapped a hand around his shoulders, leaning close to the microphone. "Thanks, Joe. Let's open it straight up to questions about the bison."

Joe stepped away from the stand, relinquishing the microphone to his boss. Was he being saved or condemned for aligning himself with Abby? He surveyed the crowd again and spotted her leaving the room. At least he'd tried. Had it been too little too late? He wanted to run after her and apologize, get her interview on record, and move on from this whole business. He felt bad about his part in the sad affair.

He wasn't a big public gesture sort of guy. But he'd tried. He hoped she appreciated the effort. The only way to know for certain would be to follow her and ask.

But he couldn't, because he had a job to do. The rest of the questions returned to the bison and the more pressing concerns about property and insurance and care. He couldn't stop thinking about her and prayed she'd endured the worst and could rebuild from here.

CHAPTER 8

As a rule, Abby avoided camping. While she didn't consider herself a particularly high maintenance person, her skincare regime relied on grocery store brands and she treated herself to two haircuts a year, she required a few basics. A mattress—not air filled—central heating and cooling, and indoor plumbing.

In the cab of her food truck, she shivered in her three layers of pants. If she wasn't so against roughing it, she might have been better prepared for her long night ahead. A sleeping bag would have been useful. She leaned her aching shoulders against the worn-down captain's seat in the front of her truck. The padding on the second-hand vehicle never bothered her much.

She wasn't in the habit of taking her truck for joyrides or road trips. Her life savings was tied up in the expenses that encompassed her livelihood. What cash she had earmarked for her restaurant would dwindle quickly if she had to purchase a place to live. She doubted another landlord or apartment complex would allow her to park her truck overnight. Then, at the minimum, she'd have to buy a car and leave the truck on her lot. Would she be vandalized as quickly as she was villainized? Dollar signs flashed through her mind with an old-fashioned cash register chime accompanying each image.

When she had purchased the vehicle, she had been thinking of a bright and shiny future. Now, she faced the harsh realities of her actions. A long night in the cab of her locked truck.

The wind whistled.

She folded her arms on the windowsill. The cold glass was inescapable. With a groan, she folded her arms over her chest. She shut her eyes and leaned her head back against the rest. The cracked leather scratched her skin. She had to hold perfectly still to avoid smelling the stale odor of degrading foam and to stop from scratching her tender skin.

Every muscle in her body ached, including her jaw from prolonged clenching. She couldn't sob if she wanted. She was utterly drained of any excess energy. The day had been an emotional rollercoaster of her own making and all she wanted now was sleep. What a joke that, in the immediate aftermath of the town meeting, she had felt heartened. Joe, of all people, had defended her. He'd used the community gathering to support her, risking his solid reputation. He, the one person in town who hated her, had spoken up for her.

Of course, she couldn't help but argue that he had no choice. The Kincaids hadn't publicly defamed her. Joe would bolster her to show his solidarity with them.

If he was only saying what he felt he had to, he wouldn't have been so eloquent. She could analyze his actions all she wanted, and she'd never reach a clear conclusion. No one was all good or all bad.

She'd been overwhelmed by his speech and had fled. She'd heard enough whispers and hisses on the streets and in the new barn to know her heart couldn't take any more public displays of either scorn or support. She'd made it into her vehicle as the call came.

After learning of the situation, her landlady had declared the contract, signed as Whit, null and void. The eviction was delivered with such succinct respect, Abby was almost glad. At least, in one instance, the situation was all business. Abby had boxed up all of her belongings and stuffed the truck to capacity and left her home.

She had spent a considerable amount of time scrubbing the furnished one-bedroom apartment and leaving a note that simply said *Thank you. I'm sorry.*

Her conscience wouldn't let her do anything less than leave the basement suite as she found it. She might have been exposed as a liar, but she had determined to prove she only deceived about the packaging and not the person. She wouldn't seek her security deposit. She hadn't thought of the ramifications of signing only part of her name. She would accept the consequences and move on.

Unfortunately, with her funds tied up, she didn't have an excess of cash to splash on an indefinite hotel stay. With her entire life now contained within her truck, she was vulnerable. She couldn't leave her worldly goods unattended. She was completely exposed now. Was this the bottom? She hoped so.

The wind picked up from a melodious howl to a sharp screech. She'd spent enough time on the plot of land beside the cemetery to know all the sounds. She'd endured plenty of blustery days. At night, however, the location became ominous. She recalled Stephanie's suggestion to host haunted events. *Please let the ghosts stay away tonight.*

Tomorrow, she'd have a plan. One night in her truck wasn't the worst thing in the world. She could do this and perhaps earn herself a hotel stay in the morning.

An insistent knock on the truck's metal door startled her.

Opening her eyes, she turned and squinted, peering through the glass to the ground and the small figure standing there. She trusted her strength. She'd easily overwhelm the mystery guest.

In the dark, she couldn't quite make out who her visitor was, other than a woman. Who was here? Why? Throw rotten vegetables at Abby and her truck?

The figure stepped back into the beam of lights from a small SUV and waved.

Meg.

Abby pressed her lips together, unsure how to proceed. Did she invite the other woman in, offering whatever meager hospitality she could? Was it better to be yelled at on your own turf?

Abby wrenched open the door and slowly lowered herself out of the truck to the ground. She couldn't hop or jump with her usual ease. Muscles in her lower back strained and tensed. With several pairs of pants on, her movements were restricted. Slowly, she shut the door, gripping her keys tight in her fingers, and crossed her arms over her chest against the chill in the night air. "Hi."

"Are you sleeping in there?" Meg asked with no preamble.

Abby's cheeks and ears burned. At least the dark hid her visceral response. She lifted a shoulder in a half shrug. Did her nonchalance land? Was it even visible?

"What happened?" Meg's features were hard to make out in the dark. Her tone sounded sincere. Meg had always been friendly. If Abby had to speak to anyone right now, she was glad it was Meg.

"Nothing I didn't deserve," Abby said.

"I doubt that. Were you kicked out of your place?"

Meg's succinct and spot-on assertions would put Joe to shame. Abby never wondered what Meg was thinking. With a second of conversational lull, Meg would fill in the blanks.

"Is that allowed?" Meg asked. "Why would she throw you out into the cold?"

"I signed Whit instead of Whittier on the contract. It's a legal issue. Don't be too hard or quick to pass judgement." *Hopefully my ex-landlady won't file a lawsuit.*

Abby would be glad to end her association with Harrison Wolff as soon as possible. She'd rather not become further embroiled with the lawyer and his sneaky tactics. He served her best interests, she couldn't argue that, but his methods seemed aligned to some other motivation.

"And you have no place to go." Meg sighed. "I'm sorry. Truly."

"Thanks."

"Where are your things?"

Abby appreciated the direct, no-nonsense line of conversation. She couldn't let any of the emotions threatening to bubble up inside her boil over, or she'd lose all her nerve. "In the back. I don't have much."

"That's good."

"Why are you here, Meg?" Abby asked, hating the crack in her voice but unable to don anymore disguises. The blackness of night was the only veil she had left. In the morning, when the whole town would learn of her situation, she would be laid bare for everyone's examination and gossip.

Rumors spread quick through town thanks to a few long-winded folks. A flicker of strong opinion flamed into an engulfing blaze of gossip after a few retellings. Most of the time, notoriety burned itself it. But she had an inkling she'd forever be a topic of conversation. For the rest of her life, she'd be another one of those Whittiers. It didn't require much imagination to summon the shaking heads and wagging tongues that would follow her every move.

She couldn't leave now. She would have to find a way forward. If anything, her refusal to remove her truck would solidify her place in the landscape.

"I was worried about you, after the meeting," Meg said. "I couldn't stop putting myself in your shoes, and I wanted to make sure you were okay. I guess I had good reason."

Abby's heart ached. She was glad to know she could count on the other woman as a friend. But she'd hoped Joe might have suggested Meg look out for Abby. "It's late you should get home."

"Late? No, it's not late."

Abby pulled out her phone and glanced at the screen. Nine ten? Really? She'd hoped it would be almost midnight. Instead, she'd only suffered through forty minutes. The night would be longer than she'd anticipated. Abby snorted. Oh, Meg's instincts were spot-on.

"What will you do?"

"Tonight?" Abby asked, sliding the phone into her outermost back pocket. "Get some rest."

"And in the future."

"I'm building a restaurant on the plot, and I'll have a two-bedroom apartment upstairs. It'll be nice." *And mine.* No one could kick her from her property. Tomorrow, she'd go to a big box store and buy supplies. A tent. A sleeping bag. She'd stay on her land.

Abby wouldn't give up on her dream. She'd called Harrison Wolff earlier. Unsure what to do next, she wanted a trusted opinion. He hadn't offered her advice; however, he'd cared only about how Ryan and Hank responded to the news. He hadn't given her a chance to ask a single question about her next steps. "If we speak any more, I'll have to charge you," he had said before abruptly ending the call.

"What about right now?" Meg asked. "Where will you go?"

Abby turned toward her truck. She shuddered, involuntarily and wished she could feel her limbs well enough to kick herself or wiggle a toe. How quickly did hypothermia set in?

She didn't know if her gas budget would extend enough to running the truck all night to stay warm. Maybe she could turn it on every hour for a little while. If she was already losing feeling in her extremities, however, she probably needed to keep the engine on until the truck ran out of fuel. And then she'd be back to sitting in her cold truck, risking her health.

"Come to my house," Meg said.

Abby faced her friend and shook her head. "I can't. You don't want to roll in the muck with me."

"I won't abandon you," Meg said and stepped forward grabbing Abby's icy hand and squeezing. "I've had my share of feeling unwanted and unwelcome in a place I love with my whole heart. I know first-hand how hard it can be. And you won't have an easier time for not sleeping."

Abby pulled her fingers out of the other woman's warm grasp. Meg had a point.

With every secret exposed, Abby could start to rebuild her standing in town with every interaction from this moment on. The entire town would dissect her comments, appearance, and behavior. Wouldn't she be better served by a night in a real bed? "Okay but only for tonight."

"No, you can stay until your apartment is ready, or you find another place to rent."

"That's too much. My building won't be ready for at least a year, and I doubt anyone in town would rent to me." Long before news of her identity spread, she had had a difficult time securing a place to rent that allowed her to park her truck outside.

"No, my offer stands. But we can work out particulars later. Do you want to follow me in your truck?"

Abby shook her head. If she was going to spend the night, she'd leave her truck in its place. She'd risk leaving everything she had out in public rather than move the loud vehicle to Meg's house where it would definitely not be hidden. She didn't want Meg to be dragged down to her. She'd leave it be and pretend everything was normal.

Could she fake it till she made it?

"Let me grab a suitcase and lock up. I'll ride with you if that's okay?" Abby asked.

"Sure. You can come back into town with me in the morning when I open the store."

As long as Abby wore a hat and dark sunglasses. She walked back to the truck, checking the locks on the exterior of the truck before entering the cab and throwing a few things in the bag. She was blessed and lucky for the kindness of Meg and wouldn't let anything harm her friend. Joe might have had mixed feelings and reasons for why he stood up for her, but she could count on at least two people's genuine support.

On Saturdays during the school year, Joe treated himself to a lazy, late start. In an area with deep roots of caring for the land, the citizens of Herd kept sunrise to sunset hours. Traditions engrained for generations couldn't be so easily forgotten. Waking up at eight was considered sleeping in.

With his self-imposed book deadline looming, however, Joe found himself pounding the slats of the downtown raised wooden sidewalk by seven fifteen. He slid a few thank you notes into the mail slot outside the post office. Gratitude wasn't a mere act of polite behavior. He carried a grateful heart with him into every day. While many in town might consider his project as superfluous or a demonstration of vanity, he understood the value in listening. The interviewees shared personal narratives, giving the town history a layer of intimacy and connection. The biggest worry was entirely out of his control. What had happened to all the stories that hadn't been collected? Were some chapters already lost to time?

He'd admit his ego played a large part in motivating him to finish the work. But his efforts weren't only to prove himself worthy. One day, everyone would understand the importance of his actions. *Is this how Abby feels about her choices? Justified?*

He released his grip on the mail slot's handle, the opening clanging shut. Her decisions weren't his business. Or anyone else's for that matter. In the heat of the moment last night, he had made her his concern during the meeting. And then spent the rest of the night berating himself. Should he have intervened? Was he wrong to do so? Had he said enough in her defense? He wasn't sure. He'd felt right in his convictions at the time. But he knew his words weren't the last on the subject. Could she, would she, stick around for long enough to prove herself?

Shaking his head, he scanned the street.

The street was nearly deserted. A few vehicles were parallel parked in front of businesses. The saloon opened for breakfast as did the General Store kitty-corner from the post office. The road was free of traffic.

He jogged across Main.

A car door slammed shut.

He spun toward the sound and spotted Abby and Meg at the end of the block. They were a curious combo. Had they decided to eliminate him and Ryan from event planning? He couldn't deny that would simplify matters. But he felt an odd pang and rubbed the ache under his breast bone.

Meg entered her store, but Abby remained on the sidewalk. She twisted her neck side to side and stalked down the street with determination. The hunch in her neck looked uncomfortable as she stared at her feet.

The door to the General Store opened, and a rush of warm air invited him in as two women exited. He stepped forward to hold open the door. The women smiled and nodded their thanks. He returned the gesture and then froze.

Abby strode past, her steps clicking in determination.

The women spotted her. In a second, their pleased expressions were wiped clean, marred with deep wrinkled frowns. And then, as if he was trapped in a bygone era, the women turned and gave Abby their backs.

She continued past.

He prayed she didn't notice.

The whole episode was over in a second.

The women departed in the opposite direction.

Abby was no doubt on her way to the food truck.

He remained in place holding open a door and gaping. His mouth could catch flies. He was too shocked by what he had witnessed.

A snubbing? He had heard enough about them from his deceased grandmother. He had never expected to observe one in action. At least the women hadn't said a word in the process. It was a small thing to be glad about, that they didn't compound their behavior with blatant pettiness, but still he was grateful.

He shut his mouth and stepped inside. He rubbed his palms together and approached the coffee station in the corner of the store.

Will Buck poured refills in several mugs at the bistro tables.

Joe waited at the counter, scrubbing his hands over his face to erase his expression. He was ashamed of his lack of reaction in the moment outside. While he was stunned by the women's behavior, he hadn't done anything to stop it or help Abby. Maybe she hadn't noticed him? He added that wish to his growing list.

"Hi, Joe. What can I get you?" Will asked.

"A coffee and a moment of your time, if you have either to spare," Joe replied.

Will darted his eyes to the side and leaned forward. "Is this about you know who?"

Joe frowned at the fervent whisper. When he had been the only person in town wary of Abby, he would have welcomed commiseration. No one wanted to discuss his concerns and worries back then. In the end, he'd been correct in his assessment and hated the end result.

He'd been so adamant against a plan Ryan Kincaid floated last fall, to partner with Abby on opening a restaurant on the ranch. And now Joe wished he could go back in time and sign the contracts himself. With a partner, she would have had what she wanted and had protection. No one would have ever needed to learn the truth.

At least she didn't know, and it had never been more than an idea. He'd always feel guilty. He'd inserted himself into her life to block and complicate her path. Could he help her somehow? He hated to be the cause of anyone's misery but especially hers.

Since learning the truth, he found himself longing for her company. She was a remarkable person.

"Actually, it's about cake," Joe said at last, breaking the awkward silence. "I'd love a coffee, too."

Will grabbed a mug and filled it to the brim. "Cakes I can discuss."

"Great." Joe reached for the coffee, letting the warm ceramic sink into his chilled fingers before taking the first sip. "I guess I need to know lead time on the orders for the ranch's big weekend. If you can make enough, all of that."

"I'd like to have the order at least two weeks out if not more. I'll accommodate, no matter what the numbers."

Joe had expected such an answer. He didn't need loyalty. He wanted truth. "We won't have a true count for either Hank's birthday or the reception. Ryan wants to invite everyone. The ranch will have around fifty guests that weekend alone. Maybe two hundred people for each event? Maybe three hundred?"

Will nodded. "For both events, my plan is to make a multi-tier display cake that can be cut for photographs. But I'll have sheet cake in the back to slice and serve. Same cake and frosting flavors but much more efficient."

"Do you need help?" Joe wasn't sure why he asked. He survived off microwave meals and takeout. Who could be of assistance? Abby?

Will shook his head. "With enough lead time, I'll be set. Cake can be frozen. My grandma is very excited to help. In fact, I'm glad you stopped by. She wanted to know if you'd be interested in interviewing her for your project. She's a few years younger than Hank so she wasn't sure if you wanted to talk. She figured you probably had enough stories from her generation to fill four volumes with your connection to Hank."

Joe chuckled, glad for the lighthearted moment. "She isn't too far off the mark. I'd love to interview her. Every perspective matters."

"Great. When can I tell her to be ready?"

The door opened, sending a gust of chilly air into the store.

Joe glanced over his shoulder as a couple strolled inside, making their way to the counter. His time was running short. "I need a few more weeks? I have to put my interviews on hold for the moment as I sort through the latest round of event planning and work with the bison introduction. But soon. I'll let you know." Maybe Joe would have more answers by then, especially as concerned Abby. He drained the rest of his coffee and left cash under the mug. "Thanks."

He turned before Will could tell him it was on the house. Joe didn't want anyone to feel awkward or obligated. As he strode through the store, however, he caught the snippet of a conversation.

"I can't believe it. I've never seen her drink. Have you?" A sharp, female voice asked.

He spotted Miriam, the town librarian, chatting with Wendy, the school secretary near a display at the front of the store and slowed his steps.

"I haven't noticed anything about her, if I'm being honest," Wendy said.

Joe stared at a display of postcards, feigning fascination while straining for every word. At least he could continue to count on Wendy's kindness.

"They say it can run in families. I suppose the Rabbitts will pay extra attention now," Miriam said the words with an edge of warning like a serrated knife blade.

"I don't want to speculate," Wendy said.

From the corner of his gaze, Joe openly stared now. He caught Wendy's eye. Miriam opened her mouth to speak. Wendy shook her head and rested a hand on her friend's arm. She tipped her head to the side. Miriam followed the direction and widened her gaze, her nostrils flaring.

Joe cleared his throat, breaking himself out of his daze, and strode out of the store. Only a few weeks ago, he would have been guilty of the same train of thought. He'd have looked for the Whittier claimant amongst the patrons who stayed too late and were cut off at the saloon. Now, he felt ashamed for his generalization and offensive prejudice.

He'd shown his public support for her, but he hadn't done enough to help her. Regardless of what came next, Abby had accomplished one thing. She had opened Joe's eyes to his own blind spots and challenged him to examine himself. He had never been more ashamed.

CHAPTER 9

Abby had never thought much about being the town outcast. In a theoretical concept, she'd tried to put herself in her ancestor's shoes. When she had first made the decision to scope out the town and learn if it was worth her while to claim the land, she had experienced such friendliness, even as townsfolk repeated folkloric gossip and hatred, she couldn't truly understand what it would mean.

Having never been shunned, she only had a hazy sense of loneliness for the prospect. Her new reality was a throwback to a bygone era. After the first time a neighbor turned their back to her and blatantly ignored her *hello*, she nearly laughed out loud at the ridiculous behavior. She'd only stopped herself because making light would not have improved her town standing.

As the days passed, she had become the center of a community-wide, targeted, snubbing, and she found less reason for amusement.

When her former part time employees wouldn't pick up the phone, she let the frustration roll off her back. The unexpected check from her former landlady was a nice touch, though. She was grateful to have her security deposit returned and to not be spending money on salary when she had no customers. Every cent added up while she began work on her future. She found, over the course of the next several weeks, she didn't mind solitude. Meetings with architects had filled her days better than sitting around waiting for no one to show up at her food truck. At least during the summer, tourists wouldn't know she was persona non grata. Their constant influx meant turnover on a weekly basis, and would keep her afloat.

Truly, she couldn't complain for her situation, but she was frustrated that no one would take her phone calls regarding the wedding and birthday celebrations. She hadn't shared the tidbit with her roommate. Every morning, Meg cheerfully marked another day off the calendar with a bright red X. She remained upbeat and unphased by the countdown to her wedding as she flipped to the month of May. Nor did she complain about carpooling into town most days.

Abby had driven the truck to the Hawke ranch only when she could be sure no one was aware of her movements. She had unloaded her belongings in the spare bedroom overlooking the back of the house and felt quickly at home. The sunny room was filled with antiques lovingly cared for and passed down. Meg had delighted in sharing the story of every item in her home. While Abby had felt awkward using family heirlooms, she had been chastised. Meg had insisted on using what she had to honor the memories of her loved ones and keep their spirits alive in the home.

Abby had never stayed in a home long enough to ever consider herself or her family tied to the space. Seeing the Hawke home through Meg's eyes, however, Abby understood the desire to cherish and hold on to the past. Every moment held a reminder of love. What a gift.

She could not wait to put down some roots of her own. In the meantime, she had taken every precaution to lock up her vehicle securely in town. When she had returned to her lot, she was mostly ignored. She hadn't experienced any physical violence or threat of retaliation, but she wasn't sure when she'd be welcomed again.

The Kincaids had remained resolved that she was their go-to caterer.

She'd have to figure out how to get more refrigerator and counter space to be able to fulfill her contract. The Rabbitts hadn't participated in any sort of active hostility. But neither had they assisted her, even when she attempted to order lunch one day at the saloon.

Perhaps they really hadn't heard her, since they had been passing each other on the way to and from the kitchen. But she hadn't wanted to cause more of a scene by raising her voice and trying again. She would give them time and space. She was more worried about someone else.

Since Joe's declaration of friendship and public show of support, he hadn't sought her company. It should be a relief to have at least one person no longer actively hating her. She missed him even if she felt judged in his presence. When she got the email about meeting up to review and finalize the menus for both events, she'd been thrilled. The hurried text that came an hour ago, however, put her on edge. Meg wanted to meet with Abby and Joe at her store. Would they mind stopping by?

Abby agreed even if she hated to drag them through the mud of guilt by her association.

From the safety of the alley on the side street adjacent to Main Street, near Finders Keepers Antiques, she watched and waited. Meg had asked her to meet to discuss the catering menu. As roommates, Abby could have easily produced a few samples in the kitchen without anyone knowing. Instead, Meg wanted a formal meeting and suggested Joe join them.

Abby would be grateful to speak with him and clarify the situation. But she didn't want to hurt anyone else's credibility in town. She'd taken great pains to conceal her residence at Meg's house by riding into town early and asking to leave late. She refused to be a liability to Meg because of her kindness.

With her ponytail threaded through a ball cap and a pair of oversized sunglasses shielding half her face, she felt more like an undercover starlet than a small-town restauranteur. Still, she waited. She wouldn't drag down anyone else.

Joe strolled down the street.

She could race inside the antique store before drawing any attention. She attempted just that. Stepping onto the curb, she took a step forward and slammed her foot into a slushy puddle. Dirty water sloshed over her ankle boot. So much for incognito. With each squelching step, she continued to the antique store. At least her ankle wasn't twisted. As she opened the front door, a bell rang overhead.

"Welcome to Finders Keepers," Meg called.

Abby shut the door and breathed in lemon furniture polish scented the air. She turned slowly and found only Joe and Meg.

The pair stared in confusion.

Abby pulled off her sunglasses, tucking the eyewear into her coat pocket. She released a shaky exhale. "Hi." Walking to the glass case and cash register, she focused only on her path forward and didn't let her gaze drift to either side.

"Thanks for coming," Meg said. "Both of you."

She said the words with significance that was lost on Abby. Frowning, she glanced at Joe for a clue.

He shrugged. "Of course. How can we help?"

"I know you have everything well in hand for the birthday celebration. I am also aware that my groom might be..." Meg scrunched her nose. "Over enthusiastic about the wedding."

"He has a lot of opinions," Joe said.

Meg laughed. "I am grateful that you two are acting as the coordinators. But I want to stress, if any of the requests are too much to handle. I'm not expecting miracles. Let me know, what is out of the realm of possibility and I'll break the news to him," Meg said.

Abby frowned. The wedding and birthday celebration were straight-forward. With the events happening simultaneously, she had a lot less work to handle. Meg's statement was ominous. Abby's stomach dropped. "Is this because of me?"

Meg had a pinched expression, her face wrinkled in concentration. "Not exactly."

Joe smiled but it didn't reach his eyes.

"If you want me off the projects, I understand. You don't have to feel bad. I get it." Abby dropped her shoulders. She felt boneless like she'd melt into a puddle of goo on the floor.

"No, I want you on the project. I love your food. So does everyone in town." Meg reached a hand out, grabbing one of Abby's limp arms. She squeezed. "Give them time, they'll come around."

"I haven't changed. Doesn't it count for anything that I was liked before?" Abby asked, fighting back the burn behind her eyes and in her nose.

Meg squeezed her hand again. "It does to me."

"If Meg didn't support you, she wouldn't have asked you to room with her," Joe said smoothly.

Abby gasped. "How do you know? Who told you?" She darted a glance at Meg but quickly sobered. Small town living. Of course he'd know. Everyone would. Secrets didn't last long. And—on the off chance they did—grudges developed.

She swallowed a snigger and studied the glass case under her fingers. Pretty, old things rested on velvet. Watches, cigarette cases, brooches, and snuff boxes. The sort of little items cherished and passed down from one generation to the next.

Her family didn't have any antiques. Growing up surrounded by other families constantly on the move, she never noticed. In Herd, where roots rand deep, she saw history everywhere.

"I was going to let the claim lapse," Abby said slowly. "Until I needed to expand for catering, I had a call scheduled to tell Harrison to drop it."

"Why don't you tell the town?" Joe asked. "If you explain, you'll be vindicated."

Abby met his desperate, wild-eyed gaze. Did he want her to be the hero? She shook her head. "Because ultimately I assumed control of the land." Could've, would've, should've were excuses. She stood by her decision. "And I have been lying. How many people only gave me business out of pity? How many people worried I was about to be evicted at any moment?" Abby asked.

"You're wrong about the pity, but I'll concede you have a point about the other thing. The town cared about you, and you hurt people that trusted you. You have to own it but also stick it out. Give them another chance," he said.

Abby shrugged, dropping her gaze to the glass case full of tiny pretty things on a velvet lined shelf. She couldn't look at him or she would break. His Freudian slip neatly explained her situation. Past tense, not present. "The moment the news came out, no one would give me the time of day."

"How are your plans?" Joe asked.

Abby lifted her head. She wouldn't wallow when she had so much to do. "I'm okay. Plans are moving forward for my new building. I'll start construction in June. I'm grateful for the ranch. Ryan is letting me park onsite for the summer. With any luck, tourist season and events catering will keep my income in a positive direction. I might never recover in town."

"You will," Joe said. "Of course you will."

His confident words, delivered without a second's hesitation, warmed her from inside out. She smiled at him. A little of his faith could go a long way.

"I also wanted to stress," Meg said. "You need to lead the tasting. Ryan would never interrupt you while you're speaking. He thinks he has an idea what he wants for the food. He has no clue. Don't let him talk you into doing something you know is wrong."

Abby smiled. She had been mostly shielded from Ryan's demands but knew tomorrow would be her big debut. "Got it."

The bell jingled overhead.

Abby froze. If she could shrink and hide, she would. In her pocket, she fumbled for the sunglasses.

"Welcome to Finders Keepers," Meg called, leaning around Abby and Joe to address the newcomer. "Please let me know if you need any help."

"I'd better go," Abby murmured, pulling out her sunglasses with shaky hands.

Joe reached for her wrist, lightly stilling her with his warm touch.

Abby fought a shudder. His kindness might break her even worse than his pity.

"Let's go to the saloon and chat," he said.

She shook her head. "I don't think that's a good idea."

"I do. I insist. My treat." He turned and offered his elbow.

Abby widened her eyes.

"Go on. Don't hide," Meg said.

Joe moved closer.

"Okay," Abby said on a sigh. She looped her hand through Joe's arm, fumbling with her sunglasses.

"Put those away. Let them see we're friends," he said.

She stared, mouth agape. Was he serious? Why would he want to be friends with her now? She had nothing to offer and he had everything to lose by association. Slowly, she shut her mouth and tucked the sunglasses back in her pocket. She let him led the way out of the store and across the street.

For the first time in a long time, she had the oddest sense of safety. How ironic that it was on the arm of the man who hated her. It felt a lot like coming home.

Until Joe walked out of Finders Keepers with Abby on his arm, he hadn't thought much about next steps. His defense of her at the town meeting almost a month earlier hadn't been enough. He should have done more. With the return to school and the frantic rush to the end of the year while also working on his new programs for the summer season on the ranch and compiling his notes for his book, he hadn't had another moment to think about what else to do. Meg's call had snapped him out of his daze.

He hadn't realized how low Abby felt until she showed up at the antique store. With her reddish-brown hair hidden under a hat, she looked diminished and anonymous. His heart broke for her. Without her in his life, his days had been a monotonous drone. He'd missed her.

"Whoa," she breathed. "Is that a bison?"

He turned and followed her finger pointing down the street towards the blacksmith shop.

A dark shadow with a big hump meandered into view. The fence was supposed to discourage the bison for their safety and the town's.

Shielding his gaze with his free hand, Joe squinted. The shape became clearer, a massive furry figure almost improbably supported by slender legs. "Yep, that's one of the bison."

Joe couldn't judge his distance away or the size of the creature. It looked like it was nowhere near the businesses. Which was good. He'd assured the town that the animals wanted nothing to do with them and vice versa.

But he wasn't a hundred percent certain that was true.

The conservation group had included some animals that had exposure to humans as both domesticated animals in private zoos and a couple from a circus. The hope was that with wide-open spaces the animals would return to their natural habitats and leave the humans alone. Of course, many of the bison had never lived in herds. Could the animals learn instinctual behavior? *Could humans?*

"Looks like he's well past the blacksmith shop." *Thankfully.*

"I know they've been in the area for a few weeks," she said. "I hadn't seen one before. It's sort of startling."

He understood. While Herd might look like an Old West town, it was as sanitized and commoditized as the rest of the country. The bison would reinstate the wild moniker to their West. "I've been out at the ranch a few times, but I haven't seen one wander close to town. The fence deters them."

"How many bison are there?"

"About two dozen, give or take. The adults are mostly females with their young. A few males were included."

"Hoping for some babies next spring?" She winked.

He liked her playful tone and the cheeky gesture. "I don't think that's the plan. Teds in charge of caring for the bison. He'll know more. I'll give him a call to let him know we have a wanderer in the midst."

She chuckled. "Maybe that one is being helpful and eating up the dead grass. Would be nice to have a little bit of natural wild fire control."

"They're not goats."

She glared, her green eyes glittering like emeralds. "Just looking for the positive."

He liked her slightly annoyed and feisty. Playing the victim didn't suit her. And she had a point. He spent too much time focused on the worst outcomes. He had a tendency to predict his own demise. Instead of the positives of a self-fulfilling prophecy, he carefully plotted his own doom. He needed to look at his life from a different perspective. She was good at reminding him about that. "I'd be a lot happier if I followed your lead."

"Glad to hear it." She lifted the corner of her mouth in a tilted grin.

He stared at her lips. She twisted her mouth to create the most fascinating shapes to express every emotion. Anger, frustration, and amusement were the three he'd witnessed the most. What else could she do?

She darted her tongue along her lower lip.

He flexed his hand at his side, fighting the itch to reach for her, pull her close, and do something inopportune like trace her mouth with his tongue.

The wind blew past and knocked her cap off her head. Without waiting, he raced after it and grabbed the hat in a couple yards. He returned with the prize, and she accepted, stuffing the cap back on her head with short, jerky motions.

"You know you'll get an earful from Ian about the animals too close to his shop," she said.

Joe sagged his shoulders. With that statement, the moment of romantic potential was officially over. But she wasn't wrong.

He narrowed his gaze for one last look at the bison, but couldn't discern if it was the troublesome male that had been treated more like a pet than a wild beast. Lover Boy had shading around his eyes that made it look like the top of a heart. Once he got to town and spotted people, pushing him back onto the prairie would be a challenge. Joe couldn't see anything from his position, but he'd shoot Ted a text, just to be sure.

Continuing across the street, he held the door open of The Golden Crown and waved her through first. As he crossed the threshold, he spotted James behind the bar. The other man lifted his chin in the tiniest nod of greeting possible. Joe smiled. He wouldn't hide now that he saw his part in her path forward. He strode toward a table almost in the center of the restaurant. If people were going to notice and talk about them, Joe would rather be seen in the open. He couldn't control other people's opinions or craft a narrative that suited his needs, but he wouldn't be accused of skulking in the corner.

He pulled out a chair for her, but she'd already grabbed the seat across the table. He frowned and scrubbed a hand over his features, not wanting the scowl to linger. Of course, she wouldn't expect him to be courteous and chivalrous. He had a lot of poor behavior to atone for.

James approached with two glasses of water. "Good afternoon." The delivery was as flat as the beverages.

Joe smiled broadly. "Good afternoon. Thank you. I know it's a little early, but could we order the spinach and artichoke dip?"

James nodded and turned his back, striding away.

Abby leaned closer. "Are you sure? That can take a while."

Her voice was barely above a whisper. "I am." He rose his voice to a normal level and said, "Are you ready for tomorrow's tasting?"

She nodded. "I think so. I've never catered a wedding before. But I have experience in accommodating a wide range of palates and dietary restrictions. My menu is both a crowd pleaser and scalable. I can add or subtract without too much fuss. I'll be able to carry it out no matter what."

He reached for his water and sipped. He hated her preparing for a worst-case contingency of no help from the town. From here on out, he had to make a bigger show of his support. A sudden thought popped into his brain. "Actually, since we're here, I was hoping I could convince you to help with my project."

"Me?"

He nodded. "Yes. You can finally shed light on what happened to your family after Hoss was kicked out of town. But I'm also asking for your assistance with some of my upcoming interviews."

"Are you sure?" Color drained from her face. "You might get the door slammed in your face."

He shook his head. "No way. Give them a chance."

"Let's see how tomorrow's tasting goes first." She lifted the corner of her mouth.

He extended his hand across the table. "Shake on it?"

She clasped his hand and shook once.

Her grip was surprisingly strong and firm. Good. He didn't like her at a disadvantage. He preferred her as a worthy foe. *Not anymore.* "Can you tell me more about your family? Do you know what happened?" He brushed the pad of his thumb over her knuckles. For someone who worked with their hands, her skin was surprisingly soft and unscarred.

She pulled her hand back. "If I tell you, you won't believe me." Her playful tone lifted the mood.

He straightened. "Try me."

She drew in a deep breath, sitting taller. "Hoss got sober. When he was kicked out of town, he was exiled from his family as well. His father never forgave him. At his lowest, he found forgiveness through religion."

Joe's jaw slackened. "Seriously?"

She nodded. "Hoss attended seminary and became a minister. He rebuilt his life and created his own family. But he never stayed in one place for long. That became my family's sort of creed. Military as far back as all the stories I've been told."

"Wow." She was right. He didn't believe it. "That is quite a story."

"I have documentation and old journals and such, if you want them." She reached for her water.

"I'd love to see everything." But he was struck by her family never putting down roots. He was glad they had survived and thrived. But to live as nomads broke his heart.

His family had been one impacted by Hoss's fire-starting accidents. It was a many times ancestor but the story sparked his interest in history. Personal anecdotes connected the present with the past in a way nothing else could. While every person was the hero of their own story, they didn't get to be the center of someone else's.

Herd had long cast the Whittiers as villains, and never let them be anything else. But that was wrong. Granting people the grace and space to change was what community should be about. And he hoped he could help her do that. Maybe they'd both win for telling a richer story and setting the record straight.

"How are your plans for your restaurant going?" Joe asked, leaning forward. "How is Harrison?"

"I haven't really dealt with him much lately. I get the sense he did his job and is happy to be done with me."

She smiled but the expression didn't quite meet her eyes. Joe had opinions about Harrison but was slowly learning the value in discretion and respecting others' assessments.

James returned to the table with small plates and napkins. Abby stiffened.

"James, I hope we can still count on your support for the Kincaid events," Joe said.

"Of course. I gave you my word. I won't let you down." James replied, his voice with a hint of modulation and emotion.

"I'm sorry if you felt that I did," Abby added. "Truly."

James folded his arms over his chest and shifted his weight from foot to foot. "I can appreciate you were in a tough spot. We didn't have any preconceived ideas about you."

"But you've lived here long enough to know how many people do," Joe said. "Come on. Casual prejudice against the Whittiers is like the town's citizenship test."

"I suppose that's true." James rubbed the back of his neck. "I guess now I should be grateful you never let me put you on payroll. Otherwise, I might have fraud issues. Let me go check on your food."

"Thanks," she murmured.

Joe reached across the table and rested his hand on hers. Her fingers were ice cold. He wanted to warm her up in both his palms. He burned where his skin touched hers. Instead, he dragged his hand away. He could be her friend. That was it.

CHAPTER 10

A beep echoed through the food truck interior.

With the metal curtain still closed, the chime rang with fervor, every surface reverberating and vibrating. Abby needed the sharp, piercing alert. She moved as slow as molasses. Up since the early hours of the morning, she'd been checking on the meat she started smoking the night before for the day's menu tasting. She'd decided to add another couple pounds in case the wafting aroma of the smoker filtered down the street and lured a few customers her way, despite their best intentions at a continued snubbing.

She shut off the timer and pulled a batch of skillet cornbread from the oven. The sweet scent filled the truck with a heavenly aroma. If she wasn't exhausted, she'd be tempted to cut a slice.

Instead, she crossed to the coffee maker and poured herself the first cup of the day in the biggest container she had on hand. She gulped the hot liquid and started to feel more in control of her day. Rituals were important. She didn't empower coffee to super-charge her in an instant, but the hot drink queued her brain to get started.

She checked on the trays warming in the lower oven and then the pre-portioned cold sides in the fridge. She was as ready as she could be. Perhaps even more so than she would have been before yesterday's meeting. Meg and Joe had restored a bit of her self-confidence. Neither had shied away from being seen with her in public. For a second on the street, after leaving the shop and before heading into the saloon, Abby had shed her troubles as easily as slipping off her boots. She had shared a moment of wonder with Joe as she had marveled at the bison in the distance. She hadn't felt so conspicuous. And she had felt like Joe saw her and not some unwanted burden.

It had been nice.

At The Golden Crown, James had slowly thawed during their exchanges. She was glad he had said what he did. While painful to acknowledge, she hadn't considered how her actions impacted others. Her occasional work at the saloon had been seasonal and sporadic. She'd been paid in cash and dealt with handling her own taxes, thus avoiding giving him her tax information. But she hated to think she'd left James vulnerable to an investigation by the IRS or anyone else because of her lie. Would some irate townsperson flag her to the federal authorities?

As they had finished the appetizer, the dinner crowd and Joe's poker group had filtered into the saloon. Joe made it clear she didn't have to run off. He was just being kind. She knew that but couldn't shake the hope that she held against her heart that maybe he could become a friend.

She raised the metal curtain and grabbed her sandwich board. Carefully maneuvering the folding sign out of the truck, she propped it open next to the back wheel. With a stick of chalk from her back pocket, she listed the day's specials.

"Mustard coleslaw with pulled pork on pretzel roll?" Hank Kincaid's deep voice boomed. "Count me in."

She smiled to herself as she stood, slipping the chalk into her back pocket, and dusting together her hands.

Hank, Ryan, Joe, Ted, and Meg approached from the parking lot.

Abby waved and swallowed the sigh building in her chest. She knew they were all coming. No sense in getting intimidated by the show of force now. "Good, that's one of the menu items for the tasting. I made extra in case I get some business today."

"You will," Hank said, nodding. Dressed in his hat and boots, the older man was every inch a cowboy. With his wrinkled, visage tanned from years in the sun, he could be intimidating. If he wanted to turn a weathered look on the town and frighten some locals into supporting her business, she wouldn't stop him.

"I've set up the picnic table with clipboards and menu sheets. I'll serve each item, and you can make notes. We'll discuss after you've had a chance to sample everything," she said.

"Very organized. I appreciate that," Ryan said.

Meg winked.

"Let me step inside to get the first course," Abby said, turning back toward her truck.

"Go and help her, Joe," Hank said, his gruff tone brooking no opposition.

"Of course," Joe replied and reached the truck first, holding open the door.

With a smile, she climbed the steps.

He shut the door behind him with a gentle thud. "Good work on the printed menu. You've already impressed Ryan with that touch."

Abby glanced over her shoulder at Joe. "I took Meg's idea seriously about setting the tone."

Joe chuckled. "He cares about details. As do you." Joe pointed to the full spread she'd prepared.

She'd probably overdone it. Would the leftover food spoil in her fridge after tasting? Was she wasting money and time? She'd need a lot of customers to get rid of it all. For the Kincaids, however, she'd spend whatever it took with a grateful heart. Their support meant everything.

"I don't take the opportunity for granted. I never do. And especially not now." She leaned against the counter. "Do you think I overdid the tasting menu?"

"Not at all. Go big or go home, right?"

They both knew she had no real home if she didn't cement her position in town. She had courage and wasn't giving up the fight. The sentiment had a casual delivery but cut through her like a knife.

He cleared his throat. "Bad cliché. My apologies." He rubbed his hands together. "I'm here to help. I worked in food service during college. I have some limited experience."

"Oh, that's great." In years past, she hired line cooks for the busy summer season. She hadn't even thought about placing an ad in recent days.

"Don't get too excited. My skills are mostly related to dishwashing."

She smiled. "I'll never turn down a good dishwasher."

He stroked his chin. "Will you pay in food?"

She nodded.

He licked his lips. "Then I'm all yours."

Her stomach tightened. He meant nothing with his accidental double entendre. "I wanted to thank you." Her voice cracked and heat crept up her checks. "You didn't need to stick your neck out for me like you did at the saloon. But I am grateful."

He shrugged. "I'm glad I could help."

She was too. Turning toward the oven, she grabbed a mitt and pulled out the first sheet pan. She set the warm tray on the stove and grabbed the coleslaw out of the fridge. Opening a drawer, she pulled out a pair of disposable gloves and a spoon. She handed both to him. "I'm going to transfer the sliders to another plate, and you can top with the coleslaw."

He accepted the utensils and gloves. "Aye aye, captain."

She pulled on another pair of gloves.

For a few minutes, they worked in silence. Surprisingly, it was companionable. With her secret now revealed, she was more of an open book than ever before. She'd shared her deepest hope with him. Establishing some place as home even when the location of her choosing seemed to be star-crossed. "Dare I ask why Stephanie isn't with the group?"

"She said she'll be along. She had to do something first. Don't worry. She's on your side."

"I hate that there are sides," Abby murmured.

He scooped the last slider with coleslaw. "Don't think about it like that. My poor choice of words is no indication of the general sentiment."

Of course he was right. Still, she couldn't shake her worry. She topped each small sandwich with the other half of the pretzel roll she'd made from scratch. "Okay, I'm all set."

"Hey, before we go out there, thanks for helping me with my interviews tomorrow."

He held her gaze and looked at her intently, not even a flicker of his lashes to break his stare. She didn't feel pity from him only reverence like she was a valued equal. She wasn't sure she was worthy of the high level of consideration, but she appreciated it all the same. She wanted a way to thank him for his display of friendship that would be organic and jotting down notes while he interviewed someone seemed the best option. "My pleasure."

He nodded and strode to the door, descending first and holding the door open for her.

She made her way carefully to the picnic table.

The bride and groom sat on one side, facing the cowboys in their midst. In the center, Abby had stacked plates, forks, knives, and napkins.

Hank tucked a bandana in his shirt and licked his lips. "I'm ready."

Heat crept up Abby's cheeks. She was glad someone was still enthusiastic about her food. "This is the special from the sign, pulled pork sliders. It's bigger than a one-bite appetizer, and you'll need a fork. So, this wouldn't be a good option for passed appetizers." She set the platter down in front. "Please serve yourselves."

The group each reached for a slider and started chewing.

Ryan lifted his head and flashed a thumbs up. He stuffed the rest of his sandwich in his mouth. Then he grabbed another off the platter.

Hank and Ted did the same.

Meg chewed slowly. She set half the sandwich on her plate and dabbed her lips with a napkin. "I think these would be great whenever we serve them. No one would mind using a fork to get every single bite."

Abby smiled. Good. Because she had brisket to serve next. "Let me run and grab some waters for you."

"I'll help," Joe said, following her. Inside the truck, he opened the oven door and peered inside. "Can I grab one? I'm not sure Ryan is planning on leaving any leftovers."

She chuckled. "Go for it. Not like I'll have to worry about serving too many customers today." Opening the refrigerator, she pulled out the coleslaw again along with several bottled waters.

"I wouldn't be so sure." His singsong tone was followed by his finger pointing to the front of the truck.

She stared at him for a long moment. He had to be teasing.

He tipped his head to the window.

Abby turned and sucked in a breath.

Stephanie appeared with Kelly Strong. Both women smiled and waved.

"Oh, wow, hi," Abby said. "Good afternoon, ladies. How many I help you?"

"Two of the specials, please," Kelly said with a grin.

"Absolutely. Coming up." Abby turned toward Joe. "Do you think you could help me run these waters out to the table? And I'll get the next course ready?"

Joe nodded and grabbed an apron off a hook on the door. He wrapped it around his waist. "Sure thing, boss. Just tell me what you need."

A lot of forgiveness and a little grace. She curled her toes in her shoes. Maybe she'd come out okay after all. His friendship was better than she could have imagined. But she'd stop her daydreaming there.

Joe had worked in food service during college. But he hadn't shared the truth of the situation with her. He wasn't embarrassed. He valued hard work.

At a fast casual restaurant, he'd been able to work around his schedule during the school year. Long hours on his feet and dealing with angry customers persuaded him to stay the course and finish his education. But he'd been grateful for the paycheck and learned a lot about diffusing an argument that came in handy for teaching.

He never stopped to consider the industry as a career path. At her side, however, he viewed the whole endeavor through another set of eyes. Inside the food truck, he marveled at her cool-head in the chaos of the lunch rush. She had seemingly bottomless energy and enthusiasm. For each order, she devoted time and care to crafting the meal.

Without missing a beat, she prepared every dish with precision. The portions were exact. The presentation was impeccable. To the soundtrack of constant motion—the clanging of utensils as served, water rushing from the faucet, and customers conveying their orders and conversing together—he was hit by an awful realization. She was an artist. He was jealous.

In a rush, he understood his earlier apprehension at the beginning of their acquaintance beyond her keeping a secret. She had attained a level of skill in her field far exceeding what he could imagine. No matter how many hours he devoted to study, he would never be as accomplished. He toiled.

By comparison, his achievements were feeble. His project was like a last grasp for respect. No wonder he'd held a subconscious grudge. Now that he saw the truth, he couldn't hide. He didn't want to. She might outclass him by miles. He wouldn't be intimidated to stay away. He wanted to help and—in doing so—earn the gratitude she had heaped on him. For too long, he'd allowed envy to influence his distrust. He was ashamed.

He hadn't noticed her focus and determination before. Because he'd been so busy looking for her faults? He could kick himself. After helping serve the rest of the tasting menu to the Kincaids, he carried their kudos back inside the truck and helped her.

He smiled at the line forming in front of the truck. While he didn't spot the Rabbitts, not surprising given they'd be handling their own business, he smiled at many familiar faces, including Miriam the town librarian.

He was glad. If he had paid even tiny bit of the debt he owed her by publicly friending her yesterday, after his proclamation at the ranch a month earlier, he did something right.

She kept her cool between serving customers and the wedding tasting. After the last customer in line was served, he faced her. "Finished."

Grinning ear to ear, she glanced over her shoulder and sighed. "Oh, thank goodness."

"And just the perfect amount of food, too." He scanned the empty trays, platters, and containers.

"Somehow it worked out. I'm glad I woke up so early."

He smiled. "I'm sure the delicious smell of the smoker wafting through town played a big part."

She untied the apron on her waist. "I owe the line to Stephanie. Thank you for helping. I couldn't have managed alone."

"I'm not done yet." He crossed to the sink and turned on the water.

"You really don't have to do this."

"I wasn't joking. You can bring me the dishes and dry." He tossed a dish towel at her.

She caught it, threw the cloth over her shoulder, and grabbed the trays.

He wouldn't have anticipated the quiet companionship he found in completing a chore with her. But every day seemed to surprise him.

He rinsed the last container, turned off the faucet, and slipped off his apron, drying his hands. He couldn't help but wonder if he'd hindered her in the long run. If he hadn't been so negative against her for so long, would she have found the courage to come out with the truth sooner? He didn't deserve her praise.

"Oh, my."

He spun back. Something in her tone was equal parts wonder and worry. He wouldn't worry about how he knew the sound. "What is it?" he murmured.

"Well. Oh goodness. It's one of the bison. And it's huge. Should I be worried?"

He stood at her side and stared out through the open ordering window. "The last orders were to-go, right?"

She nodded. "Do we have anyone at the picnic tables?"

"We shouldn't. What do we do?"

He scrambled his brain for the crash course Ted set him on recently. "We stay put. He'll move on."

"If I was a real cowgirl, I'd know what to do."

"What's this?" he asked.

"Nothing just..." She grabbed a dishcloth and rubbed the counter.

He studied her from the corner of his gaze. The stainless steel was already spotless. But the motion seemed to soothe her. He liked observing her and noticing the little things he'd missed. She never asked for someone to take care of something for her but jumped in and did hard work, figuring out if she needed help along the way.

Her open-ended statement was another opportunity to assist. "Have you been getting flack for your heritage? For not being Western born and raised?"

"Not that exactly. Herd isn't opposed to outsiders, thankfully."

He nodded.

"I hear things. Not necessarily meant as jibes but still not quite polite."

About alcohol? Of course, the biggest worry about a Whittier's return was the most unfair, that the drunkard descendant would stumble around and set fire to the town again. The community as a whole seemed to expect any descendant of Hoss would seek retribution or total destruction. Accepting the truth, someone they'd known and liked who wanted to put down some roots, didn't line up with what had been ingrained for so many years. "Are you suggesting that you should be able to go out and round up the bison purely because you're a Whittier?"

"When you say it like that it sounds really dumb." She sighed. "But shouldn't I be more of a cowgirl? Shouldn't I at least know how to ride a horse?"

"Do you want to learn?" *I'd be happy to teach you.* To his surprise, he rather liked the idea of instructing her in how to embrace her roots. He wasn't the best equestrian but knew enough for leading his tours.

"Actually, I'd hate it." She scrunched her nose. "I tried once, and I freaked out."

"Why?"

"In the saddle, I was too high off the ground. I'm scared of heights."

He had no response. Could a fear be aggravated by such a small impetus? He wanted to argue she'd be fine. With his help, he'd quickly get her comfortable and riding like a professional. But that wasn't fair. It was okay for people to know their limits. It was up to others to respect that.

"Should I close the curtain?" she asked, pointing out the window. "Is he being led here by the smell?"

"He shouldn't be attracted to meat. Bison eat grass."

She turned towards him and put both hands on her hips, glowering. "Wait, was I right?"

He frowned. Facing off against a wild animal, and she jumped onto a chance to win an argument? "What do you mean?"

"When I said maybe the bison could help with wild fire control by eating grass?"

He scrubbed his face with both hands, hiding the smirk. "You said they aren't goats."

He dropped his hands. "You're right. I'm sorry. The truth is, I have no clue." He leaned closer and narrowed his gaze.

The bison's distinctive coloring around his eyes was just visible from the hundred yards of distance. A light, irregular ring in the fur looked like a heart.

"I know that bison. That's definitely Lover Boy. He has no practical skills." Joe sighed. "He was a pet. I think he heard people and got lonely. I'll let Ted know he's out here."

"Is he friendly?"

"Very much so." Joe pulled his phone out of his pocket and pulled up his texts. "At least, for a bison. He's a wild animal. Don't approach him. Keep your distance."

She rested her hand on his phone screen.

He glanced up.

"Maybe don't tell Ted. I wouldn't mind the company for a little bit. It's lonely at my truck right now," she said, softly.

He vowed to be nicer then and there. No matter how everything played out in town. If she earned her redemption or not, if he was able to help her or not, whatever the costs, he would be her friend. Because he couldn't stand to think she was lonely and he'd been the cause. She was kind and sweet and talented. She deserved the world and way better than what he'd given.

But he had another chance, and he wasn't going to spoil it. He slipped the phone back into his pocket. "I'll let him know in a bit. Do you suppose your affection for a bison is your ranching ancestry coming out?"

She giggled. "Not in the slightest. I can't twirl a lasso."

"I don't think—technically speaking—lassoes are twirled."

She pursed her lips.

Joe laughed. The expression highlighted her perfectly kissable mouth. No, he tamped that down. Spending time with her had nothing to do with attraction, and everything to do with righting his past behavior. Her fun personality made the situation a bonus. He saw no harm in prolonging their encounter for another hour. "How else may I help?"

"You've done more than enough."

Not nearly. He had a lot of apologizing to do. Manual labor was one way to repay his debt. Maybe he had a better reason to spend time with her again under the guise of friendship. "Will you join me at my interview tomorrow?"

"Do you think I'd be welcomed?"

"I do." Because he wanted her company. He suspected the more time he spent with her the more he'd want to see her. He might be making a big mistake. If Hank Kincaid caught a whiff of their changed status, he'd push his matchmaking again hard.

"I'd be delighted."

And—to Joe's surprise—so would he.

CHAPTER II

Abby smoothed her hair behind her ears and shifted on the passenger seat in Joe's SUV. She should have worn a ponytail or a bun. With the weather warm enough she could leave her knit hat at home and the humidity still low enough not to inflame her naturally wavy mane, she couldn't resist leaving her hair down. But now she worried for another reason.

She stood out. Everyone knew the auburn hair was the mark of a Whittier, enemy to town. Some might have forgotten about the family's coloring but once her identity was known they'd all be sure to notice. One good day wasn't going to be enough to suddenly atone for her sins. She wasn't a fool.

Joe parked the car in the driveway and cut the engine. "Ready?"

She smiled, not feeling the emotion but desperate to fake it. She patted the purse in her lap. "All set. I've got a notebook and pens. I vow to sit quietly and take diligent notes."

"Well..." He wrinkled his brow. "I didn't invite you to be silent. If you have a question, you are free to ask as long as you don't interrupt. And I've learned over the past few years, you need to pause for longer than you would in a normal conversation. Once the interviewee starts reliving their memories, they need time to process. A comment or question asked too quickly can throw the interview off track."

She nibbled her bottom lip. She was famous for fast-talking and jumping into conversations. Essentially, she'd have to bite her tongue to give anyone enough time.

"Can you do that?"

She flashed a thumbs-up. "I'll do my best. I should be an expert in waiting for others to speak first after the last few weeks."

He nodded. An air of solemnity heavy in the vehicle.

"Besides," she said, rushing ahead before silence ensued. "I used to be obsessed with a kid detective TV show on public broadcasting. Patience solved those cases."

"*Ghost Writer?*" he asked.

"Word."

They both chuckled at her invoking the show's catch phrase.

"I cut my teeth on those episodes," he said. "I sent in a self-addressed stamped envelope to my local public TV station for the sticker for my notebook and everything."

She smiled. She'd done the same, anointing one wide-ruled single subject as her official casebook. It was nice to learn how much more they had in common than she'd ever suspected.

Their mutual respect for the other's abilities warmed her, too. She'd do her best to be an active, but unobtrusive, participant. "Who are we meeting?"

He grabbed his phone from the cupholder and scrolled through the lock screen to his calendar. "Will Buck's grandmother."

"Will Buck? Like owner of the General Store?" She drew in a sharp breath.

"Yes. He didn't grow up in Herd, but apparently his grandmother did. She moved away when she got married and then Will wandered back." Joe lifted a shoulder. "Doesn't seem so odd, all things considered."

"I suppose not." She rolled her eyes at his playful tease. But the smile that followed was genuine. Still, she couldn't fully shake her trepidation. It clawed at her with an icy burn.

"Will is at the store. And, according to Ted, Will is taking Jennifer out on a date after work. He shouldn't be here today. If it makes you feel better."

"Thank you. I'm not trying to avoid anyone. I just don't want to make your project awkward for you." And in a small town, everyone seemed to know everyone else's business. Will was dating Ted's sister so those in either orbit would know his plans.

"I'm grateful. But you are fine," he murmured. For a moment, he held her gaze and smiled.

The crinkles at the corners of his eyes reflected his sincerity. Her stomach flipped. She craved his gaze only to squirm under his focus.

"He'll come around. He's not a bad sort. And trust me, the rest of town will forgive you, too. We better head inside."

She unbuckled her seatbelt and exited the car. Rounding the bumper, she followed him up the front path to the door of a snug colonial revival home.

Joe rang the doorbell.

She glanced over her shoulder, taking in the neighborhood. Built in the seventies and eighties, the homes in the subdivision were the most recent, major construction project in city limits. An apartment complex with a strip mall had popped up off the highway a little further out of town. But with no great demand for housing, no one had broken ground any closer to Herd despite plenty of available land. Her restaurant's construction would have been the subject of scrutiny regardless of ownership.

The front door opened.

"Hello? Mr. Staunch?" A petite, silver haired lady dressed in a sweater set, pearls, and pressed chinos answered the door.

Abby felt shabby in her jeans. She should have dressed in nicer clothes.

"Yes, good morning, Mrs. Buck. Thank you for taking time to meet with me," Joe said smoothly.

"Are you Abby Whittier?" Mrs. Buck asked.

Abby drew her shoulders up tight, hoping the sneer or whatever else she'd come to expect of the townsfolk would bounce off her. When she met the pleasant expression of the older lady, she relaxed. "I am." Answering to her real name felt almost as foreign as those first few months using the alias.

"Don't suppose you've brought any food?" Mrs. Buck licked her lips. "I love your brisket. Willie brings it home for me when you have your specials in the summer."

Willie? The nickname soothed a little of the sting from the grandson's continued anger. "Oh, that's so sweet of you to say. I'm sorry. I didn't know," Abby's voice cracked.

"It's okay. Next time." Mrs. Buck winked and held open the door. "Please come inside. I'm very pleased to have both of you here."

Joe waved Abby through first.

She passed the threshold into in a short entryway leading to a living room on the right and stairs to the left. She followed Mrs. Buck into the living room and settled on the sofa. Beyond the next open doorway, sunlight spilled in from a sliding glass door, illuminating a large eat-in kitchen with a southern exposure backyard.

Joe settled down next to her, rifling through his messenger bag.

Mrs. Buck sat in an arm chair, facing the sofa.

Abby pulled out her notepad, silenced her phone, and studied her surroundings. The fully furnished rooms had bare walls. No knickknacks or commemoratives took up space on a table, shelf, or cabinet. The khaki color carpet blended into the beige wall color and cream tiles in the connecting kitchen. Joe told her the home belonged to Will and that his grandmother moved in. She didn't see any personality to the space.

Perhaps Mrs. Buck had a suite of rooms decorated to her taste, with warmer colors and specific details. Will's home was bland. Because he spent so much time at work? Abby wouldn't have to worry about making that mistake, when the time came. She'd be living just above her business and decorating as she chose.

"Mrs. Buck, do you have any questions for us before we start talking?" Joe asked.

"I am curious, if I change my mind and want to redact some of what I've said, how I'd be able to do that?"

Abby's eyebrows stretched into her eyebrows at the woman's question. How many scandals had Mrs. Buck witnessed? Abby came to the right interview.

"Is there anything in particular you are worried about?" Joe asked. "To be honest, no one has brought this up. I haven't been trying to uncover gossip or old stories, if that's your concern. My interest is purely in trying to understand how the town has changed. You're not being interrogated."

"I know you're friendly with the Kincaid family. And… I just don't want to say anything that might upset any of them," Mrs. Buck said.

Abby shut her gaping mouth. She was brimming with follow-up points but silently counted to ten. As neither Mrs. Buck nor Joe said anything, Abby inserted herself into the conversation. "Mrs. Buck, I can assure you the family are very reasonable. They've been forgiving and welcoming of me. You won't need to fear retribution."

Mrs. Buck smiled. "Well, it's nothing damaging. I've known Hank a long time. I doubt he'd remember me. I had an opportunity to see him over Easter, but I caught the flu. Not that he would have known I was absent."

"How did you meet Hank?" Joe asked. He hadn't turned on his phone's voice recorder and made no move to uncap the pen in his hand.

"My maiden name was Everson. I'm the kid sister of Hank's high school girlfriend, Ava," Mrs. Buck said.

"He dated someone before Susie?" Joe asked.

Mrs. Buck nodded, interlacing her fingers, and lowering her chin.

Wide-eyed, Joe met Abby's gaze. *What?* He mouthed.

"And you are concerned Ryan might be hurt by stories about his grandfather's first love?" Abby added.

"Exactly. I don't want to upset him," Mrs. Buck said, pressing a hand to her heart. "I lost my sister about a decade ago. Hank and Susie came to the funeral. They were very kind. I went to Susie's service. I kept telling myself I should reach out to him for a chat. It would be good to catch up. I didn't want to force myself on him."

She looked wistful and girlish. Abby smiled. "You should call him. You can never have too many friends, right?"

From the corner of her gaze, she scanned Joe's grin. She relaxed. She feared her instantaneous response betrayed the code she'd agreed to follow.

Joe reached inside his pocket for his phone. "Do you mind if I record our interview? I can type up my notes and send them to you. Anything you want to strike from the conversation, you can."

"Yes, please," Mrs. Buck said.

Joe turned on the dictation app and set the phone on the coffee table. "Mrs. Buck, wherever and whenever you want to begin."

"Hello, I am Lana Everson Buck."

The older lady continued, but her words became almost white noise to Abby. Instead of participating, she found herself content to observe. Joe was a thoughtful, patient, and considerate interviewer. Treating Mrs. Buck with respect, he earned the same in return tenfold. His reputation in town was well-deserved. She knew he wanted to be an expert, a trusted historian. He didn't need credentials or accolades. He already was an important member of their small society.

The more she learned about Joe, the more she valued and liked him. Maybe being scorned by the town had provided the unexpected chance to become allies. But she was almost glad for it.

His friendship had come to mean so much. She had the urge to reach for his hand and squeeze. But she wouldn't risk asking for too much. Instead, she'd just sit in the comfort and warmth of his companionship. She wouldn't ask for more. Even if she wasn't sure what she felt as far as Joe was concerned.

Joe drove the SUV down Main Street as the sun started to dip on the horizon. The sky was washed with pink and orange and blue. It looked sugar-sweet just like his day.

They'd ended up spending the entire afternoon with Lana Buck. She brought out old yearbooks, scrapbooks, and more memorabilia from the high school and town than he'd ever seen. She had buttons and bumper stickers from Herd's celebration of the American bi-centennial and even more saved from Herd's big party in the 1990s. He'd been too young to think about keeping anything, and his mom wasn't the nostalgic sort.

The talk was illuminating and charming. And not just for the bygone tales Mrs. Buck told. Whenever he was at a loss for words or the next question, Abby jumped in.

She was never flippant or off the cuff. She thought quickly though, faster than he did. Her statements were insightful and encouraging. She enhanced the interview. He almost wished he could re-interview everyone with her at his side. What would he learn now with his new double act?

He drove slowly through town. The lights had turned on, spilling onto the street, and raised sidewalk. He hoped someone would see them. He didn't want to hide their association anymore.

He drove past the General Store. Will should be heading home soon. Lana was making his favorite meal, chicken pot pie. Joe envied him having someone there who cared. Joe had been as eager as anyone else to leave home for college and hadn't ever truly returned to living with his family. He hadn't missed it. Until the past few months or maybe even the past year, when his friends started to couple off and had less time. Then he'd envied those who had someone else—whether romantic or not—in their lives.

"Do you think she'll call Hank?" Abby asked.

Her voice was soft and sweet, almost wistful. Joe smiled. "I'm going to make sure I give Hank her number, too. They should spend time together and catch up."

She turned in the seat and arched an eyebrow.

From the corner of his eye, he spotted the incredulous look. "What?" He continued to Church Street and turned into the parking lot. "What's that look for?" He pulled to a stop.

"No look." She shook her head.

He rolled his eyes. She wore every single expression like a costume. Happy, sad, mad, and confused were broadcast with her expressive eyes. And yet, somehow, she'd concealed her identity, hiding in plain sight.

"Oh, okay, fine." She exhaled a heavy sigh, turning towards him and loosening the seat belt. "I can't help but wonder if you're turning the tables and setting him up now."

He grinned. "Turnabout is fair play. They both still have a little spark."

She tapped a finger to her chin. "I hadn't thought about it like that. Maybe we should be careful. Those two are both feisty. Together, they could start a fire."

He laughed, the chuckle flowing out of him with ease. Being with her had shifted so abruptly from pain to pleasure. Joe wouldn't mind a little heat as long as he wasn't engulfed in the flame. Since Hank backed off of setting him up with Abby, Joe finally came to understand what would have inspired the old cowboy to make the match in the first place. Unlike the match Hank had engineered for his friend and boss, Ryan, Joe hadn't known Abby forever. Sure, he'd gone a year and a half without seeking her out. But was Hank's push really what prompted him to change his opinions about her?

He wasn't so sure.

"I think it would be nice for Hank to have a companion. But Ryan might get jealous," Abby said.

"He doesn't have the time. Between his wedding and his business and his new wife, he should be able to let his grandfather do what suits him. Hank should enjoy himself too. He raised two kids almost thirty years apart. He should relax now while he can."

She shuddered.

"You okay?" He turned the key in the ignition, warming up the engine and restarting the heater.

"Sure, I'm not cold so much as... I guess it all just hit me. Everything Hank's lived through. So much pain and loss. He's so steady and so positive. A lesser person would have keeled over from any number of his hardships. But he's still here. That's..." She sniffed and swiped at her eyes. "Inspirational."

Joe fumbled in the glove compartment for his stash of tissues and handed her one.

"Thanks." She accepted the square and blew her nose.

"Herd will come around and accept you. You haven't done anything unforgivable. Your reasons are understandable. The town holds its prejudices. You've made them all wake up and realize what they're taking for granted."

"If you say so," she mumbled.

"I do. In fact..." He shouldn't do it. He'd barely had a chance to update it over the past few weeks since learning of her claim. But he wanted her to see she had a friend. "I want you to read what I have in my manuscript so far."

She widened her eyes. "Are you sure?"

"I am. I have some hard facts about your family in there. I need to edit and compile all my recent notes. But I want you to see what my goal for the project is. If you have time?"

She nodded. "Of course I do."

He reached behind her seat, unzipping the front flap of the messenger bag. He grabbed the stack of two-hundred recycled paper sheets bound with a thick binder clip and pulled them out. In his hands, he scanned the neat, white stack. This latest version hadn't had his red pen and sticky note treatment yet. "You can mark it if you want. This is not the final edit by a long way. But I'd appreciate your thoughts."

She accepted the pages and held them to her chest.

Her actions were tender. She cared and understood the enormity of his vulnerability in handing over his work for her critical inspection.

"Will you have another interview with Hank? Now that you've met with Lana?" she asked.

"That's a good thought. I have follow-up questions about his high school days." Joe stroked his chin. "If I do speak with him, will you come?"

"Depends when it is. I'll do my best. I'm meeting with Harrison Wolff and an architecture firm this week. At least, Harrison is supposed to be there. I rather think he might have changed his plans."

"How do you like working with him? Has he been treating you well?"

She lifted a shoulder in a shrug. "I know you don't like him."

Joe scrubbed a hand over his face. He wouldn't pretend he hadn't publicly railed against the aggressive lawyer. But that didn't mean he wasn't concerned that she get the full benefit out of the association since she'd already pursued it. "Don't put any stock in my opinion. I don't matter."

"Well, the price for working with Harrison is right."

"It is?" Joe had been turned off by the lawyer's website stating his fee as *market price.*

She shrugged. "Hard to beat free. That's why I think I won't see much more of him. I can't afford his time."

Harrison waved his fee? Joe had misjudged the lawyer. Not that she gave a glowing review. But perhaps the disgruntled Kincaid rival had another, better side. "I'm wondering if I should get a legal opinion about my project before going too much further."

"Like to determine if you can be sued? What are your writing?"

He chuckled. "I like to be prepared for the worst-case scenario. I appreciate advice."

"Oh, then he's definitely got that." She smiled. "He's good at what he does, but he can be determined. Clients and other parties don't know what's best. As far as he's concerned, his opinion is the only one that matters." Abby rolled her eyes. "Are you sure you need him?"

No, Joe wasn't. The problem was his need for validation outweighed every other consideration. He wanted someone—anyone—to approve of what he was doing and encourage him to keep going. "I don't know what I need."

"You're a smart guy. Can't you do it on your own?"

"Self-publish?"

She nodded. "That's one path, sure. Or reach out to publishers on your own."

"Maybe." Perfectionism held him in its sharp talons. If he made the wrong move, would he doom his career and his future? He had spent a lot of time imagining worst-case scenarios. "I want to be sure I'm not putting myself in a bad spot. Legally speaking." Libel was a handy excuse for the real source of his professional procrastination.

"Don't you need to build a presence in your field? Get a reputation as an expert? Or do you publish first?" she asked.

"Again, a good question."

"I believe in you. Whatever you choose."

He held her gaze and for a second, something changed. The air electrified, full of a charge that might zap them at any moment. It was a heavy moment like the lead-up to the final seconds of a game. He almost had the urge to kiss her. He stared at her lips, berry pink and full, slightly parted. He might have leaned forward.

A low moan, deep and rumbling, carried in the air.

"What is that?" he asked, turning toward the windshield.

"Oh, it's just Lover Boy. He likes to hang out by the truck. You're right he loves people."

Joe frowned. He wasn't sure the pairing was for the best. What if the huge beast decided to knock against the food truck? What if the creature ran at her vehicle when she left?

The door opened and shut.

He turned toward the sound and frowned. She'd hopped out of the car?

He rolled down the passenger window. "Hey, are you okay?"

"I'll be fine. Good night and thanks for this." She held up the pages. With a wave, she unlocked her food truck and strode inside.

Lover Boy stood near the picnic tables, keeping watch.

Was Abby running away from one or the both of the men outside? He wasn't sure. But it wouldn't last. If something was going to happen between him and Abby, it would have a long time ago. Before Hank's meddling and during, they had never rubbed well together. Her needing a supporter changed the tenor of the relationship but that wasn't sustainable. She was a confident, capable woman. And if she'd been interested, she would have kissed him moments ago.

He backed the SUV out of spot and drove home. He knew Ted's advice so he wouldn't bother with the call. Ted would tell Joe just to leave the animal, and he'd learn. Animal instinct would kick in. Lover Boy would go back where he belonged without any unnecessary human intervention. Maybe—in that respect—the bison was smarter than him.

CHAPTER 12

"Of all the wedding tasks," Joe said. "I would never have imagined Ryan delegating this one."

Abby smiled. Seated at a folding table set up to one side of the General Store, she surveyed the eight-foot surface. Slices of cake with buttercream frosting set on small plates filled the tabletop.

"Right? I would have thought tasting the cake was his top priority," she agreed.

Ryan had been an eager participant in her food tasting, firmly stating his selections. She wouldn't have thought he'd pass off the cake sampling. But she wasn't going to question her good luck.

At four o'clock in the afternoon on a Friday, the General Store drew a steady stream of traffic. When she'd received the text from Joe about meeting up, she expected to find a space carved out in the back so Will could hide her away from the public. Instead, he'd welcomed them both warmly and invited them to sit as he started to bring out the cake samples. Perhaps his grandmother convinced him. Or he decided on his own to give her another chance.

The third option, however, was Joe had a hand in this change of heart. It seemed the most likely and the one she hoped had caused the change. Joe was finally, and truly, her friend. Every meeting, she learned something new about him and enjoyed a fun, sparkling conversation.

Abby scooted forward on her chair and reached for a plate. "I'm not going to complain about being asked to do this job."

Joe chuckled and grabbed another. "But," Joe said, dragging the word. "In his defense, it isn't surprising he doesn't have time. He's too busy trying to source potted wildflowers. I don't think he took Meg's request to get married in the field of wildflowers seriously until this week. He wants to fill the barn with enough that she won't mind the locale."

It was a sweet sentiment, even if it took the groom a while to appreciate the bride's sincerity. "I'm certain Meg will love his efforts. He isn't quite the over-the-top, grand gesture guy like Ted. But it'll be perfect."

"Until last fall, I would have pegged Ryan as the public display guy. But Ted, standing in the middle of Main Street and reenacting multiple romcom cliches, proved me wrong."

"Yeah." Her single word reply was delivered more breathless than she intended. Her cheeks burned.

"Do you like public displays?" Joe asked, studying her.

She shrugged. "I've never had one. I guess I don't know." She stuck her fork into a slice and stuffed the cake bite into her mouth. Glad for an excuse to stop talking. She'd never been in a serious enough relationship to warrant such an idea. But in her gut, she knew. She'd love it.

As she chewed, a bright burst of lemon cake hit her tongue first followed by the raspberry curd that cut through the tart bite. She chewed and swallowed, setting her fork to the plate. "Well, that's the winner for me." She slid the plate to Joe.

He frowned, hovering his fork over the cake, reading the plate. "Ryan said no citrus."

Will had used paper plates and written the cake and frosting flavor on the rim in permanent marker.

She slid the plate back over. "Then I claim this whole slice."

"We don't need to act like pirates, laying siege."

"Do you want some?" she said between bites, sliding the plate between them.

"I'm just giving you a hard time." He shook his head. "I'll give the chocolate cake with chocolate fudge filling a taste." He slipped his plastic fork into the cake and it stuck. "Well, maybe not. This is thick. The fork isn't budging."

"Are you sure you don't want a bite of mine? Lemon cake is my absolute favorite. I can attest to the superiority of both the crumb structure and smooth filling." She forked another bite and stuffed it in her mouth.

"I'll trust you since you sound like an expert. Good to know your favorite."

She smiled as she finished chewing. His sincerity warmed her. "What's your favorite?"

"Pie."

She giggled, but the laugh turned into a snort. She covered her mouth and nose with both hands, her cheeks burning.

He grinned broadly.

"Did someone say pie?" Will asked, wiping his hands on his apron.

Joe turned away.

She felt sort of sad to lose his attention. She liked being under his focus. He had a depth of caring she hadn't even guessed at. For two years, she thought she knew him, and she'd been flat wrong. The only saving grace was that she could say the exact thing about him regarding herself. At least they got a second chance.

"Ryan wants cake for the wedding," Joe said.

Will pulled a chair over and sat down opposite. "Understood. He is very traditional."

Abby snorted again. "Sorry, allergies."

A cheeky grin tugged at the corner of Joe's mouth again. "Sure, of course."

"I was wondering if we could have a little more freedom for Hank's celebration?" Will asked. "I know it's the same event. But after the cake cutting, couldn't we do something different for Hank? He won't mind as long as we sing happy birthday."

It was a good idea. While she had spoken with him enough to have heard he didn't mind, she still wanted to make Hank feel special and not like an afterthought. The whole weekend had been all about him, celebrating in grand style after a health scare landed him in the hospital on his birthday last year. Ryan had slowly usurped Hank's event.

Abby cleared her throat. "Sure, what do you have in mind?"

"I wanted to have a dessert bar. I'll have a cake for Hank to blow out his candles. But I wanted to display a variety of sweets," Will said.

"Like fudge?" Joe asked. "Was that real fudge in the chocolate cake?"

Will nodded. "Yes, it was. Our signature dessert."

No wonder Joe couldn't move his fork through the slice. The fudge had the reputation as the go-to pulling solution for kids eager for a visit from the tooth fairy.

"The General Store's fudge has many fans. I love to make pies and bar desserts. If the events do take off at the ranch, I'm hoping to expand my bakery business," Will said. "I guess I figure might as well take this moment to really showcase what I can do, besides standard cakes."

"Good idea," Joe said.

Abby nodded. "I agree. Hank would love whatever you came up with and especially if it's something you're passionate about."

Hank was the town's encourager-in-chief. He hadn't always been. Stories told about him thirty plus years ago showed a man very stringent and stuck in his ways. But at some point, he'd become flexible and open to new ideas. At the time when most people would have doubled down on their old patterns, he became someone new. Hank showed an example of how Abby hoped she'd be in the future too.

"I will." Will smiled. The bell over the front door jingled. "If you'll excuse me?" He walked away to help the customer.

Abby turned to Joe. "Okay, which flavor is next?"

"Right... here's the thing. I know which cake Ryan wants."

"You do?" She gazed at the table full of sweets, darting her tongue over her bottom lip. Will had baked twenty cakes and whipped up different flavor frostings and curds for a full sampling. Had his work been in vain? Could she eat a few more slices before fessing up?

"I do," Joe said. "Ryan wants chocolate cake with white frosting. Meg agreed to it."

"Well... Now I feel bad. Are we wasting Will's time?" She drummed her fingers against the table.

Joe reached for her hand and squeezed. "I couldn't think of another legitimate reason to meet so I agreed to go ahead with it."

His touch sent a shiver along her arm. She licked her lips again. This time, the action had nothing to do with sweets. She stared at his mouth, his full lips curving into a mischievous expression. She'd thought he might kiss her the other day and felt the same charge between them again. "Do you need an excuse to see me?"

"No. But I worried you'd be too busy otherwise."

Good answer. She should hide her smirk. He knew her, and she was glad. "I had a chance to read your manuscript."

He drew back his hand and scrubbed his face. His actions were slow and deliberate. "Oh? What did you think?"

"It's good. Really good. I think you should talk to someone. If Harrison Wolff can help, let him." She managed to keep her voice even.

With time to think, she had accepted the lawyer's curt behavior in the immediate aftermath of her exposure was to be expected. He had been right. She couldn't afford his fee. She would have appreciated his help, but he had never pretended to be her friend. "He has all sorts of contacts in a variety of industries. Or you could strike out on your own. I'd help if I can."

"I don't know that Harrison would want to work with me. I'm close with Ryan."

She wanted to assure him she'd put in a good word with Harrison. But she wasn't sure he'd be at the meeting in an hour. Instead, she reached a hand into Joe's and squeezed. "I know he would. People can change, right?"

He squeezed her hand in return and then lifted her fingers and kissed her knuckles. "You are too kind."

The light touch sizzled her skin, like he'd branded her. A strange and searing feel but not unwelcome. She grinned. She hadn't imagined anything good coming out of her public outing as the big bad Whittier. But then everything worked out better than she could have imagined. "We better get to work eating all these cake slices, so Will won't feel put out."

He winked. "Your wish is my command."

A little thrill zipped along her. Reluctantly, she dropped his hand and reached for another plate.

She hadn't given him any notes.

Joe sat behind his keyboard and stared at the blinking cursor on the computer screen.

The wall clock flashed seven pm, but it might as well have been midnight. The hours had dragged as he mentally berated himself.

Without anything to change or delete, he had no other reason to stall in his writing. He still had to finish adding in Lana Buck's stories as well as figuring out how to restructure the early chapters to include the history of the Whittiers that Abby had shared.

But she hadn't told him the manuscript was garbage, and he should throw it all away. She hadn't offered any critique whatsoever. He'd prepared himself that she might hate his words. Instead, she had praised him. And now he found himself almost immobilized.

Because if it wasn't awful, if the work might be okay, then he should finish and present his study to the world. Maybe that was the whole point she'd tried to get him to. He needed to take a chance with no guarantee of success or the greater reception.

He smiled. She was a leap *whether or not she looked* sort of person. He wanted to be that brave. He hadn't realized how he envied that quality until the past few weeks. She wasn't sure her best was good enough, but she still tried.

While he found the thought terrifying, he witnessed her give each day her all despite the unknown. How much of his perfectionism was imposter syndrome? And how much born of cowardice?

He reached for his water and took a long sip. After cake tasting, he'd grabbed dinner at her food truck, pleased to join the line. The town had again embraced her.

She had rushed to unlock the truck and start cooking.

He had waited patiently at the back of the queue. He bounced on the balls of his feet. The plates of cake provided an overwhelming rush of sugar to his bloodstream. He'd crash hard soon. But he wouldn't regret it. He could have called in the order but then he wouldn't have had the chance to learn her favorite flavor or hold her hand in public.

When his turn had finally arrived, he stepped up to the window and heard the now familiar low moan of the town's lonely bison.

A breeze swept through.

Joe bundled deeper into his jacket and placed his order.

"Would you look at that?" she had asked in wonder.

He turned and spotted the bison.

The wind had blown a hat onto Lover Boy's head. Now a permanent fixture at the food truck, he had looked almost jaunty with the accessory covering one horn.

"You said he was a pet. But I wonder if he wasn't in the circus or in the movies," She had asked with a tone full of such wonder as she.

"I don't know of any celebrity bison."

"He has presence. If any animal deserved their turn in the spotlight, it's Lover Boy."

The statement encapsulated her sweetness. He envied and longed to share her optimistic view of the world. "You're really something special. Did you know that?"

She blushed and handed Joe his order.

He almost kissed her then. Their location, however, had kept him in check. He wouldn't have the whole town as an audience for their firsts, so he held himself back. He had walked around to a picnic table and eaten his dinner, pleased to see a wide variety of faces both familiar and foreign.

School only had a few more weeks until summer break. While she'd told him of counting on tourists to keep her business running, she must be at least a little relieved the town wouldn't abandon her totally, despite their initial reception. When her restaurant opened, she'd have year-round business.

He set the glass to one side and scanned the document again. He still needed to make changes. He hadn't formally interviewed Abby yet and hadn't added her story into the manuscript. The history he presented on the page remained the one-sided version everyone had grown up with. It was time for the town to get comfortable with being uncomfortable.

He grabbed a pen and a legal pad. Writing longhand wasn't the most efficient choice. Often, he had trouble reading his penmanship when he typed his work into his saved document. But he liked the freedom of expression, the connection between his brain and his heart that only the pen conveyed.

What if the ending we've accepted didn't capture the entire picture? What if Hoss's exile ultimately started the man on a path to redemption? Would this explain why his father remained in town for several years following the departure, hoping for a day he could welcome his son back into the fold?

Hoss Whittier left Herd and took a surprising path, finding faith alongside his sobriety. He raised a family. But he never felt a connection to another place, relocating often. His legacy lingered through his own family until one brave descendant returned to challenge the town's myth-making of the early days.

He wasn't sure he quite captured the spirit and gravity of what had occurred in the past and the impact being felt in the present. Would he ever? If he didn't establish some sort of external deadline, he'd never finish the work.

His cell phone rang.

Frowning, he grabbed the device off his desk and swiped his thumb to accept the call from the unknown number. "Hello?"

"Joe? It's Harrison Wolff, calling."

Joe's mouth dropped.

"Listen, I heard you might have a book, and I might have a contact."

In his icy grip, Joe lost his hold on the phone. The device slipped and clattered to the floor. He dropped to his knees and reached for the device. "Sorry. Can you back up?"

"I had a call from Abby this evening, and she shared that you might be in touch. We've never worked together, but as you can imagine I don't like to beat around the bush. If you're serious about your work, you should send me what you have, and I'll put you in touch with my contacts."

For a fee? Joe didn't know much about the publishing industry but Harrison's proposal sounded all sorts of backwards and out of order. Was he going to act as an agent? Approaching Joe felt sort of aggressive? Was this his first moment to test his new found resolve to try?

He'd want a lawyer to review any contracts on his behalf but hadn't anticipated the attorney would seek the sale. What percentage would Harrison expect as both legal counsel and pseudo manager? Fifty percent? An even more outrageous rate?

Trusting someone else for guidance was meant to ease the pressure. But Joe had leaned on someone he expected to stab him in the back. He had set himself up for this moment. A self-fulfilling prophecy. He dragged in a shaky breath.

"Listen, I know this is unexpected. Both that I would call you and that I would want to work with you," Harrison said.

Joe was glad the lawyer couldn't see his smirking face.

"But," Harrison continued. "I'm expanding my practice and looking into pursuing IP in any capacity."

"IP?"

"Intellectual Property."

"Isn't that more like patents? I'm writing a book."

"You need to think broader. Your writing could launch into a variety of media."

Joe doubted the commercial appeal of his work. Harrison wasn't known for his flattery, and he didn't waste his time on any venture without some personal or professional gain. If anything, Harrison surprised Joe by meeting with Abby. Joe had the impression the lawyer had washed his hands of her association since she hadn't managed any vengeance against the Kincaids.

"And I wouldn't mind seeing the Kincaids taken down a few pegs." Harrison chuckled.

The lawyer had read his mind.

"I'm kidding," Harrison said. "It's a joke."

In Joe's experience, the people who had to point out their mean comments were meant to be funny had very little sense of humor.

"I grew up in Herd, too. I mean no offense to the Kincaid family, but I am glad your work will highlight the entire community's history and not focus solely on the last legacy ranchers. People like you and me count, too."

"You're absolutely right about the scope of my project," Joe said, calming down. While he didn't entirely trust the lawyer's motives, he vowed to keep his wits through the process. "If we move forward, what's the next step?"

"You send me a copy, and I reach out to my contacts. A few editors and a couple agents. We get a feel for the interest."

Literary agents? Or film industry professionals? Would that be realistic? A big screen adaptation hadn't been part of his plan. That didn't mean the path was meritless. Joe was getting ahead of himself. He swallowed. "I'm not finished."

"You don't need to be. This is more of a proposal than anything else. Let me see if it's even worth your time to complete the work."

Joe furrowed his brow. If his life's work wasn't deemed valuable, he walked away. From a logical standpoint, he understood. But the black and white nature of the prospect skewered him through the heart.

Was Joe really going to consider involving himself with someone who'd make that sort of comment? Harrison never understood Joe and that hadn't changed. Joe pinched the bridge of his nose. What would the Kincaids think about this?

Hank would encourage him to do what he needed. Ryan wouldn't like it but he'd never begrudge anyone a career opportunity. "Okay, what exactly do you need from me?" Joe asked.

"Write up a couple paragraphs, like the back of the book. Then I need two to three pages of synopsis. Send me those along with the manuscript you have so far. By Monday."

Joe almost chortled. Oh sure, no problem. The number of pages was overwhelming. How to sum up all of his interviews and research into an enticing couple of paragraphs and a synopsis? He'd devote his weekend to the work. At least he had a deadline now. On his own, the project would never be completed. "Okay. Fine. By Monday."

"Great."

Are you sure you want to work with me? Joe held back the insecure question. He knew the lawyer never did anything he didn't want to do. Joe's lack of confidence wouldn't endear him to the person he turned to for help. But his imposter syndrome lurked just behind his smile. "I'd better get to work."

"Please do. We'll be in touch," Harrison said and ended the call.

For a few seconds, Joe sat in silence. He'd probably been oversold. Abby's enthusiasm for his work had been relentless. He wanted to trust her opinion about the value of his project.

He pushed off the floor and strode the length of the room. Harrison made the entire process seem simple. Joe wanted to trust the path wasn't as complicated as he'd been making it in his head. Regardless, he had his work cut out for him if he was going to update the manuscript with what he'd learned from her and Lana. And only so many hours in the weekend.

CHAPTER 13

Abby opened the front door of the Hawke house, bracing for impact.

Colby loved to greet everyone at the threshold. The mutt didn't particularly care if a person had only stepped outside for a moment to check the mail. If a human walked inside, the human must submit to a thorough sniffing as Colby happily wagged her tail.

But today, Abby walked in without an elaborate welcome.

She frowned and peered over her shoulder through the still open doorway. She'd driven herself home, not wanting to hold up Meg. Since everyone knew where Abby now lived, she saw no purpose to the subterfuge besides reinforcing the town's opinion of her behavior as sneaky.

Meg's car was in the driveway.

Where was Colby? The pair were always together. Or almost always.

A lump caught in Abby's throat and her limbs were heavy. She hadn't grown up with dogs. In the short time since moving in to the pretty white ranch house, however, she'd become accustomed to the pup and glad for the freely given kisses.

"Meg?" Abby called, shutting the door, and slipping off her shoes. She padded through the empty first floor, from the front door through the living room to the dining room.

"Colby? Are you here?" The dog loved to sleep. Perhaps she'd curled up on her dog bed in the kitchen.

The kitchen was empty too.

She returned to the front hall. "Meg? Are you home?" Abby tried again and climbed the steps.

On the second floor, she heard movement. Tiptoeing down the hall, she kept her back against the wall. Her pulse pounded. She wasn't going to walk into a crime scene. She attempted to reason but couldn't fight the bile rising in her throat.

At the front bedroom, she eased the not quite shut door open with her fingertips, holding her breath.

Inside, Meg danced around her bedroom.

Abby entered and sighed.

Meg shrieked.

Abby jumped.

"Abby?" Meg removed a tiny earpiece. "Gosh, you startled me."

"You startled me," Abby said, bracing her waist with both her hands and dragging in deep breaths. "Where is Colby? What are you doing?"

"I'm packing." Meg held out her hands.

Abby assessed the stacks of fresh, never folded cardboard boxes near the window. Several large wardrobe style boxes sat open near the closet. "Packing? Already?"

Meg patted her bed. "Colby is spending the evening with Hank. She gets worked up whenever I pack, even for a weekend. She'll be happy once we are there. But the process overwhelms her."

Abby crossed the room to sit on the soft mattress, her hands gliding over the worn quilt. She knew Meg planned on moving into the Kincaid ranch house. During the summer, the ranch house operated as the lobby for guests, not offering privacy for newlyweds. But moving one person versus two was preferred.

In the past few weeks of cohabitating, however, Abby had blocked the knowledge from her mind. She liked living in the gracious, warm, welcoming home. More than that, she enjoyed Meg's company. She hadn't started to look for another place yet. She wasn't sure anyone in town would rent to her again. Moving to the apartment complex outside town would give her more of a social life. Stephanie and many of the other young, single people lived in the modern building stocked with amenities. But the drive would be burdensome. Abby wasn't sure any complex would have the parking necessary for her vehicle.

Meg grabbed a flat box and began to assemble. "Are you okay? Everything go alright today?"

"Yes, it did. Sorry." Abby shook her head. "Didn't mean to give you the wrong impression. I just...forgot about the move. I really shouldn't. I was cake tasting for you today. I know you're getting married."

Meg chuckled. "Were you pleased with the options? Were the cakes good?"

"Will had a lot of choices. I wouldn't have been able to narrow it down." Abby could still taste a hint of lemon. She licked her lips. "I'm surprised you didn't want to join us at least to enjoy free dessert."

"I agreed to whatever Ryan wanted so I didn't want to change my mind with options. Ryan is the picky one in the relationship," Meg said, her right eye twitching. "I can't believe he didn't join you. I'm slammed setting up the framework for future weddings. I want to use our big day as a test run for clients so I spend my time looking at the big picture, getting samples, reviewing contracts. I can't get lost in the details. I'm glad you and Joe are taking care of the minutiae." Meg finished taping the bottom of the box and crossed to her dresser, grabbing sweaters by the armful. She dropped her pile into the box and repeated the motion. "I'm glad we are starting our events business with our own. I'd rather not use a paying customer as a test run."

"How do you think it is going?" Abby shifted on the bed. She hadn't had a chance to pick Meg's brain about the new business. The success of the ranch impacted Abby for better or worse. While they might not be true partners, they each felt the consequences of the others' choices.

"Slow but steady. I'll know a lot more after the event. Thank goodness we won't have another wedding until next year." Meg sealed the full box and set it on the ground, pushing it to the wall. She assembled another box.

"I can help you build some boxes." Abby held out her hand.

"Thanks." Meg carried a stack to her along with the tape.

Abby began to fold the first box and secure it with the clear tape. She slid the completed box onto the ground and started on the next.

"I can't believe I'm leaving," Meg said, sighing.

Abby glanced up.

Meg didn't stop moving.

Abby reasoned she couldn't. The countdown calendar in the kitchen now flashed with a warning. "What will you do with this house?"

"In the long term? I'm not sure. My mom owns the house. I don't think she has any intention of selling. But houses need to be lived in. They need care and maintenance. I don't want this place sitting empty."

Abby nodded and moved on to the next box in the stack. After growing up in Chicago, Meg had relocated to Herd. The house was her mother's childhood home. Meg craved the small town her mother had escaped. Would her children do the same? Or would they love the land like her husband-to-be's family?

"Would you want to stay?" Meg asked.

Abby met her gaze. "Does that mean you'll let me pay you rent?"

Meg bristled.

"I can't keep squatting on your property." Abby hated being treated like a victim.

Meg scrunched her nose. "I hate that word."

Abby shrugged. She didn't have a better word choice to define what she was doing.

"Until your restaurant opens, you'll need a place. Construction might last a year. I'd be happy for you to stay here. I hate to think about it empty."

"I won't stay unless I pay you something."

"Fine."

"To be honest, I wonder if it's too much for me." Abby shivered remembering the chill that snaked up her spine when she thought an intruder was in the house. Without the dog to greet her, she hadn't entered with the same sense of homecoming she had begun to take for granted.

"Why not ask Stephanie? Her lease is up soon."

"That's a great idea. She's swamped with studying. I bet she hasn't even looked into what she'll do next. I'm sure Ted would like having her close."

Abby agreed. Stephanie's long-time crush turned boyfriend was the lead cowboy on the Kincaid ranch next-door. "I'll give her a call."

Meg stuffed another box to bursting and taped it shut. "What about you? Any changes to report?"

Abby's cheeks burned. Hank Kincaid, Meg's soon to be grandfather in law, had made no secret about his matchmaking. He'd had Abby and Joe in his sights for over a year. But it was moot. No matter that Abby liked Joe. Until recently kept himself slightly removed. He was a historian and, by default, an observer. He wasn't the type to get in and live. He'd study and analyze.

Sure, over the past six weeks or so, he'd changed and become a friend. But he'd always have a separation, like he looked at her through a pane of glass. She didn't always mind his gaze. What would it feel like to be in his arms?

A low, deep moan sounded from outside.

Abby hopped off the bed and joined Meg at the window.

Outside, Lover Boy nudged the side of her truck and grunted. The bison must have traveled at top speed to follow her. They were a surprisingly fast animal. Abby hadn't noticed a lumbering animal running behind her. But she was more than a little distracted lately.

Abby chuckled. "That's all the romance in my life I can handle."

"Is that okay?"

"Ted thinks so. But I better start leaving the truck on the ranch to keep him safe," Abby replied.

Lover Boy didn't quite fit. Despite his best efforts, he remained misguided. She was exactly the same. What a pair they made.

At the kitchen table in the snug cabin, Joe stared at the cards in his hands. Unseeing. He blamed his location for his lack of focus.

Ted lived across the lake from the spa barn, guest cabins, and the bunk house for employees on the Kincaid ranch. With the arrival of the seasonal employees, the ranch was coming alive once again. In a few more weeks, the summer would kick off with the resort's Memorial Day weekend opening. And then the big celebration.

Final details for the celebration as well as his summer tour guide job demanded much of his time. Coming to the ranch was no longer the peaceful break in an out of the way location. The ranch was—once again—the center of the local universe.

And Abby's.

She could distract herself with her restaurant all she wanted, but she couldn't hide what was so clear. She didn't have enough customers to keep going in the off-season. She'd need the support of everyone in town, and she wasn't quite there yet.

It hadn't occurred to him before how much the Rabbitts had kept her afloat at the saloon in the colder months. Should he intervene on her behalf with the couple? Would the return of the summer guests be enough to sustain her? She planned to build on her lot but how feasible was the endeavor. He didn't know her financials and worried about how quickly expenses could add up. Because he didn't want her to leave.

"Well?" Ryan asked, arching a brow.

Poker night wasn't the time for his mind to wander. He knew better.

Or at least he used to.

He used to be sure of so many things. The longer his project continued, and the more twists and turns he uncovered along his path to prove himself, however, the more doubt crept in. He should welcome the emotion like an old friend and pull out a chair at the table. They were already a man down. They could use another player. "I fold."

"Call," Ted said.

Ryan laid out his cards and crossed his arms over his chest, leaning back and raising his chin.

Joe examined the hand. A royal flush. At least the other man earned his smugness.

Ted tossed his cards to the table.

Ryan collected his winnings, neatly stacking the chips into a tidy pile. "I feel as lucky as Hank. Not sure if either of you has noticed his chipper moods lately. He practically started singing today."

"What's he up to tonight? Why isn't he joining us?" Joe asked. Hank loved to challenge the younger men to any sort of competition. With each passing year, however, he preferred sitting down events to level the playing field. He rarely missed a card game.

"Trying to get Colby comfortable in the house," Ryan said.

"She isn't?" Ted asked, gathering the cards, and shuffling the deck.

"Not according to Hank. He made her a steak dinner and bought her several dog beds. I think he's concerned she'll sleep in my room after the wedding," Ryan answered.

Joe wasn't sure what to say in response. Before Colby came into Hank's life, the older man treated animals like animals.

Colby softened him. Now he bribed a dog for affection. Love was remarkably powerful at changing hearts and minds.

I should know. Mentally, he kicked himself. The tenderness he felt was the appropriate amount for friends to share for one another. He wasn't a lovesick fool. "Is Meg officially moving in?"

"She is." Ryan grinned. "I wouldn't mind a little separation from work and home over at her place. But I know better than to ever suggest Hank move."

Will Abby be back on the streets? Joe hadn't known about her momentary homelessness until long after the fact when Meg let it slip. She'd stepped up. Thank goodness for her kindness. But learning about Abby's plight—no matter how short—filled him with a despair and hopelessness he could never have guessed. She mattered to him, and he hated that he hadn't realized her precarious situation. He should have been the one to help.

"Stephanie and Abby are going to rent the house together," Ted said. "Steph called with the news a little while ago, all excited. She's stressed about continuing her education and keeping up with all her other tasks. I'm glad she won't be on her own anymore."

"Oh, that's nice," Joe said. "A good solution for everyone."

"To get back to Hank," Ryan added, clearing his throat. "He's acting strange. I'm telling you. Do either of you know why? Does he have a new scheme afoot? Are you two taking his advice about something?"

Could the secret source of Hank's happiness be Lana? Had the older woman kept her word and called him? Joe kept his mouth shut. He wouldn't seek to poke the bear and Ryan was no less wild and grizzly than the massive beasts.

Ted stroked his chin. "Maybe he's happy because Joe is finally being nice to Abby."

"That's the extent of it. No romance. I don't have time." Joe sighed. "I can barely sleep. I'm focused on the wedding slash birthday and school and my tours and the book. That's it. That's more than enough."

"What about your amateur detective agency?" Ted asked. "No more cases to solve?"

Joe shook his head and reached for his cola. Investigations were his forte. But he also came to appreciate that he'd let bias and prejudice keep him from the truth. Or had that been his heart?

"Ted, you ever notice how someone swears off love and then falls head over heels?" Ryan asked.

"No, not me," Joe's refusal was adamant and immediate. "I don't hate her, and that is enough." His mouth filled with an awful sour taste and his stomach churned. He hated denying his feelings to his friends. But he couldn't have more focus on what was happening. Or he worried nothing would change. Pressure made diamonds, but it also cracked glass. Could what he shared with Abby become more than friendship if given space and time?

"If you say so..." Ryan said from the corner of his mouth.

"Are we going to play?" Joe asked.

Ted dealt and the sounds of cards sliding against the wooden table and ice cubes clinking in glasses restored the balance to the room. Joe couldn't find his equilibrium so easily. He hadn't been helpful when she'd needed him. Could he step up in another way?

He grabbed his cards and studied them, shielding the view of his hand from the others. A queen and a king weren't any guarantees of success. In this as in all things, he must make his own way. "I did want to ask about the bison that keeps wandering into town."

"Have we had complaints?" Ryan frowned.

"Not that I'm aware. Why won't he fit in with the herd? Is there a reason?" Joe asked.

Ted shrugged. "Some animals are loners. Can't force everyone into a mold. No matter how it might make your life easier."

The words reverberated within Joe's soul like the clanging of a bell. Joe wanted to make sense of his world by framing it within the larger scope of his moment in history. He wanted to know what would happen next so he could take away the uncertainty of having to make his own choices. He grappled for anything to hold onto.

"I could call the conservation group. Let them know we're having trouble," Ted continued. "But he isn't a nuisance. I worry that the solution suggested will be final."

Ryan dragged a finger across his throat.

"No, don't do that," Joe said quickly. "The town hasn't really opened for the season yet. Maybe we can find a solution."

"Is he attracted to Abby or the truck?"

"I'm...not sure."

Ted stroked his chin. "Huh. Maybe it doesn't matter. As soon as she moves the truck out here, the herd will take him in. Problem solved," Ted said.

If only Joe's issues could be so easily resolved. He'd have to give himself the permission to succeed and finish first. "She's moving here?"

Ted nodded. "Yep. Figured we'd give her some space away from the construction on her lot. Once the crew begins, she'll have a tough time keeping dust and dirt out of her truck. Her customers won't appreciate the noise, either." He stroked his chin. "Actually, she could settle here now."

No. The word was an immediate, knee-jerk response.

Ryan nodded. "Makes more sense than what she's doing at the moment. She lives at Meg's. Would be easier on everyone if she didn't have to run back and forth all day. Might give the bison a chance to get used to the ranch and move on."

I'd miss her. How would Joe stop by and see her without notice? The plan was sensible. But not for him. "Don't you think you should let her make her own decisions?" Joe asked.

Ryan leveled a steady stare. "Of course. I'm not a dictator. Why are you so bothered?"

"Hey, cool down both of you," Ted said. "Abby can make up her own mind. She's an adult and a business person. Ryan will give her a choice."

Joe stroked his chin. "Under pressure, she won't have a choice. To keep everyone happy, she'll agree."

"Fair enough. You ask and give her the option," Ryan said. "She has no problem saying no to you." He chuckled.

"Great," Ted added. "Now pick up your cards and let's play."

Within a few seconds, the tension evaporated in the room as bets were made and laughter shared. Joe wasn't sure if he'd defended Abby or passed some sort of fidelity test with Ryan. Or both. But at least he had another reason to seek her out. That was a good win from a tense round.

CHAPTER 14

Abby frowned at the spray-painted lines on the ground and slowly meandered around the outline. Somehow, ten thousand square feet better resembled the chalk shapes on police dramas. She shuddered. She sure hoped not. What was the crime? The murder of her dreams?

At least the weather was mild for mid-May. She turned her face up to the sun and let the warmth sink into her for a moment. The land near the cemetery was peaceful and quiet.

The air was sweetly scented by lilacs planted near the entrance. Typically, her food truck's cooking overpowered the location. Taking a break from her smoker and ovens, the natural aroma of her plot sank into her, reminding her of the first day she'd come here. When she'd felt like she'd known the landscape by heart because she'd found home.

By the end of the month, she'd witness the ground breaking as long as she approved the architectural plans. After a few changes to allow more privacy in her proposed two-bedroom apartment upstairs, she couldn't think she'd change a thing. Of course, she'd been surprised a lot lately.

She turned toward the picnic tables and approached the builder.

Corey came highly recommended from the over-booked architecture firm. She liked his no-nonsense demeanor. Maybe she should have gotten a second recommendation, but she trusted him. Besides, she wasn't sure who she could have asked for their opinion. Harrison stopped returning her calls. At the ranch, the Kincaids trusted Ted and a work crew of tradesmen to help patch up and fix things. What she wanted was a little more specialized than a barn raising.

Corey spread out the blueprints across the top of one of the picnic tables, weighing down the sheets with rocks and condiment jars.

"Thanks for mapping it out. I still can't exactly visualize it. But that's on me, not you," she said with an apologetic smile. While she'd hired the man, she couldn't shake the trained good girl instincts to make amends for any hint of a slight.

He chuckled. "I should thank you for feeding me first. You've definitely given me the encouragement to get your kitchen up and running."

Making a wrap from leftovers taking up her limited fridge space helped her more than him, but she'd accept his thanks for her hospitality.

She crossed her arms and studied the plans spread on the table. The proposed build lurked at the top end of her budget.

She was paying a premium for speed as much as anything else. The sooner she was officially up and running, the better. Business was slow and the only major events slated for the summer were the opening week birthday celebration and wedding double act.

She hoped she wouldn't have to content herself with utilizing the food truck and the limited kitchen space in the rebuilt barn. She needed to make time to meet with the Rabbitts and discuss their collaboration. Would the meeting be civil? Had enough time passed to move beyond hurt feelings and deal with each other in a strictly professional capacity? At least, after her building was complete, she wouldn't need their help so desperately.

"If I want to expand?" She tapped her finger on the blueprint.

The proposed two-story building would be in the Western style with a high-false front stretching a half level above. The curve to the roofline would differentiate it enough from the appearance of the rest of Main Street to be unique without off-putting. Her goal was to compliment the town and not stand out.

But she didn't want any comments about *if you can't beat them—or burn them—join them.* She wanted tourists to view her business as a natural extension of the rest of the town. Without the raised sidewalk, she'd already be separated. She didn't want any more distance.

"You'll have plenty of space." He pointed to the back of the building. "You could always add a patio. The kitchen is set to the eastern wall. If you wanted to expand the building, you could add another wing and create an L-shaped footprint with a semi-courtyard in the back."

She liked the idea. She could string lights between the two halves outside. It would be like magic during the summer. She could almost feel the warm breeze and smell the sweet grass. Anything was possible with enough cash.

A low groan shook the ground.

She smiled at Lover Boy, standing a few yards away. Of course, she'd need to establish some sort of bison defense system. She wasn't concerned about the tourists' safety. Lover Boy needed protection.

"Whoa, stay back." Corey grabbed a rock and shook his arm.

"Stop, no." She jumped in between the builder and the bison. If she didn't physically block the animal from the man, she worried what either's next move would be. "He's a sweet animal. He's harmless."

"He's a bison. No such thing as harmless."

"I know and don't approach him. But he'll wander away. He doesn't get close," she said.

"If you say so..." Corey eyed the bison and—without looking away from the animal—pulled the blueprints off the table and rolled them up.

The tension dissipated. Her breathing slowed to normal. She really did need to take precautions.

Corey stuffed the blueprints into a cardboard cylinder. "I will get these submitted. I don't anticipate any issues."

"Neither do I." She smiled at the sincerity in the statement. The restaurant would succeed. She'd prove her sincerity in putting down roots.

"If the Kincaids can keep their wildlife under control, then we won't have any problems."

She frowned. "I'll speak with their lead ranch hand about Lover Boy. Let me assure you, the animal is fine. He is passive."

"He is, until he isn't. You don't want to use up your liability insurance before you've even opened your doors." Corey capped the cylinder and extended a hand. "Have a good day, Miss Whittier. I'll be in touch."

She accepted the brief hand shake and dropped her arm to the side.

He strode away toward his car in the parking lot.

She gazed at the horizon, studying Lover Boy. Why did everyone want to see him as the villain? He was a misguided animal struggling with a life many couldn't comprehend. Joe had called the animal a pet. Had he been discarded by his owner for growing to full size? Was his crime reaching his potential? She worried that was becoming her fate. Building on her ancestor's land meant establishing herself and not budging. She refused to be shoved aside, and she'd fight for Lover Boy, too.

Pulling back her shoulders, she strode toward Main Street. With her chin held high and—she hoped—a pleasant expression on her face, she walked with purpose, her steps clacking against the raised sidewalk. If anyone noticed her, they'd glimpse a woman standing tall. She wasn't shrinking anymore. She pushed into The Golden Crown, nearly deserted at ten forty-five.

"Good morning, we aren't..." Heather said behind the bar, pausing with a rag on the walnut top. "Oh, hi, Abby."

Abby wouldn't let herself be deterred by the flat delivery. She owed too much to the Kincaids to disappoint them. *Joe would approve.* The rightness of the stray thought sent a shiver down her spine as she approached the counter. "Hi, Heather. I was hoping for a minute to speak about the wedding?"

"We promised our help. We're always true to our word." Heather focused on polishing the wood.

Abby refused to flinch or otherwise react from the verbal slap. "I hope I have shown the same. I want us to move forward with mutual respect for each other."

Heather didn't reply. But she lifted her gaze and scanned Abby's face.

What did she find? Her former friend? Abby hoped so. She hadn't really apologized. Time might diminish the immediate pain of her betrayal, but she hadn't spoken honestly and from her heart. She owed the Rabbitts better.

"I am sorry. Truly," Abby said. "I lied to you and James. You have always been so good to me as a friend and occasional employee. And for all your trust I rewarded you with deception."

Heather nodded; the firm set of her mouth wobbling. "I suppose you were scared."

"I was. But I should have had faith in you and James. You both have been kind and respectful. I can't apologize enough for my behavior."

Heather picked up the rag and rubbed the bar top again.

From her winter-time stints at the restaurant, Abby knew the gesture wasn't a brush-off but a sign of consideration. Heather needed time to process. She valued giving thoughtful responses.

"If you can send me your menu, I can see what we can prep here," Heather said.

Abby released a heavy, stuttering sigh. "Thank you. I'll be running the smoker almost non-stop starting in the days leading up to the wedding. I'll be driving my truck out to the ranch to get set-up."

"Is it a buffet? Or plated?"

"Plated."

Heather whistled. "That'll take some planning and organization."

Abby chuckled, the laughter both a release and a nervous response.

"Would it make sense to use the truck's kitchen for the appetizers?" Heather asked. "We could plate dinner more efficiently in the barn's galley if so."

Abby nodded. "That's a great idea. I will send you everything I have. Thanks."

Heather extended her hand.

Abby shook and offered a shy smile. The gesture wasn't a complete thaw. But it was the start she needed.

Joe took a sip of his iced tea. Seated at the large farmhouse table in the Kincaid's kitchen, he shifted on the hard bench seat. Only one person could claim the comfortable high back and padded chair at the head of the table. And Hank Kincaid wasn't likely to stop holding court from the throne-like position.

At the moment, Hank steepled his fingers together, pressing the hands under his chin.

With sunlight streaming into the warm room, Joe was almost tempted to remove his sweater. But he didn't want to do anything to disturb the old cowboy. Instead, he sat patiently waiting for Hank to jog his memory.

Joe sent the paperwork as requested by Harrison Wolff on Sunday night and spent the rest of the week grading papers and playing catch up on the hundred other tasks he'd let slip. The end of the school year might be a slippery slide for students. But teachers had no let-up on the work.

What free time he did have, he devoted to finishing the project. If nothing else came from the outside interest, he'd at least use the push as the motivation to complete what he had by the end of June. He had plenty of things he wanted to do, changes to implement and edits to tackle. He couldn't keep letting the roadblocks he created impede his path. Done was better than perfect Or so he hoped.

"Ava Everson. Oh, she was something," Hank said, his deep voice gravelly. "She was beautiful, sure. We had a town full of pretty girls. No, Ava was almost like a cat. I always had the sense she was playing a game. Letting everyone chase her until she caught them."

Joe widened his eyes. "And you dated her before Susie?"

Hank rubbed his chin. "I did. The ratio back then was about three girls to every guy. But Ava had everyone chasing after her. As the quarterback and captain of the football team, I was her prize."

"Football? Ryan says you're against tackle sports."

"I sure am now." Hank shook his head. "We didn't know too much. I'd never risk Ryan's health. But back when I was a kid, we all played. Ava was a cheerleader." Hank's eyes sparkled.

"So..." Joe darted his gaze through the room and strained for any noise above that of the dog snoring on the bed in the patch of sun in the center of the slate tile floor. He didn't want to have the conversation around Ryan. "What happened?"

"We never had..." Hank dragged out the moment. "Zing."

"Zing?" Joe asked.

"A spark. You know? An undeniable chemistry together," Hank continued.

Joe understood. The air sizzled between him and Abby.

"Ava was bold and brash," Hank said. "She captivated me. But when we finally dated, it sort of fell flat. Maybe two big personalities are too many."

Joe nodded. Hank was more than enough to fill up a room all on his own.

"We were better friends. In fact, we were still dating each other when we met our spouses," Hank said.

"Really?" Joe asked.

"We went on a double date. I sat across from Susie and next to Ava. Wouldn't you know, I couldn't keep my eyes off Susie. She was so sweet and so different. She only said maybe two sentences. But one was the funniest thing I'd ever heard. And the other was so insightful." Hank stared past Joe, resting a hand over his heart. "She was always the smartest and most thoughtful person in any room. But never showy. She wasn't a braggart. She saw the world with clarity and joy."

Often, when speaking of the love of his life, the cowboy seemed to enter a different plane. What would it feel like to so cherish and adore another person that—long after they'd gone—a memory could still bewitch? Joe envied him.

"I did call Lana. Thank you for the number," Hank said.

"Oh, good. I'm glad," Joe said. He wasn't sure if Lana approved. She had asked for Hank's phone number. Perhaps she had wanted to take the lead in their friendship?

Footsteps echoed off the tiles.

"You're glad about what?" Ryan asked.

Joe turned and smiled at Ryan and Meg entering the kitchen. With an under the breath woof, Colby scrambled to her feet and padded over to Meg. Meg knelt on the ground, scratching the dog under the chin. Colby's tail swished like a propeller.

"Glad that I have a date to the wedding," Hank said, lifting his chin and crossing his arms over his chest.

"Excuse me?" Ryan gasped. "What did you do? What did Joe put you up to?"

"Oh, Hank, really?" Meg beamed. "How lovely!"

Ryan twisted his neck from the table to his fiancé and back again. "What? What? What?"

Hank grinned. "Thank you. I wasn't looking for anything special. But I got a phone number out of the blue and figured only a fool would miss a chance with a fine woman. Something Ted and I talked about recently really resonated."

"Ted?!" Ryan almost squeaked. "What did he say?"

"That I shouldn't give up on living," Hank said.

The group fell quiet.

After Hank's health scare and the old barn's fire, none of those present took a single day for granted. As the silence stretched, however, the lack of noise became oppressive.

"She's a real nice lady," Joe interjected. He'd witnessed enough moments where Hank pushed his grandson to exasperation to revel in this one. The wedding had Ryan truly on edge.

"What?" Ryan glared at him. "You know who he is talking about? What did you do? Give her the number?"

Joe almost turned away. How else could he hide his guilt from his friend?

Hank dropped his hands to the table. "Don't get yourself all worked up. It's Lana Buck. She'd probably be at the wedding anyways as Will's date. I'm claiming her for myself."

"And how do you know her? Since when have you been dating?" Ryan glowered.

Hank rolled his eyes. "I'm not dating. Although, maybe I will be. She's an old friend. She was the kid sister to the first girl I ever dated."

Ryan flared his nostrils.

"Long before your grandma gave me the time of day," Hank added.

"Well... well... good for her," Ryan sputtered. "Grandma had a lot of sense."

"How lovely to reconnect with someone," Meg exclaimed. "I can't wait to meet her." She pushed off the ground and approached the table. "How about you, Joe? Any date for the wedding?"

"He's working." Ryan frowned, wrinkling his brow even more.

The lines could be etched in stone. Unfortunately for Ryan, he was in a room surrounded by those who knew him too well to be fooled by one of his bad moods. "I might. I have to ask her first."

"Maybe you should," Ryan said. "I've decided on a change of plans. You and Ted are no longer groomsmen."

The back door opened and Ted strode in, his boots loud against the tiles. "Morning. What did I miss?"

Joe gritted his molars and shook his head, trying and failing to grab Ted's attention.

"I no longer require your services, or Joe's, as groomsmen at the wedding. You won't be standing up at the front with me. You'll both be sitting in the first row," Ryan bit out.

Fired? Joe wasn't sure if he should be offended or relieved. With any luck, losing his official position meant he wouldn't have to perform the dance for Meg. Neither would Ted. Joe didn't dare ask for confirmation or dart his gaze at Ted. Was he expected to sit between Hank and his date? Whatever Ryan wanted, he'd get.

Joe flashed a thumbs up.

"If you're sure, boss," Ted said.

"I am." Ryan lifted his chin. "Meg didn't have a second attendant, only her mom. I think this will line up better. I'll ask you both to please be ushers and help seat everyone. But I only want Hank standing up for me."

"Do you mean it, boy?" Hank asked, his voice thick with emotion.

"Oh, Ryan." Meg sniffed. "How sweet. My mom and your grandpa as our attendants. I love it."

Hank leaned forward and covered his grandson's hand with his big palm. "I'd be honored."

Joe watched the tableau and couldn't help but analyze the touching scene. Ryan was quick-witted and had no doubt come up with the alternative on the spot as a way to keep his grandsire away from a love interest. If Joe could be finished with the dance lessons, however, he wasn't going to be cynical about the change of plans. He could hardly wait to commiserate with Ted out of earshot.

Joe drank the rest of his iced tea and slid off the bench. "Thanks for meeting today, Hank. I think that'll be it. I'm all wrapped up on the interviews for my project."

"Congratulations," Meg said.

"Really?" Ryan asked, dropping his jaw.

Joe would feel put out by the expression if he hadn't shared the opinion that he'd never finish. "Thanks, Meg. And yes, Ryan. I wasn't sure I'd ever be done." *But then Abby stepped in*. He was glad she'd made him set a deadline. "I've already be in contact about reaching out to publishers with the help of Harrison Wolff."

"Are you sure you can trust him with your work?" Ryan asked.

"I'm keeping my options open. But I can't ignore an opportunity if he really has the network he claims," Joe said. He grabbed his messenger bag off the bench seat and slung the strap over his shoulder.

"You'll be great," Meg replied. "You're smart. You won't be a pawn. Besides, Harrison is a professional. He's done right by Abby. I guess we need to give him the chance to do right by the rest of us. He wouldn't want a whole, growing community mad at him."

Joe nodded.

Ryan dropped his shoulders. "What she said. Sorry. I'm on edge. I just want everything perfect. No mistakes."

Meg wrapped her arms around Ryan's waist and leaned her head against his back. "It's one day. Don't stress about perfection. That's boring. It'll be wonderful no matter what happens. We're starting our lives together."

As she cooed, Ryan relaxed.

Joe watched, transfixed by the transformation. Could he have a love as deep and unending as Hank's for Susie and as life-affirming as Ryan and Meg's? Joe wouldn't find out standing around the kitchen and letting life happen without him. "Good afternoon. Thanks."

The group waved.

Joe saw himself out of the kitchen via the hallway and the front door. Now he needed to push himself. He owed Abby a proper date. He didn't care who knew or what they thought. For so long, Hank pushed them together and Joe resisted. If he hadn't been determined to avoid the meddling man's snare, would he have reached the point of almost being happy earlier? He wouldn't get mad worrying about would've, could've, and should've. Instead, he'd be glad for second and third and fourth chances.

As long as he had breath in his body, he had an opportunity to go after what would make him happy. Joy was a choice. He'd been setting up so many stumbling blocks to prevent him from truly enjoying his life. He was done with nonsense.

CHAPTER 15

Abby draped the cloth napkin over her lap and crossed her ankles under the chair. She scanned the interior of the upscale restaurant again. For the past hour, she'd marveled at the building, absorbing every detail to see what she could apply to her business. Her restaurant would be far more casual, but she appreciated the high-end without feeling snobbish ambiance created through a mix of custom and box store furnishings. After she spent the rest of her week touring a tile store, picking options for flooring, backsplashes, and the bathrooms, she more easily spotted what she would have previously overlooked.

In fact, she'd perhaps spent too long detouring from the table to the washroom. She was at the bistro on a date. Or, at least she hoped it counted as a romantic dinner. From under her lashes, she glanced at her companion. "Sorry, if I was gone too long."

"Everything alright?" Joe asked.

"Yes, fine. I was being a little nosy. The kitchens are on the way, and I was curious about their set-up."

He chuckled. "I understand. Professional curiosity. I get that way at any place with even a hint of history."

"Really?" She leaned forward, closer. Despite over two years of acquaintance, she was only beginning to know him. She rather hoped he'd always be a little bit of a mystery.

"Oh, yes. Museums, homes, public buildings, heck even a field. If it has a hint of historical significance, I'm there."

Every new fact drew her in with another chance for an inside joke. They had developed a sort of easy, friendly intimacy she couldn't have imagined. While they had never been true enemies, their frenemy status had created a barrier. She was only too glad to dismantle it one conversation at a time. "Don't go to the East Coast then, or you'll never leave. George Washington has supposedly slept and stepped foot in so many locations, you'd be utterly absorbed. Even parking lots have historic markers."

"I already have a favorite, significant parking lot. Very close to home." He winked. "And plenty of reasons to stay here."

Her cheeks burned, and she reached for her water.

"I take it the construction is off to a good start?"

"It is. I was picking out floors and finishes this week. I guess I almost feel like this dinner is a celebration."

"Mission accomplished. I have so many questions about your restaurant, but I don't want to overwhelm you."

She shrugged. "I'm sure I can handle a few. But I can probably guess. Yes, we will be open for breakfast, lunch, and dinner. Yes, I will continue to serve a mix of barbecue and Tex-Mex style flavors. Other than that, I'm still figuring out details."

"Fair enough. You are so incredibly talented and creative. I admire you a lot. To be honest, I'm a little jealous of your talent."

A moment of silence fell between them. She liked the pauses in their conversations equally as much as the chatter. Time to absorb and reflect on what the other had said somehow strengthened the trust she put in him.

She darted her gaze through the bistro. Taking in the white linen topped tables and customers in dressy clothes. Her business wouldn't be nearly so upscale. But dressing up and putting in an effort about her appearance felt nice to do for a change.

She exhaled a sigh. "This is really nice. You didn't need to take me out."

"Of course, I did." He smiled and raised his wine glass. "And you deserve it."

She clinked her glass against his before sipping.

"What don't I know about you?" he asked.

She flinched, carefully setting her wine glass on the table. Had anyone ever asked a more loaded question? "I think we've covered it all."

"Sorry, that came out all wrong. I meant like...first date small talk." His cheeks turned bright red.

She liked him off-balance and unsure. It was a refreshing change from the man who always had an answer. *First date?* She liked the categorization, too. With candles on the table and chandeliers overhead, the dim lighting set a romantic mood. The occasional titter of laughter rose above the low din of private conversations lured her to lean close and speak softly.

He reached for his water and gulped.

"I supposed this could be a chance to talk about hobbies?" she asked, offering him a reprieve from the hot seat. "I don't really have any. I was knitting for a while at the saloon. I liked spending time with the group. I haven't really continued on my own. How about you?"

"Same," he agreed. "Not about the knitting. I have a poker group. We don't play for money, and I'm terrible at cards. I like the companionship, and I'm glad it doesn't revolve around sports. I am clueless about professional, collegiate, or high school teams."

She'd tried softball in third grade and only lasted half the season in outer outfield, a position created for her. "I suppose we could join forces and start a P.I. firm, now that we're aware of each other's lifelong passion for solving cases."

He chuckled, shaking his head. "I'm happy to put my sleuthing days behind me. Learning your secret was the biggest mystery I ever cracked. And that was all intuition."

She smiled but didn't feel the expression. "I guess the truth wasn't very exciting. I came here to assess the situation and the value of the land. I didn't want to put down roots when I came. Now I can't leave."

"And aren't we lucky?" He held her gaze with an intensity that sent a shiver down her spine.

She wanted to belong to Herd and maybe to him, too.

The server approached, topping off their glasses of wine and setting a lava cake in the center with two spoons.

Abby smiled at the man as he retreated before turning her attention back to her surprising date. Nothing about the evening had been typical. Then again, she wasn't sure she'd ever expected to join him on a date at the steakhouse midway between Miles City and Herd.

When he had called and invited her out, she'd been speechless. Sure, she hoped he'd ask her to dinner but thinking wasn't doing and it had been little more than a silent wish. She hadn't prepared for the call but stammering her way through her acceptance.

She'd managed a little better through the meal, returning to the table after she slipped the server her credit card during her washroom and kitchen detour. "How did you know I liked lava cake?"

"A good guess, and they didn't have anything lemon."

She slid the spoon through the ice cream and warm cake, scooping a little of each in equal parts. The gooey sauce poured onto the plate. "This is a promising sign. If my spoon stuck like Will's fudge cake, we'd be in trouble."

"Don't remind me."

Raising her spoon, she savored the first bite. Sweet and rich, the dark chocolate was neither too bitter nor too sugary. The dessert provided the perfect finish to the meal. She swallowed and dabbed at her mouth with her napkin. She'd have to take notes for her menu.

"Good?" he asked

She slid the plate closer to him past the imaginary dividing line. "Dangerously so. Maybe even addictive."

He scooped up an oversized bite and moaned as he chewed.

She laughed. When had she ever enjoyed a first date? She knew Joe. Their conversation had flowed so easily all night, she almost forgot this was any sort of start.

"You're right," he said, his voice muffled through the napkin covering his mouth.

"I usually am."

"You are." He nodded. "Did I tell you Hank is bringing Lana to the wedding as his date? They spoke over the phone, and he asked her out."

"Oh, that's so lovely." She was glad for Hank. If nothing else, he'd appreciate companionship with a peer. He was so spry and witty; it was easy to forget his real age. Everyone needed somebody. Maybe she had found her someone? "And fast."

"Hank doesn't waste time. Ryan was a little annoyed. But he'll come around. Speaking of Kincaid business," Joe said. "Ryan says you can move the truck to the ranch anytime."

"I hate to ask my customers to drive out of their way. But I can't operate on a construction site. The noise is impossible to escape and dust seems to slip in through every crevice. It's not very appetizing."

"It's only a temporary change. Your food is worth the road trip." He winked.

"And I'll update all of my social media feeds. Maybe I can ask Ryan to add me to the ranch's website too."

"Might help with Lover Boy, too."

"Oh, that's one of the big selling points for sure. That would be a big help." She breathed a little easier.

If the bison needed a little encouragement to explore the wide-open prairie, she'd be glad to assist. But she'd miss the chance for a run-in with Joe under the guise of needing advice. In a few weeks, he'd be at the ranch every day leading his tours. Could she go that long between their run-ins?

"Madam? Sir?" The server asked, stopping by again. He moved silently. "Can I get you anything else this evening?"

"Just the check," Joe said.

The server met her gaze and smiled. "Have a good night." He backed away from the table.

"You paid?"

"My treat." Now she had the chance to wink. "I guess you'll have to take me out again."

He reached for her hand across the table and squeezed. "I guess I will."

Inside her heels, she curled her toes. This was the start of something special. She was excited to see what happened next. "After the wedding?"

"Sure, I'll offer a raincheck."

"I can't believe how fast time is going."

"It's only another week and then we get our lives back. Won't that be nice?" he asked.

Then she wouldn't have any excuse to hold her back or any reason to hide. She wasn't quite sure what to make of that. Was she ready to fully step into the next phase of her life? If she focused on her restaurant, she was ready. With Joe, she was in no rush. She enjoyed the toe-curling excitement of every encounter.

"Abby? Joe?" A familiar voice called, booming in the space, and drawing all the attention.

She turned toward the sound and almost deflated. Such a lovely evening, full of firsts on a road to forever, should only have one possible ending. The man striding toward them promised nothing like a happy resolution.

Joe might have growled. He wasn't the sort to lean into his animalistic urges. He was enjoying his night and didn't appreciate the interruption from Harrison Wolff.

When Joe had selected the restaurant, he had accepted the possibility the flashy lawyer might be here. Arguably the nicest place for a few hundred miles, Joe wanted to pull out all the stops to show Abby what he thought about her. He'd told her plenty of times. But he wasn't sure she really heard him. Until tonight.

Their conversation had been relaxed. Despite being on a first date, he had none of the usual apprehension. It had been a long time since he'd taken a woman out to dinner. Perhaps the most surprising of all was how natural the night felt.

"Harrison, hello," Joe said, instilling the two words with polite curtness. He didn't want to engage in a conversation.

Harrison faced him, turning his back on Abby.

The move felt unnecessary and cutting. Joe frowned. What was that about? Would Harrison throw Joe away as soon as their project together was completed? Abby hadn't brought about any sort of revenge for Harrison against the Kincaids. It was an unfair assessment, but Joe couldn't shake his conviction.

"Glad I saw you. I might have a lead on your work," Harrison said.

"Wow, already?" Abby asked.

Joe heard the disbelieving upspeak in her tone. He shared the same sense of wonder and smiled across the table at her. "You move quick." He addressed Harrison but focused on his date.

She covered her mouth with a hand but couldn't hide the shake in her shoulders.

Harrison glanced down his nose. The effect was almost a sneer. Like he'd noticed a pest. Joe wanted to be wrong.

"What do you need from me? Sample chapters? Should I refine the pitch?" Joe asked.

"I'll take another look at what you sent. I might make a few notes, and I'll share those with you later in the week," Harrison said.

"How lucky you have so many connections?" Abby asked.

Harrison bristled.

Joe didn't like the man's continued snubbing of his date. Of course, after the past month, Abby must be used to being ignored. Her comment had been delivered kindly if somewhat questioning, and she deserved an acknowledgment of her presence. The other man had interrupted their date after all. "Yes, how lucky," Joe said. "Thanks to Abby for putting us together. I wouldn't have approached you without her encouragement."

She blushed slightly.

"I'll be in touch. Have a good evening." Harrison tipped his head to Joe and strode away without another glance.

Joe didn't like that the lawyer had no manners for Abby. Was she no longer of any value and thus below his notice? Maybe. That's how Ryan had always described the man. Joe wasn't sure getting into business with Harrison was a good idea. He hadn't signed anything yet. He wasn't tied into a legal tangle. He still had options. "Shall we leave?"

She nodded.

He pushed back his chair, left his napkin on the table, and quickly came around to pull out her seat.

She stood inches away. "Thanks."

The murmured word hung in the air between them. He stepped to the side.

With a soft smile, she passed, brushing his shoulder, and continuing through the restaurant to the host stand. He handed over the coat check token and a tip. The maître d bowed and made quick work of grabbing the coats. The maître d returned. Extending Joe's coat, the man retained hers, holding it out for her to slip into.

Joe didn't comment, but he was a little disappointed. He wanted to take every opportunity to be chivalrous. He pulled on his wool overcoat.

Abby thanked the maître d and buttoned up her coat.

Joe reached the door to the vestibule, holding it open for her and then quickly crossing ahead and grabbing the front door.

A chilly breeze blew in like a wave crashing against the shore. She stumbled back. He reached for her elbow, steadying her.

She chuckled. "I don't know why I'm always surprised by the cold weather."

"Because it's May, and you're longing for warmth." He tucked her arm tight against his body and steered her toward the parking lot, careful to navigate around the slushy puddles. "On the bright side, we're almost done with the current cold snap. And at least it's a clear night."

She snuggled closer to his arm. "I suppose so. I do love stargazing in Montana. No other sky comes close to matching the visibility."

Big sky country. The catchphrase was apropos. And he'd prepared for just this moment, on the off chance it came. With his free hand, he pointed overhead. "Do you see the cluster over there?"

She nodded.

"That's Andromeda, and if you follow up the chain you reach Pegasus."

"Really? Are you sure?"

"Of course. I didn't spend an hour of my day on the internet for nothing."

She laughed, her whole body shaking. "I know nothing about stargazing. I look up and see a bunch of spots. I have always wanted to see the Northern Lights."

"You should. Glacier is a good spot."

"Did I miss it this year?"

He opened her car door and held it as she hopped inside. "Not necessarily, we could go in the late fall." He shut the door hoping she'd take the hint.

He filled his lungs and slowed to his normal gait as he rounded the vehicle. He felt like he stood on the edge of something, and he'd never been much for patiently waiting. He opened his door and slid inside, turning the key into the ignition. "I think I need to let the engine warm up."

She snuggled into her jacket with a shaky thumbs up.

"Oh, I'm sorry." He hit the heated seat dial to max and turned toward her, holding out his hands.

She put her icy fingers in his warm palms.

He encased her hands, rubbing quickly to jumpstart her circulation. "Nights like tonight make me wish I had splurged for a remote start car or heated steering wheel."

"Not on my account." Her teeth chattered. "I'm always cold."

"I would like to do better for you," he said, unsure whether he should be honest about his upset at what had just happened. Keeping secrets had erected a stone wall between them at the start. He didn't want to risk what could develop with any more omissions or little white lies. Every tiny untruth was a pebble in another barrier. He had to share his feelings. "I don't like what just happened back there."

She stiffened.

"Not you. You're perf..." He cleared his throat. "I meant Harrison." Joe ran a hand through his hair, tugging the ends. "That behavior doesn't sit well with me. How he treated you was abhorrent. I should have called him out."

"For acting like himself?" She lifted the corner of her mouth in a sort of wry-sad smile. "I'd be tempted to use our newly established, fictional P.I. firm to get to the bottom of Harrison's problem. If it wasn't so lame and obvious as a high school grudge."

Four years younger than Ryan and Harrison, Joe never witnessed the rivalry first hand. "At the risk of sounding smug," Joe said. "I am always shocked some people can't stop living in the past." Because if he hadn't shaken off his misconceptions, he wouldn't be here now with her. He'd be just as bitter as the lawyer.

"Regardless, Harrison wasn't outright rude. You couldn't have called him on snubbing me without risking your project. I'm glad you're pushing yourself and seeing this through. Good things will come to you. But..."

"But what?"

She drew in a shaky breath, the inhale almost as loud as the winter wind.

He gritted his molars. He hated preparing for the worst but couldn't stop his instinct for self-preservation.

"I've done a little research on the internet."

He relaxed. "Ah, yes. Search engines tend to rule our lives, don't they?"

"I was curious about the steps to become a non-fiction author. And I really don't think you need Harrison. I'm not saying that because of what happened in the restaurant." Her words tumbled out in a rush.

"I wouldn't accuse you of that."

"Most non-fiction authors get book deals after they've established themselves as an expert in their field. You could do that. Easily. You start by building a platform. Get yourself credentials by sharing your knowledge."

He stopped rubbing her hands and held her fingers in his. "How?"

"First, you need to set up a website and social media. You could share selected excerpts of your interviews or interesting facts you've learned. For official documentation, you could link to the Kincaid Ranch's website, ask to be listed as the resident historian. Then start getting out there. Interviews, podcasts, lectures. You have what it takes to be a big success. You don't need Harrison."

"My social media feed is pretty lame. I don't think anyone wants to follow me."

"Luckily for you, you have an expert on your side." She winked. "I've learned how to utilize hashtags and posts to advertise for the food truck without a marketing budget. You've got this. Trust me. You're the real deal."

"I feel the same about you." He stopped rubbing her hands and held her fingers in his. "I'm glad you're moving forward, and that you're staying put."

She leaned forward. "I'm glad you are, too."

With only the center console between them, the setting was intimate and comfortable. The distance shortened from inches to centimeters to a breath. Her warm exhale tickled his nose. She was as near as a person could get.

But he didn't want to take any chances. Now that he found someone who really mattered, he wouldn't ever act like he knew best. He wouldn't ever do anything without her consent. "Can I ask you a question?" he murmured.

She nodded.

"Would you want me to kiss you?"

She darted her tongue along her lower lip. "Hmm. Why do I feel like I should be circling something on a note passed during class?"

He chuckled. His approach wasn't smooth at all. "I suppose I spend too much time around middle schoolers. I have no game."

"I think you're smooth enough." She squeezed his hand. "And yes. I'd like you to kiss me. I'd like that a lot."

He pressed his lips against hers, still clasping her hands in his. She sighed and deepened the kiss, opening her mouth slightly. He cheered inside. It was like coming home at last, and he couldn't understand how he'd ever been lost in the first place.

CHAPTER 16

For most of her life, Abby felt time was not on her side. In the past, she had come to ideas too soon and lacked the self-confidence to execute a plan only to learn of another's success with a similar concept later. Or, and perhaps worse, she had arrived at a conclusion too late and missed the benefits of the idea by years, months, or days.

With Joe, however, she couldn't help but smile.

She had, for once, met someone at the right moment.

Maybe two years of barely concealed animosity had—in hindsight—served a purpose. Neither of them had been ready for anything serious. She had been lost in discovering who she was, if the sum of her experiences was enough to subtract the infamy of her family's past, and so had he, in his own way.

He had been on a journey to establish himself as an authority. While she understood the thrill of power, she had lived a life almost in the shadow of such figures. She trusted he wanted to use his position for good.

Of course, the start of any relationship was easy and lovely. And she was probably jumping way ahead by even declaring an attachment after one evening and a perfectly swoon worthy kiss. Inside her newly purchased cowgirl boots, she curled her toes.

He had been so sweet and earnest. Not pushy. Not demanding. When she had pulled back, she hadn't been greeted with a frown or mark of frustration. He had kissed her hands and driven her home.

Dating him wouldn't be casual, but he had already showed he could be patient. She was glad for his calm demeanor. The timing worked in her favor because of her packed schedule.

Their date had occurred the week before Memorial Day weekend. She was simply too swamped with business and preparation to stew over their encounter. Between final tasks for the combination birthday wedding and serving the first wave of tourists at the ranch, she didn't have time to think let alone overanalyze about their shared meal. All she could do was savor the memory of his lips on hers and smile whenever she saw him. He returned the expression with a quirk of his lips that sent a tingle down to her toes.

On Wednesday, she had an especially overscheduled day. Meg's mom arrived that evening, and Abby had to make it home to help clean and prepare a welcome meal at the Hawke house. She had agreed to close her truck tomorrow to enjoy a bridal shower spa day with Meg, her mom, and Stephanie. Without any wedding attendants, Meg had avoided any sort of bachelorette shenanigans at the hands of her friends.

Stephanie had balked at Meg's insistence she didn't want to do any more celebrating besides the wedding. Abby had joined forces with Stephanie. Meg was happy to share her wedding with her grandfather-in-law's birthday. But she deserved a little spoiling. And especially with all of her kindness, Abby wanted to pamper her friend.

She rang up her last order and handed the change to the customer. She fought the urge to sigh. She was grateful for her welcome on the ranch. She hadn't had a chance to stop by the restaurant site all week but had placed a sandwich board with news about her temporary location. Hopefully very temporary.

At her station, she made quick work of frying the hushpuppies, loading the last of the pulled pork on the pretzel buns, and topping with a heaping spoonful of mustard coleslaw. "Order up," she called at the window.

The husband and wife approached, an older couple who talked Abby's ear off about returning for the wedding of the century. Or, at least the wife had. Marcia and Clayton Ford were a pair who swore they couldn't miss the wedding when they were the first to see the spark between the pair. Abby rather doubted the truth but wouldn't argue with a customer.

Marcia and Clayton accepted the baskets with thanks and retreated to the picnic tables.

She lowered the window and began to clean. While her truck would be closed, she wouldn't be taking a day off cooking. She'd need the extra time to start smoking the brisket for the wedding. The Rabbitts had volunteered their ovens as well, and Abby intended to take them up on their offer to roast chickens. Cooking for an undetermined number of people was daunting and nearly impossible. She was grateful for the help of the Rabbitts and Will Buck. Without their assistance, she would be totally lost.

Herd rallied when it mattered. And she hoped she'd shown her heart hadn't changed just because her name had. She scrubbed a sticky corner off the griddle. Focusing on her work was all she could control. She'd learned that lesson well over the past few months.

Her feet ached in the tight boots. She'd let Meg talk her into embracing her cowgirl roots with the purchase. Abby would have been better off finding an already worn-in pair at Finders Keepers, the antique store. But Meg didn't have many leather goods in stock at the moment.

Abby had bought the boots online and decided to break them in today. In a few minutes, she could head home and slip off her footwear in favor of soft loafers. If she wanted to connect with her past, she'd be better off sticking with the riding lessons Joe had promised. And she wouldn't mind another excuse to spend a day together.

A low moan almost shook her off her sore feet.

With a jerk, she glanced at the clock hanging on the back wall. Couldn't fault the timing. She hopped out of the truck and made her way around.

Lover Boy had returned. His custom on the ranch had been to stop by for a visit in the late afternoon. While he seemed to like people, he was smart enough to be wary of crowds. He preferred when only a handful of humans gathered near his truck.

Abby was glad someone loved the vehicle as much as she did. She worried about the bison. In the weeks she'd been relocated, she hadn't seen him close to any other of the free-roaming herd. Being on one's own was great, she'd attest. But she hadn't realized how much she had been missing out on until she'd made a friend in Meg. She was grateful to continue on with Stephanie as a roommate. She wasn't ready to go back to being alone.

"Wow, look at that," the woman said, her voice breathless and wary.

"He's okay as long as you don't approach him. Or feed him," Abby rushed to add.

She put herself between the guests and the bison.

Lover Boy stopped in front of the truck, as was his custom. He faced the grill.

Could he see himself reflected in the chrome? Was he in love with his reflection? Abby shook off the ridiculous thought. Not everyone was motivated by romance.

"Can we take a photo?" the woman asked.

"If you stay where you are, yes. You may. He won't react to the noise or a flash," Abby said.

"Was he someone's pet?" the husband asked.

The question was delivered in a tone of wonder. The very idea was awesome in the clearest definition of the word. That a giant creature capable of destruction could have been domesticated was almost too fantastic to be believed. And it was the absolute truth. "I think so. But we don't go near him."

"Oh, of course not," the man replied.

Abby pulled her cell phone out of her back pocket. She needed to call Ted. With the tourists returning, the situation regarding Lover Boy took on more urgency. While the beast's presence on ranch land wouldn't shock anyone, the animal's safety could be compromised by his seeming docility.

Her grip on the cell slipped and she opened her inbox instead of pulling up her contacts list. An email from Harrison Wolff appeared at the top of her messages. What could he want?

He'd made his dismissal of her quite clear with every interaction. She was sure the Kincaids embrace and encouragement had frustrated the lawyer with a grudge. She opened the message. Within seconds, her skin chilled and her palms went clammy and cold.

"Great angle. How backstabbing built the West."

She raked her gaze over the pitch. No one was spared. The Kincaids were greedy and ruthless, grabbing land like a mad board game. The Hawkes acted as double agents, befriending one side and then the other, never staying loyal with their support. And the Whittiers were fools, easily manipulated by the more clever families and townsfolk. How could Joe write such an attack piece? And why? What did this history serve but to disgrace the entire community?

"Are you feeling okay?" the woman asked.

At the hint of concern, Abby raised her watery gaze. She swiped at her lower lashes and glanced at the husband and wife. "I am perfectly well. But I unfortunately need to ask you both to grab your food and walk slowly to safety. I need to head to the barn to get the lead cowboy. He'll handle the situation." *And I'll handle mine.* "Follow me, please."

And without turning to be sure she was followed, Abby pulled back her shoulders and strode forward. Hyping up the founders' feuds. Replaying the past so many wanted to forget. Why? She wanted answers.

If Joe thought his troubles had been solved by Ryan's abrupt wedding changes, namely firing the groomsmen, Joe couldn't have been more wrong. He wouldn't explore being a medium, palm reader, or any other sort of psychic channeling energy and auras. He didn't know people as well as learning their family's history had led him to believe.

Standing in the barn with only two days until the wedding, Joe held as still as a statue. If he didn't move, perhaps he'd escape detection.

Ryan certainly stalked around like an ancient predator. From one corner to the next, he jerked his gaze so hard his neck cracked. He grabbed a ladder leaning against one wall.

Ted ran after him, holding onto one end of the sixteen-foot steps to keep it from swinging around and crashing into the tables that had already been set up.

Ryan stopped in the center of the room and, with Ted's help, set up the ladder. He climbed and glared at the ceiling.

Ted held the ladder in position.

It shouldn't be possible to fix an inanimate object with an evil eye. But Ryan found a way. Joe shuddered. At least he wasn't the one standing closest to the groom. Falling off a ladder a few days before a wedding was probably a bad omen even for a witness. The closer to the incident the worse off the luck.

"How did this happen?" Ryan asked.

The question was rhetorical and more moan than query.

"We didn't think we'd need a chandelier, boss," Ted said slowly.

Joe tried to meet the cowboy's eye.

Ted avoided him.

Probably the smart move. Any show of commiseration between the pair would only rile Ryan more. He was practically a peacock the way his non-existent feathers stood at attention.

"Well, now we do," Ryan sputtered, climbing down the ladder.

Joe pressed his tongue against the roof of his mouth. He knew better than to counter that the bride to be wanted to get married in a field. She didn't need a chandelier.

"The deck is set. We have the poles in position on the railing and the lights strung up in between. You'll have plenty of light. It'll be magical," Ted said evenly.

Joe widened his eyes. Ted wasn't one to speak with such whimsy. But Ryan was too overwrought to notice.

"What if it rains? What if we can't have the ceremony out there?" Ryan spun in a circle.

"The wildflowers are still in pots. We can move them in as needed," Joe interjected.

Ryan's concession to his bride had been to create a field of flowers on the deck. Meg had expressed her disappointment that they wouldn't be married outside with quiet resignation. In Ryan's defense, he had been correct that the field wouldn't have been much more than grass at the moment. But that was the only argument Meg had brought up. Ryan had won of course but his victory looked hollow from the outside.

"And the paint? Is it too white in here? Will it be blinding? Should we put up darker paneling? Re-paint?" Ryan asked.

Joe widened his gaze.

This time, Ted did meet his eyes.

After a fire last fall, rebuilding the barn had been a herculean task. The town had united to get the structure built before the snow came. The activity had been a callback to the long-ago days of barn-raising. Hurdles, including local bureaucracy and state laws, hadn't existed when the structure had first been built. The community had rallied to overcome those, too.

The fact that the building had paint on the exterior—let alone paneling inside—at all was a miracle. But Ryan wanted perfection. His clear-eyed focus had transformed his ranch and helped rebuild the local economy. Getting in his way was never a good idea.

"The forecast is bright and sunny all week. You could still get married outside like Meg wanted," Joe said. "You won't even need to take everyone. Just the pastor, Meg's Mom, Hank, and the dog. By the time you get back here for the reception, you won't even notice the paint. The sun will start to dip and the color won't be so strong."

Ted rolled his eyes.

It had been a low blow. But Joe felt the need to remind everyone the scale of the event on a day that was supposedly the bride's had ballooned. Abby didn't even know how many people she'd be feeding. She'd shared her attempts at meal planning over a few stolen moments and phone calls.

He hated that he couldn't sweep her off her feet. Following the best first date of his life, he wanted to repeat the experience. He wanted to spend every second in her company. He'd dated women in the past but Abby was different. Their connection was more special. And more fragile.

With a rough start behind them, he wanted to solidify his place in her good graces. He wanted to wash her dishes, take out her trash, hold open her door, and help in any way he could.

"I know," Ryan said, hanging his head. "This is a little more public than either of us understood. But we'll do it for Hank."

Joe wasn't sure that was quite right either. Hank's birthday celebration had morphed into a joint event. Once he had made his intentions to bring a date clear, he had been forced into the bridal party. Nothing about the event lined up with Hank's wishes. But Joe wasn't going to say anything else.

Ted clapped a hand on Ryan's shoulder. "We'll help. Everything will go smooth."

"Even without a rehearsal?" Ryan asked.

"What do you need a rehearsal for? You don't have any kids involved, and you only have two attendants," Joe said.

"And the dog," Ryan replied.

Colby was better behaved than many adults. "You'll be fine. It's better without a rehearsal. How would you feed them all? Abby wouldn't have time to smoke enough meat for that dinner too."

"Yeah, Abby. How is that going?" Ted asked.

Joe gaped, darting his gaze between his friends. "Excuse me?"

"I understand you've taken her on a date," Ted said.

"Did you tell him?" Joe asked Ryan.

Ryan shrugged. "Didn't have to. Meg, Stephanie, and Abby are friends. They chat."

"Maybe they shouldn't," Joe murmured.

Ted howled with laughter. "Hey, I didn't say anything in front of Hank. I didn't put you on the spot."

"Thank you. Although I'm sure he'd appreciate hearing he was right," Joe said.

"Oh, please save me from that," Ryan added. "Don't give him another ego boost. At least let me get on my honeymoon before you start building him up."

Joe smiled. Hank had been right. Abby and Joe were a good fit. While he was frustrated the busyness of the past few weeks had meant no quick follow-up date, he had been glad too. They had known each other for so long, they weren't going to be casual. They were destined to go from enemies to friends to committed relationship pretty fast.

And they'd avoid some of the inevitable sanding down of each other's rough edges. Perhaps the past two years had been the worst of the conflict they'd ever have. Now they could go forward and just be happy.

He found a wonderful woman and his big project was nearly complete. After years of doubt, he'd finished his book. He had found the self-confidence to tell the story. He had silenced his imposter syndrome, in large part thanks to her. The pair weren't mutually exclusive. Life didn't get much better. If he had to deal with a little taunting and a little decorating, he could take it.

The barn door slid open with a whoosh.

"Speak of the devil," Ted muttered with a grin.

Joe spun and spotted her. He waved and froze. Her face was pinched and drawn. Her posture was tight.

"Excuse me," Joe said and crossed the room. He held his arm out as he approached, and lightly grazed her upper back. "What's wrong?"

"We need to talk."

Under his palm, he noticed the tremors. "Of course, come on, let's head outside."

She nodded and spun, stalking back to the still open door.

By the time he got outside, he couldn't find her. He shut the door and strode around the barn to the deck on the side.

She paced the boards, her body radiating with energy.

"What's wrong?"

She approached and thrust a phone into his hands. "This."

He squinted and read the screen.

Harrison Wolff's email didn't make sense. The pitch he presented didn't represent any of the material they'd discussed. "What is this? Why do you have it?"

She snorted and crossed her arms. "Good questions. I don't know. I have no answers."

He didn't like her defensive stance or the snark in her tone. He turned back to the email. Harrison hyped up the founding feuds against every family. Why would she assume Joe wanted this angle? She'd read his manuscript. She knew what he had to say about the town.

"That isn't what I read. I can't believe you would re-write the whole thing to be a hit piece."

"But you do," he countered. "You do believe it or you wouldn't have come storming into the barn."

"Just tell me you didn't do this." She dropped her hands to her hips. "Tell me you haven't been twisting everything."

No, I shouldn't need to. In every draft, he had worked hard to create balance. Sure, at the beginning without another side it was a classic western good guy versus bad guy scenario. But he'd changed his opinion and so had the work. He struggled to establish the nuance of the situation. The end result still wasn't perfect but allowed for more interpretation. He had faith a good editor would help him hone the tone.

"No response?"

"What do you want here? What are you really looking for? Do you want me to rewrite the history of what happened?"

"I expected fair treatment and an understanding that winners write history, but that isn't the whole story."

Her words were measured and logical. Her delivery, however, pricked deep like a burr to tender skin. Was she picking a fight?

"Come on, give me answers," she said. "Tell me you didn't write the book with my family as the scapegoats."

You should know I didn't. He hadn't given her any indication of duplicity or subterfuge. But she had.

The long simmering frustration bubbled up from the depths inside him. If anyone had the right to feel betrayed, it was him. He'd been magnanimous and kind. Did his treatment not matter? Weren't his actions stronger than a few words?

"Why? Why are you confronting me?" he asked. "Are you here seeking your own validation? Are you looking for me to build you up and tell you you're good enough for this town?"

She scoffed.

"I'm serious. I don't appreciate your accusations, and I'm going to walk away. But I need you to know. You don't need to be good enough for me, for Hank, for the town, for anyone but yourself."

"My self-confidence isn't on trial here."

"Isn't it? Bye, Abby." He walked away while he could. He had phone calls to make regarding his intellectual property, he needed to reframe his understanding of the situation because maybe the last jibe wasn't only meant for her. Maybe he needed to be enough for himself as well. He might never be the expert he needed to be to prove himself worthy. What came next?

CHAPTER 17

Abby didn't consider herself a spa person. Sitting around, sipping flavored water, and listening to new age music in a robe while waiting for a stranger to rub her body held no appeal. But, until Thursday, she'd never had the chance for the experience. And she had to admit, don't knock it until she'd tried it, might be her new mantra.

In the private waiting room, Abby reclined next to Meg and opposite Meg's mom, Carole, and Stephanie.

The water was chilled, the room warm, and the air lightly scented with eucalyptus and lavender. Abby hadn't enjoyed a massage or pedicure yet and was already a me-time convert.

"This is so nice," Meg's mom, Carole, said for the hundredth time.

Meg sighed.

"It really is," Abby agreed, hoping to distill some of the nervous energy rolling off Meg. With each hour closer to the wedding, the more Meg tensed.

After Abby's confrontation with Joe, she had waited at her truck until she had calmed down enough to close up her business and put out her closed signs in a safe perimeter. She didn't want Lover Boy spooked by any curious tourists while she was gone. She had called Ted for a ride to the Hawke ranch, and he had promptly picked her up and driven her back.

They had not spoken.

She had been grateful for his silence. She wasn't sure if he had overheard any of the conversation between herself and Joe. She wasn't sure if she cared. She needed space to process what had been said.

Joe's shock at the email had seemed genuine. His parting words, however, had been a jab. If she had been congratulating herself on timing hours earlier, she had been mistaken by her afternoon.

She had reached the house only a few minutes before Meg's mom. The house had been full of energy, both good and bad. Meg's mom fussed and fretted. Each mention of the wedding had visibly aggravated the bride to be.

Meg had drawn her shoulders together and flinched. She had grown quiet and reflective. The stress of the wedding had finally caught up and infiltrated her calm.

Abby hadn't had the heart to run upstairs and shut herself off, to focus on her hurt. She had to be there for a friend who had gone above and beyond for her. Maybe she was simply delaying the inevitable. Maybe she was once again guilty of living a lie. But she couldn't let Meg down.

"When you're on the ranch," Meg said, "do you ever feel like you've set foot onto the set of *Hey Dude*?"

Abby chuckled. She hadn't thought about that TV show in years. "Too much grass here. Wasn't that filmed in Arizona."

"You're right. But I wonder if we shouldn't embrace the nostalgia a little bit more," Meg continued.

"What is *Hey Dude*?" Stephanie asked.

Stephanie's lack of pop culture knowledge wasn't only due to being eight years younger than Meg and three years younger than Abby. Stephanie didn't watch TV or many movies. Moving into the ranch house and further away from the hustle and bustle happening close to her current apartment building wouldn't be an inconvenience. If anything, relocating to the middle of nowhere made perfect sense for someone oblivious to trends.

"Thank you for inviting us to join you," Stephanie said. "I haven't used the spa before."

"Neither have I," Abby added and leaned forward, catching Stephanie's eye.

Stephanie gave a barely perceptible head tilt.

"Have you had a chance to sort out your something old, something new?" Abby asked, slowly, deliberately enunciating each word. She didn't want to push the morning into another stressful meltdown.

Carole leaned forward.

"The dress counts as new. I'll probably have my nails painted blue. And I have plenty of options for old and borrowed at the store," Meg replied. "Mom, did you remember to bring the six pence penny?"

Carole flashed a thumbs up.

Perhaps the mother had caught on to some of the off-vibes from her daughter, finally, and wasn't jumping into any more conversations.

"Abby and I brought you a few things," Stephanie said and reached behind her chair for a tote bag she'd insisted on bringing with her. "Something new, something blue, something old, and a special something borrowed." She handed the bag to Meg.

Meg accepted the cloth bag, scrunching her nose. "You didn't have to go to so much trouble for me."

"Of course we did," Abby said. "And this is all Stephanie."

"Abby helped," Steph replied. "You'll see. Open it."

Meg reached inside and pulled out a lacy, bright blue skirt slip. She threw back her head and laughed. "Good thing the skirt has plenty of layers. Otherwise, you'd be able to see my something blue from space."

Abby dropped her shoulders a fraction of an inch and grinned. The merriment dispelled the ever-present threat of a meltdown. The bride could crumple at any moment. "That's from me. I had to dye it. Many times." She was glad she'd had the foresight to get an old pot from the donation store or she'd have ruined her cookware.

"Thank you." Meg smiled, tears in the corner of her eyes.

"Keep going," Carole urged.

Meg opened the bag again and pulled out a pressed hand-kerchief, embroidered with her new initials. "Oh, wow," she breathed and met Stephanie's gaze.

"I can't take credit. Kelly is a master with a needle," Stephanie said.

"One more," Carole murmured.

Taking a deep breath, such a large gulp she nearly sucked all the oxygen out of the tiny room, Meg looked in the bag one final time. Her nose twitched, and she sniffed. "I don't want to cry."

"What is it?" Abby asked, sitting on the edge of her chair.

Meg retrieved a faded, blue velvet box and opened it, displaying a strand of pearls.

"Wow," Abby gasped. She had done her part but hadn't asked about the other items.

"These belonged to Susie Kincaid," Meg said slowly.

The significance of the moment created an air of solemnity and awe.

"And these," Carole began, producing a box from the pocket of her robe, "are from your grandma. She wanted you to have these on your wedding day. Your borrowed and old." She handed her daughter a box.

Meg opened the last box, revealing pearl and diamond studs. Tears streamed down her eyes.

Carole embraced her daughter, kissing the side of Meg's face. "They are watching. I know it."

Abby sniffed and dabbed at her own eyes.

"How?" Meg asked, her voice muffled against her mom's shoulder. She pulled away from the hug and wiped her tears with her hand.

"Stephanie wanted you to be fully prepared for your big day," Abby explained. "It was all her brainchild. She approached Hank about the pearls."

"He was very happy to lend them," Steph said. "Abby had to jot down your mom's number so I could call and fill her in on the plan."

"I can't believe you all went to such trouble for me," Meg said.

"It's your big day, sweetie. You have to make every moment count," Carole said. "Trying to start a business around weddings can take some of the excitement away." Carole patted her daughter's hand. "We won't let you miss a moment."

A knock sounded on the closed door.

"Please come in," Meg greeted, her voice still lower than normal but slightly above the whisper their surroundings invited.

"Miss Hawke and Ms. Hawke?" Two women dressed in the pale blue kimono uniforms greeted them. "Are you ready for your massages?"

"Yes, please," Meg said on a heavy sigh. She shut the boxes and put everything back in the bag, clutching it to her chest. "Thank you all. Truly." She stood and crossed to the door with her mom. "We'll meet up with you two for lunch before our nail appointments."

Abby wanted to say it was too much. That Meg didn't need to go to so much trouble or expense on their behalf. But the slightly frantic look in Meg's eyes, the twitch of her pinched smile, told Abby to hold her tongue. Meg was trying to hold on to every ounce of control she could. Abby wasn't going to disagree. She nodded.

Stephanie flashed a thumbs up.

"See you two in a bit," Carole said before exiting behind her daughter.

The door shut softly behind them.

Abby turned to Stephanie.

The other woman widened her eyes.

Abby released the nervous laughter she'd been holding in for eighteen hours.

"Wow," Stephanie murmured.

"Seriously," Abby agreed. The tension could be sliced with a cake knife. Weddings brought up all sorts of emotions, dealing with heightened feelings. "Hopefully Meg will relax with the massage or as soon as the wedding is over. I know I'll be glad for a break. Luckily, James agreed to keep an eye on the smoker so I could sneak out here."

"That was smart." Stephanie nodded. "I'm glad you're here and I know Meg is, too. She is under a lot of pressure. I wouldn't want to get married with the whole town watching."

Abby shrugged. "I can't see their big day going any other way. I anticipated a much more elaborate and involved weekend. Their plans seem tame."

"True, but I'd need a head count at least." Stephanie chuckled.

"Are you thinking about weddings?" Abby asked.

Stephanie blushed.

"Sorry, I shouldn't tease." Abby didn't want anyone poking around her love life and knew better than to do the same to others. Especially when, despite his accusation that she needed to be enough for herself, she couldn't stop missing him.

His words didn't even make much sense. Of course she was enough for herself. She believed in herself. She invested in a future with everything she had. How much more did she have to show to prove she wouldn't ruin the town?

On further reflection, she hated her immediate antagonistic response. Of course, Joe wouldn't be involved in bashing everyone in town. The proposal from Harrison left no one in a good light. She had reacted irrationally, ready to strike before she was hit. She should know better than to trust anything from Harrison. He used and discarded people. She was proof. But how could she apologize when Joe cut her so deep with his words. Better to push it aside and get through the wedding the best she could. They could go back to being strangers as soon as the event was over.

"How are you?" Abby asked her friend instead. "How is everything going?"

"Good, but busy," Stephanie replied. "Although, I don't know how to function without being overbooked."

"I'm glad you're moving into the house with me. I didn't realize how much I liked having company." *Until I lost it*. Abby wasn't letting Joe ruin her day.

"It'll be nice to have someone to talk to," Stephanie agreed. "How has business been treating you? Welcomed back into town?"

"Summer season isn't a good indicator of local popularity." Abby shrugged. "I have had a nice, steady business." She didn't want to unload on Stephanie. With her own packed schedule, Stephanie didn't have time to work through all of Abby's problems. But they would be roommates soon. They would need to understand the other. "It's okay. I'm on better terms with everyone in town. Thanks to Joe."

"No, I don't think so. You've done the work on your own."

"Joe helped pave the way."

"Maybe. But you stand on your own merits. You aren't the sum of the people before you or town opinion."

Abby hoped so.

Joe was grateful Ted had suggested heading over together. Instead of cards at the saloon, as Joe had anticipated, the groom had requested a campout. Joe wasn't a huge fan of sleeping under the stars. No matter how much padding he brought, he could never seem to get comfortable sleeping on the ground. But he wouldn't mind a night away from town and his mistakes. He piled his gear into the four-wheeled gator and headed out.

You don't need to be good enough for anyone but yourself. His harsh accusation echoed in his mind.

He'd been talking more to himself than her. His whole endeavor with the town history had been an exercise in establishing his identity and his role. He wanted to be an expert to solve his own inferiority complex. None of that had anything to do with her and yet he'd looped her into the situation. He'd been hurt that she'd jumped to the conclusion he was in cahoots with Harrison Wolff. Joe should have avoided the weasel. He should have known better. Even if he hadn't only believed the stories told him by Ryan and Hank, after witnessing Harrison's abhorrent behavior of Abby, Joe should have steered clear. Instead, he'd entertained the idea of working together and he'd ended up with what he deserved.

But he shouldn't have said what he said to Abby. And now he didn't know what to do next. Ted drove further and further away from the ranch. Into the unknown. The green hills against the blue sky were an endless sea of possibilities. The gator climbed a hill and finally the campsite came into view.

Two figures sat on collapsible chairs.

With an hour until sunset, they didn't have too much time to spare for setting up their tents.

A large fire burned, the orange flames licking the sky. Surrounded by huge stones, the blaze was well contained.

After losing the barn, Joe was surprised Ted had approved the evening's plan. Helping put out the fire and cleaning through the mess that followed, both physically and emotionally, had strained Ted. Witnessing it had been a lot for Joe. But his friend came out the other side all the better.

Joe stopped the vehicle several yards away, hopped out and grabbed his tent and sleeping bag.

Ted did the same.

"What are we in for?" Joe asked under his breath.

"You'll be pleasantly surprised," Ted said and strode to the other men.

Joe followed, leaving his tent and bag in the pile of gear, and taking an empty seat. "Hey, are you two fighting yet? Or have you decided to take a night off?" He asked Hank and Ryan.

"Ha. What would we fight about tonight? Hank's getting his way, and I'm not against it for once. He was right about Meg. And I'm happy to say he told me so." Ryan reclined in his chair, hands behind his head and legs spread wide. "Glad you could make it."

Joe didn't detect any warbles or intonations. From the corner of his eye, he studied the groom. Ryan was the picture of contentment. No tension, no sighs, no frowns. How strange. Joe couldn't remember a time he didn't witness a big reaction out of the legacy rancher.

"Were you taking a nap?" Joe asked.

Hank guffawed.

Ryan rolled his eyes. "No, just taking stock of the landscape before it changes."

"What is this spot?" Joe asked, turning to Hank. "I've never been here before."

"The old barrier between Kincaid and Whittier land. It's the last vestige of the ranching past. The cowboys used to have to set up a vigil out here, keeping an eye on the Whittiers. After the Whittiers left, the cowboys maintained the spot. Hauled out the stones and built the firepits, kept the ground level and worked on drainage." Hank poked a toe in the dirt. "I used to take Meg and Ryan camping out here."

"That's a generous assessment," Ryan said, lifting the corner of his mouth. "Meg never lasted a whole night out here."

"True." Hank grinned. "I'd have to leave Ryan out here and haul her back to the house. Good thing he wasn't afraid of the dark."

"Of course I was. I'd stick close to the fire until you came back. I probably ruined my vision staring into the flames. But won't have to worry about that anymore. We're thinking of developing this spot into a med spa," Ryan said.

"You'd need a new building," Joe said.

"We would," Ryan said. "We'd need a lot we haven't required before." He held up his fingers one by one. "An architecture firm. A land survey. Collaboration with medical professionals. All sorts of certifications. Running utilities all the way out here won't be easy or cheap."

To Joe, the process sounded complicated and unnecessary. Constant change overwhelmed him. He'd thought Herd escaped the rat race. But by staying the same, the resort risked becoming tired and obsolete. "What would a med spa offer?"

"Cryotherapy. Vitamin IVs. Infrared sauna. Blood analysis. Naturopath stuff," Ted replied.

It sounded sterile and clinical. Not exactly fitting with the rough and tumble West image they sold guests. Joe flinched after every word. "Huh. Really?"

Ryan shrugged. "It's the next level in high-end spa services. We'd build out here though. Wouldn't want people on cleanses smelling the barbecue. It would need to be self-contained."

Joe didn't disagree. He scanned the horizon again. The spot was secluded. Establishing utilities would be its own headache and hassle. "How would you staff?"

"My sister has friends that have left traditional nursing to pursue alternative medicine. She'd be a big help," Ted said. "Early days and all that."

"First events and now a new spa," Joe said. "Never any rest for the boss, is there?"

Ryan smiled. "I wouldn't want it any other way."

"Glad to hear it," Hank said. "Does that mean you are building pickle ball courts, too?"

Ryan groaned.

Ted shook his head.

"Pickle ball?" Joe asked. The gym teachers taught the kids how to play the popular sport at school, but Joe hadn't realized how far the pastime had spread.

"Don't," Ryan bit out.

"Lana and I play together," Hank said with a grin. "We've joined a league. It's one of our favorite activities."

"And, your doctors cleared this activity?" Joe asked. He waded into dangerous, fast-moving waters. After Hank's health scare last summer, however, he wasn't allowed to do a lot of things. Like eat candy. Not that a disapproving doctor stopped him.

"No," Ryan said at the same moment Hank replied, "of course."

"Whatever keeps me moving, keeps me going," Hank added. "And you should be supportive. The alternative is I could be spending all of my time at her place, or parked in front of the ranch, necking."

Ryan shuddered.

Ted stood and threw another log on the fire. "Everyone good with hot dogs and s'mores?"

Joe was glad for the break from the sudden discussion of Hank's love life.

"Not quite the bachelor party I expected," Hank replied.

He wasn't kidding. While the typical bar hopping slash strip club bash wasn't an option in Herd—or appealing to any of the group—Joe imagined he'd find Ryan pacing and pulling out his hair. Joe anticipated heavy lifting with calming last-minute nerves. Ryan was sedate. Joe scanned for empty beer bottles or cans, anything to indicate the cause, and spotted nothing.

"Everyone ready for tomorrow?" Joe asked. He hated to poke the seemingly calm bear but was taken off-guard by Ryan's complete nonchalance.

"Absolutely," Ryan said.

"No rehearsal needed?" Joe asked.

Ted glared at him.

"Nope. Not as long as Hank is on his best behavior," Ryan answered.

Hank grinned. "I've got Lana to keep me in check."

Ryan rolled his eyes but didn't otherwise rise to the bait.

"And the honeymoon is all set?" Joe asked.

"They'll be in a yurt for two weeks, giving me and Colby plenty of space," Hank said. "I'm looking forward to some me-time."

"We'll go on a trip in January. I want a week of sun and sand with Meg. When the weather is unbearable here, and there isn't too much for us to be doing, we'll be gone," Ryan answered.

On the ranch, there was never an off-season. Joe would have to follow up later with Ted to see if he needed help watching the herd or Hank.

Ted stood again and moved to the cooler, grabbing a package of hot dogs, and tearing it open. "Why don't the rest of you work on your tents? I'll start dinner."

Joe nodded and walked to the pile of gear, grabbed his tent, and headed to a clear spot.

Ryan picked a spot beside him.

"Ryan, I have to say I'm shocked and impressed with your demeanor tonight," Joe said, glad for Ted's back so he couldn't experience another withering look. He unzipped the bag and pulled out the poles and fabric.

"I'm not stressed at all. I wanted everything perfect. I've done all that I can. Now I can sit back and just enjoy the moment. I'm marrying the love of my life. I couldn't be more ready," Ryan replied.

Joe wanted a simple life. Make a choice, be confident in the decision, and let everything play out. He had made a mistake, lashing out at her with words meant for himself and in doing so had cut her deep. He saw her pain. He knew the consequence his action had earned. She'd give him space. They'd be worse off than before. He'd be lucky if she ever spoke to him again.

Joe finished laying out the tent and started slipping the poles into position. He'd bought an easy to assemble pop-up tent from a big box store. The first time he watched Ted and Ryan put up the tent with a pole, stakes, and sheet of canvas, he had decided to opt out of future camping. Today, he made an exception.

"I can almost guarantee you that Meg is spinning her wheels now," Ryan said. "I plan and work out all the details in advance, looking for the issues before they arise. Meg is calm because she knows I'm taking care of everything. But now she has plenty to do that I am in no way involved with. Now she has to worry about details. Have you heard from Abby?"

"No." *I'm not likely to.*

"They were having a spa day today. Wasn't sure if you heard any updates about Meg?"

Joe shook his head and pulled the rain cover on to the tent. He moved to stake the bright orange shelter.

"Anything you want to talk about?" Ryan asked. "I know we've been focused on me and my life. I'm not completely oblivious to the rest of the world."

"I rather hoped Lana and Hank were enough of a distraction."

Ryan groaned. "As long as she doesn't move into the house, she can date Hank. I won't get in the way. What's going on with you and Abby?"

"A fight. A big one."

"Don't waste time stewing. Tell her you're sorry."

Joe drew back his chin. "How are you sure I'm the one at fault?"

Ryan didn't reply, too focused on the canvas for the tent.

Joe needed to apologize but in a big way. A gesture so undeniable she'd understand the depth of his feelings. He glanced back at the group as he finished assembling the tent, before staking the construction into his spot. An idea sprang into his mind fully formed. This group of men that had rallied for each other could be counted on. "Do you mind if I ask for a favor at the reception?"

"Make it a good one," Ryan grinned. "And I'm in."

"I need a grand gesture. I have to show her how I feel," Joe said. "Whatever I do, it has to be at the reception. I don't want anyone to question my loyalty."

"Then we'd better loop in Ted. Although, to be honest, I'm a little afraid of what he'll come up with." Ryan chuckled.

Joe was too. But Abby deserved a big declaration of love. No matter how much ridicule he'd earn from the public display.

CHAPTER 18

For the better part of three years, Abby had bemoaned her place in the town history. Her family's loss over a century ago had started a chain of events no one could have known. From Hoss to her siblings, no Whittier had ever found a permanent home. Their curse was inherited. She wondered how different their lives could have been with generational wealth. While owning land in the past was no guarantee of the future, property did set some people ahead of others and gave a head start on reaching their greatest potential. Some people built their lives off each victory until almost guaranteed a positive outcome in the future. Not everyone had that chance, but she wouldn't bemoan the hand of fate today.

In Herd, three wealthy families from the East Coast had been lured west by a false gold claim. Three families had plotted and backstabbed one another. In the end, only one had been left standing.

From the deck off the barn's kitchen, she watched a perfect punctuation mark to one of the town's enduring chapters and the start of a new legacy. Instead of crowing over past victory, however, the winning family had held out a hand to lift the other two up. The Hawkes and the Kincaids would now be forever linked through marriage. And the Whittiers would have their chance at a return through Abby. She couldn't help but cheer for it all. Today's wedding was a healing of old wounds.

"You may now kiss the bride," the pastor said.

With a stunning sunset backdrop, standing amidst pots filled with colorful wildflowers on the barn's deck, Ryan wrapped his bride in his arms and kissed her, dipping her slightly.

To either side of the happy couple, Meg's mom, and Ryan's grandpa grinned. Seated in a chair, Hank held Colby's leash and petted the dog on the head. The black and white mutt woofed. The crowd seated inside the barn, watching through the pushed open accordion French doors, swooned, clapped, and cheered.

Abby swiped at her lash line and got to work, striding into the prep kitchen. "Ready to start?" she asked James and Heather Rabbitt at the counter.

Near the oven, he raised an oven mitt clad hand in salute. "Sounds good."

"I'll send the wait staff out to bring in the appetizers," Heather said.

"Great. I'll head to my truck and then I'll come in here to help with the entrees." With a smile, she exited and made her way to the foot truck. For the next hour, Abby operated without thinking. Moving by rote helped her finish trays and pass them off to the servers in a never-ending line.

Occasionally, laughter poured out from the celebration inside the barn, carried on the wind along with a contagious joy Abby wanted to soak in. She wanted the happiness to wash away every last ounce of longing and hurt. But she couldn't so easily turn off her emotions. Luckily the crushing chaos of catering kept her busy.

When the appetizers were finished, she lowered the curtain over the window, and locked up the truck.

Fortunately, Lover Boy had stayed away.

She scanned the horizon but couldn't see much of the prairie past the cars filling every available spot. Perhaps he couldn't spot his love, the food truck, in the crush. Or maybe he had found company among the herd and was safely away from the noise.

As long as he wasn't hurt somewhere...

She pushed the thought from her mind, dusting her hands on her pants, and strode around the side of the deck again.

She appreciated the care that had gone into the barn's construction, to allow for her to enter and exit more easily. Today, however, she was a little sad to miss a chance to see the crowd. A glance at her watch disavowed her of any idea to sneak into the reception. She didn't have time.

Entering the kitchen, Abby checked on the brisket, pulled pork, chicken, and began to position the sides for the assembly line. While a buffet was the typical style of service at the barn, Ryan had requested a sit-down dinner for the reception. The barn could comfortably—and safely—seat two-hundred.

"Ready?" Heather asked.

With a nod, Abby took her spot at the end of the row and using an assembly line began plating. In wordless unison, the four moved through. Abby felt like she engaged in a dance or meditation. More than that, she felt like she belonged. She'd offered to hire more staff to help with plating but the Rabbitts and Will had balked.

Once again, she was part of town. She'd take the baby steps to regain her foothold. She wasn't going to make a misstep again. She wished Joe was at her side. One perfect kiss was all they'd be to each other. She had to accept it and move on graciously.

Heather handed the final plate to Abby.

Abby dished a helping of all three meats and passed the plate to the server. Turning to the group, she exhaled a heavy sigh and rolled her neck. "Anyone hungry?"

The trio laughed and grabbed plates, serving themselves.

Abby dished herself a heaping pulled pork sandwich and savored the bite. She ached from the marathon cooking and serving. She had left the boots at home. All the work of the spa staff to alleviate her aches and pains was in vain. But it had been worth it to make her friend's day special. The kitchen crew still had to plate and serve dessert. They'd earned at least a few minutes break.

"How is your restaurant?" Heather asked, standing next to Abby as she leaned against the wall.

"We're making progress. The plans are approved, and the footings poured. Thank you for asking," Abby said, touched. She had never thought her business would be competition to the saloon. If so, she wouldn't have pursued it. But in the time since she'd been painted as a villain, she wasn't sure what anyone's perception of her future brick and mortar business were. Construction noise would keep her in some people's complaints. But she couldn't do anything about that and was almost confident only Miriam would bring it up.

"About a year do you think?" James asked.

"Hopefully," Abby replied with a tentative smile.

"Good," Will added. "We need more businesses downtown to help us all to keep visitors in the off-season. Will you open for breakfast, lunch, and dinner?"

"That's my plan, unless that's difficult for you," Abby said.

"Not at all. We will welcome it. The saloon traditionally never served breakfast," James said. "We added it on in the last couple of years to keep pace with the demand. To be honest, I'd be glad to give it up if you took it over."

Abby took a huge bite of her food. She was heartened by the sentiments but still a little hesitant. *You have to be enough for yourself.* She hated him for saying the words. The more she had time to consider what he'd said, however, the more she had to give him some amount of credit.

Without taking away anything from those around her, she could be enough. *But what about pursuing a romance with him?* She wasn't seeking external validation from his approval. She missed him.

"How is your blanket coming?" Heather asked.

Blanket? Abby furrowed her brow and then remembered. Her life had changed since she'd been wordlessly kicked out of the knitting club. It was almost hard to recall what she had been doing. But not the reason why. She'd been looking for friendship. When she'd been at her lowest, however, she'd found connection from other—some surprising—people. "Not very well," she said, blushing. "I might end up with more of a shawl. The loom is hard to manipulate. I've made very little progress."

"Whenever you want to come back to knitting club, you'll be very welcome. Kelly mentioned she could help you work off the loom. If you're interested on progressing to knitting needles, you'd have our full support."

Kelly and Heather had discussed her. Abby wasn't sure she wanted to leave the safety of the plastic figure eight pegs for the freedom of traditional knitting. If she put her work down, she knew exactly where to resume. Working with needles was a few levels ahead of her skills. "Oh, that's nice. Kelly did a beautiful job embroidering the handkerchief for Meg."

"She is quite talented," Heather said. "I hope you will come back. Even if you don't want to test your skills, you are still very welcome. A little positive peer pressure might be a good push to finish your project."

Abby took another bite and flashed a thumbs up. Anything to save herself from a response. Or she might say something embarrassing about her gratitude.

"Is Abby in here?" Stephanie asked, appearing in the doorway.

With a walkie talkie and a clipboard, Stephanie wasn't quite a guest either. The town's go-to events queen couldn't sit still long enough to simply enjoy the day.

Abby stepped forward, swallowing her bite, and raising a hand. "I'm here. What's wrong?"

"You'll see." Stephanie grinned. "Come with me. You're needed."

Abby had never heard a more ominous phrase. Was something wrong with the food? Were the bride and groom unhappy? Was Hank? She fought off a shudder. "I'll be back to help with dessert."

The other three nodded and flashed thumbs up before dishing themselves seconds.

At least she knew the three toughest food critics in town didn't take issue with her food. But what could she have done wrong? Stephanie dragged her through the crowd to the edge of the dance floor next to the bride. With a leashed Colby at her side, Meg looked serene. Appearances could be deceiving.

Abby's stomach clenched. "Meg, is something wrong?" Abby whispered. "Where are the tables?"

"No, everything has been wonderful. The food was perfect. We pushed everything back for dancing before dessert. Look." Meg pointed to Ryan, Joe, and Ted in the center of the dance floor with their heads down and their hands clasped in front of them.

"What are they doing?" Abby asked.

An orchestral song cut through the noise of muted conversations. Abby twisted her neck from one side to the other. Guests had cell phones angled at the trio.

"Baby, baby, baby, baby, baby, baby," K-Ci and Jo Jo sang. The piano music began for *All My Life*. Abby hadn't heard the song in years, but the hit of nostalgia from her youth overwhelmed her. Her skin prickled with goose bumps from a sense of anticipation for what might follow and a hint of worry she'd be involved somehow. She did not love the spotlight.

In the center, Ryan turned on his heel and strode toward his bride. Joe and Ted raised their chins and copied the pivot turn sequence. Ryan led Meg to a chair they'd blocked from the crowd's view.

Meg darted her gaze around at the three men dancing around her, holding tight to Colby's leash.

The dog wagged her tail against the ground, the thump thump thump a loud addition to the bass line.

When Abby's gaze met Joe's, she was hit by a wave of amusement and second-hand embarrassment for his nineties dance moves.

"What is this song?" Stephanie asked loudly, leaning close to Abby. "What are they doing?"

Abby grinned. If she used the term cabbage patch, she wasn't sure Stephane would be enlightened. She probably wouldn't even ask if the dance had to do with the stuffed dolls of the eighties and nineties. She'd miss that connection, too.

"Is this the electric slide?" Stephanie followed up with earnestness.

Abby shook, her whole-body shuddering from holding in laughter. Stephanie's lack of pop culture awareness didn't faze her. But she spotted the annoyed expression on Joe from the loud comment.

Ted shrugged.

Hank ambled onto the dance floor to grab Colby's leash and led the dog away from the crowd. The guests clapped for the pair. Ryan reached for his bride's hand to help her up and twirled her into his arms, slow dancing to collective oohs and aahs.

Joe and Ted strode forward.

Joe held out his hand to Abby.

She hesitated, pressing her lips together.

"Please?" he asked. "This is all for you. To show you and everyone else what I'm feeling and where my loyalties lie."

She widened her gaze. "For me? Based on the choreography and music, I figured this was another Ted special."

"He helped. But it's for you," he called back. "I couldn't find the *Ghost Writer* theme song."

His voice carried over the music, loud enough for everyone to hear. But he didn't hesitate. He was making a show of his feelings in front of the whole town. She offered him her hand.

As the song finished, he led her through the crowd on the dancefloor to the doors leading to the deck. "Harrison's pitch was heavily edited and had nothing of the actual text in it."

"I know," she sighed, dropping his hand to cross her arms over her chest. "Or, at least I guessed after I calmed down and had time to think."

"Thank you. But I want to be honest. He did capture the spirit of one of my earlier drafts. At least, as far as your ancestors were concerned. I am sorry for that."

She shrugged. "You didn't have all the facts. I can't blame you for the correlations you made."

"No, but as an aspiring historian I should be more aware of bias and should fight against it harder. History shouldn't be so one-sided but it is. We can at least change that with the real project. I won't be working with Harrison."

"It's fine. We're fine. You don't need to miss a chance because of me." Her voice warbled. She wanted to keep the emotion out of her responses but she struggled.

He shook his head. "No. I will pursue another partner on the project. I was flattered by Harrison. I don't want to be a pawn, and I'd hate for him to make money off my hard work. I'll query literary agents. Or better yet, I'll take you up on your advice about building a platform. There are a lot of paths to success."

"If you're sure..."

Joe reached for her hand and raised it to his lips, kissing her knuckles. "I am. I shouldn't have agreed to work with him anyway. He fed my ego and gave me an easy path. I know better. Getting published might take longer on my own, but I'll do it. I don't need him." Joe cleared his throat. "And no, we aren't okay. I don't want to go back to being acquaintances. I said some hurtful words to you that I didn't mean. I wanted to be taken seriously and the only person who did that I pushed away."

"But you weren't wrong. I do need to be enough to myself. I need to stand on my own." She turned up the corner of her mouth. "I think I am."

"Can I be part of your future?" he murmured. "Did my grand gesture sufficiently demonstrate my feelings for you?"

Tears stung the back of her eyes. Emotion caught in her throat. He held her gaze with a steady intensity, conveying so much more than the words he spoke. She saw flashes of what they could have together and how much better they both would be as partners. She'd come to Herd to claim her family's land and find out if a second chance was possible. Ultimately, she'd discovered herself. Along the way, she'd found him, too. She wouldn't give up this chance. "Do you want to be?"

He stepped closer, narrowing the space between them from feet to inches. "I would." He tipped up her chin, a soft smile playing across his lips in the second before he pressed his mouth against hers.

He wrapped her in his arms like she fit. She wasn't letting go, ever. They'd have plenty of disagreements in the future. They'd probably always have some sort of fire burning that needed to be stoked or put out in equal measure. And wouldn't life be better for it.

A low, deep moan shook the deck.

She pulled away and drew back her chin. "Was that... you?"

He gaped. "What?"

The sound came again.

"Oh no, Lover Boy is back," she murmured. She broke free of his arms and raced around the side of the barn. No one else was outside. Yet. But in seconds, guests would start filtering out onto the deck to enjoy the evening breeze. Some might leave. If the animal got spooked by the crowd and vehicles, he might charge and endanger someone. Then he'd risk himself.

She raced to the food truck, twisting the back door, and diving inside in a swift motion. Her shoulder ached. She'd probably pulled something but she didn't stop. She had to get up to the driver's seat and steer away from the crowd.

The truck shuddered. Lover Boy must have bumped into it. Utensils clattered and pots clanged as drawers and doors opened and spilled their contents onto the ground. She kept going, squeezing through the door into the cab and climbing behind the wheel.

The bison moaned and nudged the truck with his shoulder. The vehicle shuddered and rocked side to side. While guests had been directed to park their cars some yards away from the truck, the truck falling over could crush a few sedans in the best-case scenario and start another fire in the worst case.

She patted her pockets and pulled her keys out, slipping them into the ignition. The engine wouldn't start. "Come on, come on," she pleaded as she twisted the keys again and again to no avail.

"Where is Abby?" Ted shouted.

"Abby!" Joe yelled.

She was in trouble. Joe sounded worried. Lover Boy knocked the vehicle again with more force than he'd ever attempted. She'd made a bad choice and had to hope she would have the chance to never repeat this mistake again.

"What are you doing?" Joe yelled from the passenger side, his voice cracking.

"I wanted to move the vehicle. I don't want him to get hurt," she shouted through her open window. "But the battery is dead."

Now she was going to be hurt. Or worse.

"What do we do?" Joe shouted behind him.

Ted must be behind the truck. He couldn't see the bison. Both men were at risk and it was her fault. "Lure him away," Ted shouted.

Lover Boy kept up his assault, moving to some sway of his own beat.

"How?" Joe sounded frantic.

If he was nervous for her, she was scared. She darted her gaze through the cab. She needed anything that could distract the bison. Her emergency kit with road flares was in the back next to a fire extinguisher. Could she throw something out the window for him to chase? Did bison fetch like dogs?

A higher pitched moan carried through the window. Abby turned and stared at the prairie. A pair of bison stood nearby, the closest any of the other herd had ever come. The larger of the two grunted and snorted.

Lover Boy stopped rocking the truck. Slowly, he turned and grunted at his comrades.

The smaller bison grunted.

Lover Boy walked away.

Without a backward glance, he followed the pair, and, after several minutes, the trio disappeared into the dark night.

Joe rushed to the cab and wrenched open the door. "Are you okay?"

"I am. How bad is the truck?" she asked, letting him help her to the ground.

The side of the truck had dents, and the back tire was flat. "Not as bad as it could have been."

"Do you think he's found love? He's moved on for good?"

Joe pulled her into his arms. "I think everyone has earned a happily ever after."

"Your heart is racing," she said.

"A bison rammed your vehicle. Of course, my heart is racing." He held her tight, resting her head against his pounding chest. "Are you okay? Really?"

She nodded, her hair brushing his chin. She was glad for his strength. Her limbs felt boneless and without him holding her up, she'd have melted into a puddle on the ground. But this wasn't a moment for recrimination. They'd finally reached understanding and she wasn't about to ruin it with apologies and excuses. She pulled back and lifted her chin. "Kiss me and find out."

EPILOGUE

ONE YEAR LATER...

In front of her bathroom mirror, Abby smoothed her hair back into a bun.

She loved her bathroom mirror with the polished chrome frame that she had selected and purchased for installation in this very spot. It was a small detail. For many, it was an afterthought. By that point in the construction timeline, she shouldn't have cared what she selected, but to Abby, everything mattered and deserved her full attention.

A lump caught in her throat. Or maybe it was her heart leaping out of her chest. Her blessings were abundant. The living situation was only the most obvious—and biggest payout—of her struggles to claim her legacy. She had never owned anything new before. Her truck was second-hand. The two-bedroom, two-bathroom apartment was not only brand-new but designed specifically for her over her restaurant on her land. Hers, hers, hers.

A knock shook the door.

"Come in," Abby called.

Stephanie appeared through the crack, slowly widening it. "Hey, are you almost ready? We have to head downstairs soon. Everyone will be here in the next ten minutes."

"Yes, I'm glad it's only the soft launch for friends. I made it easy on myself."

"Easy?" Stephanie bulged her eyes. "You've been cooking non-stop for the past three days. What about *that* is easy?"

Abby chuckled. All things were relative. And in Herd, the tight-knit community was like a giant extended family, stepping in when needed without much notice. After the building was ready, she had gratefully accepted the keys. Ted and Joe moved their boxes over from the Hawke farmhouse. Stephanie's friends, Kelly, and Lauren, painted the apartment. And thanks to the Kincaids recommendations, the restaurant booked reservations two weeks in advance.

After nearly a year as roommates, Abby couldn't imagine being alone. She might have to figure it out soon. According to Joe, Ted was getting very close to a proposal. Although, knowing Stephanie, Abby was almost sure Stephanie would be the one to ask the big question.

No sooner than they had moved out and Meg's mom Carole had settled back in her childhood home. The sudden relocation had been shocking and the biggest news in town. Abby had been grateful to finally be shoved out of the gossip circle.

The speculation reached a near fever pitch until the announcement of Ryan and Meg's impending bundle of joy. Of course they had shared the news on Hank's ninetieth birthday.

He had gladly shared his day once again. With Lana as his date, he was glad to avoid some of the limelight.

With one last glance in the mirror, at a happy face Abby almost didn't recognize, she smiled at her friend. "Let's go."

Abby led the way through the apartment and down the spiral stairs reaching the main floor of the restaurant. She opened the employees only door that would—as soon as the business officially opened—be locked to all except those with keys and crossed down the back hall to the main open dining room. With dark paneling, oversized crown molding, historic photographs, and a few tasteful touches of antlers, she had decorated with a Western Cowboy chic look she hoped wouldn't date the restaurant too soon.

The clattering of metallic utensils and low conversation from the open kitchen spilled into the main room. The sounds of cooking filled her with gratitude. Staff had been easy to find. Cooks were eager to work. High school aged kids applied for busser jobs. She'd hired college undergraduates home for the summer for front-of-house staff. With more employment opportunities, the community thrived. Her family's historic misdeeds officially erased from current local memory.

At the front, Abby spotted the small crowd gathering outside the plate glass windows. "Come on inside," she greeted, pushing open the door and held it with her back as they poured in.

"Wow," Meg said as she passed. "If I'm not careful, I'll lose our events to you."

"No, I'll leave the big productions to you," Abby replied, hiding her shudder. Meg's idea to expand the ranch's offering to include weddings kept a steady stream of tourists in town through the fall. Occasionally, a big event popped up on the calendar in mid-winter too. After assisting with the Kincaid wedding and birthday celebration, however, Abby didn't want the stress of being actively involved in day-of logistics. "I'm happy to cater but that's it."

Abby had moved her food truck there in a semi-permanent spot to help with catering events. That was the official reasoning and it made sense. In truth, she'd been worried about Lover Boy. Since he nearly flipped her truck, however, he hadn't ever gotten close again. Every so often she'd spot him with another pair. He'd found his place too. He belonged.

"Actually," Joe said slowly, pausing to kiss Abby's check. "You've already lost one. I'm hosting my book launch here."

Abby let go of the door and waved her guests to the large table in the middle of the room. "Just the one."

"Maybe a few more," Stephanie added. "Not weddings. I promise. The restaurant will be part of Frontier Days this year. Joe is a featured lecturer, and Abby is hosting his talks here."

"What a great idea," Meg said.

"Don't forget anniversary dinners," Hank said with a cheeky grin. He hadn't brought Lana as his date tonight. But the pair were quite the couple around town. "It's a nice, romantic spot."

"Please stop," Ryan muttered.

Abby shut the door and scanned the room, warmth filling her from heart to hands at the scene. Under the brass sconces and hanging fixtures, the dark stained paneling held depth in the grains. Dotted with historical prints of the town, sourced by Joe, the décor was a mix of past and present, inviting and familiar and new all at once.

Cheerful chatter from friends who had become family added to the atmosphere. Herd was worth fighting for. She was so happy she'd stayed in the battle and—ultimately—won the war.

"Are you okay?" Joe murmured, reaching for her hand.

She hadn't moved from the doorway. She didn't want to disturb the picture-perfect scene by inserting herself into it.

She squeezed his fingers. "I'm great. Never better." Her voice cracked, and she cleared her throat. "Did you see the sky tonight? I thought I saw something green and wavy."

"The Northern Lights? This early?" His face crumpled.

"I assume so. Pretty cool, huh?"

He scowled.

"What's wrong?" she asked.

"I planned a trip at Glacier for the fall. I already booked it."

Her heart swelled. "For us?"

He nodded and, his mouth down turned. "I figured it would be a nice way to celebrate the end of my lecture circuit and thank you for all of your help with building my platform and getting my book published."

"I'm pretty sure your agent gets the credit for that."

"Without your hard work getting my social media visible and reaching out to libraries to get me notice, I never would have had the confidence to approach a literary agency. You get all the credit."

She stepped close and wrapped her arms around his waist. "In that case, yes, I'll take you up on your offer. It's a date." She leaned into him, kissing him until she was breathless. She'd come to Herd unsure of what she wanted for her life. Along the way, she'd been unmasked as a cowgirl. Now she was more than ready to ride off into the sunset and live her happily ever after.

CHECK OUT THESE OTHER GREAT TITLES FROM ROWAN PROSE PUBLISHING!

Rachelle Paige Campbell writes contemporary romance novels filled with heart and hope. She believes love and laughter can change lives, and every story needs a happily-ever-after. Check out her blog for updates on current projects, and sign-up for her newsletter to learn about upcoming releases and announcements: rachellepaigecampbell.com